Diary
of a Stressed Out
Mother

Madness

(Part Two)

NICOLA KELSALL

Little Studio
Publishing Company

Diary of a Stressed Out Mother:
Madness

First published as an eBook 2017

This first paperback edition published 2017

Cover Illustration by Nicola Kelsall © 2017
Cover designed by Fiona McIntyre © 2017

Nicola Kelsall
Visit my website at www.lspublishing.co.uk

First Printing: Oct 2017
Little Studio Publishing Company

ISBN 978-0-9956685-1-5

Many thanks to all my friends and family who have inadvertently inspired the content of this book, and a special 'thank you' to Fiona at Fiona McIntyre Designs, for her work on the cover design.

DEDICATION

To all the mothers I know and love.

"It's not easy being a mother. If it were easy, fathers would do it."
(Bea Arthur – Golden Girls)

PROLOGUE

It's all very well, people suggesting a holiday is what you need when you're feeling stressed, but in my experience, holidays can fall well below expectations. My husband Andrew thinks that any trip away is better than none, but after my recent holiday debacle, I would definitely dispute this. If he'd made the mistake of booking a week on a Japanese island full of toxic chemical sites, poisonous bunnies and barbarous fish, I'm sure he would agree with me. But his little excursions away usually consist of posh hotels, gourmet dinners and lashings of champagne – all expenses paid of course. So, I think I'm entitled to feel short-changed, especially when not only did my luggage go missing as soon as I arrived, I had to endure a particularly distressing encounter with an old adversary from my past, and then, worst of all, I nearly died from a vicious fish attacking me with its poisonous prongs. I've been a fan of all things Japanese since Jess bought me a bonsai tree for my birthday in 1978, but I must say - now I'm wavering.

Anyway, I'm now back in the safety of my own home, thank goodness! Things like this do make you appreciate your family, even if they are quite taxing at times. I can't remember the last time I was able to relax completely. Now Flora is eighteen, there's a whole new set of things to worry about, Tom at sixteen seems to be regressing at an alarming rate, and Luke and Billy (11 and 6 respectively) are a constant source of distress, magnetically attracting trouble wherever they go. Infuriatingly, Billy's arm will be in plaster for another four weeks, after his latest misadventure. At least Andrew is fairly predictable in his shortcomings. Mind you, after his recent altercation involving a particularly unpleasant individual at a school rugby match, and a large quantity of discarded bricks, I'm now not so sure. Oh well, "KBO", as Churchill would have said.

APRIL

Monday 1st April (Easter Monday)

In Hungary, on this day, it's traditional for people to throw their spouse into a pond. If there isn't a suitable one nearby, they resort to buckets of water – preferably ice-cold. I was very tempted to do just that with Andrew this morning, but more out of malice aforethought than high jinks. I don't know what possessed him to suddenly decide he wants to give up his job.

'But what will you do instead?' I shrieked, slightly hysterically.

'What's going on?' asked Flora, joining us in the kitchen. 'I heard shouting.'

'Your father's gone mad,' I told her.

'No, I haven't, Dora. I've been thinking about it for a while now.'

'So why didn't you say something before?'

'Because I knew you'd freak out.'

'That's not a good enough reason!' I said.

'It is!' said Flora and Andrew in unison.

'But you're a really good lawyer – why would you give it up!'

'I'm bored,' he said.

'Well, I could say that about my life – I could beat you, hands down,' I said, - 'but I've got responsibilities you know! Like looking after the children, a house to pay for, food to prepare, laundry to do, and dealing with a difficult husband who plainly needs to see a therapist!'

'Hey Dad, you could be in a band again like in the olden days,' said Flora helpfully. 'And go on the road – the Beach Boys are about your age, aren't they? They're still doing it!'

I was relieved when Andrew laughed at this, because the way he was behaving was very unnerving, and I could almost imagine him deciding to do something as ridiculous. As it happened, Flora's suggestion was not a million miles away.

'I'm going to take a six-month sabbatical.'

'And do what?'

'Write.'

'Really? What kind of writing? You've never mentioned this before!'

'Well, I'm mentioning it now.'

Oh my God! I thought, panicking – he's going to be at home! All the time! Frying lots of things in pans! Making loads of extra washing up! Using up all the milk! Shouting at the cat! Shouting at the dogs! This can't be allowed to happen!

As if reading my mind, he said, 'you'll be out working in your new job at Pooch Parlour, Dora. You won't even notice I'm around.'

'It's only part-time,' I said, looking seriously perturbed. 'What are you going to write, Andrew?'

'I thought I'd have a go at Crime Fiction. I've always had a yen to write that stuff – it can't be too difficult! Look at that farmer! What's he called? Oswald isn't it? Anyway, he was an overnight sensation with his e-Books - people couldn't get enough of him.'

'But he's really good though,' I said, somewhat unkindly. Andrew looked undeterred.

This is it! I thought – this is his mid-life crisis. I've seen the signs: The lycra cycling shorts, the covert glancing at unattainable women half his age, his pathetic attempts at 'getting down' with the kids… Where will it all end? As if I haven't got enough to worry about at the moment.

'Don't worry, Dora, I'll be a better person to have around – less grumpy and less tired. I'll have lots more energy – I'll be a new man!'

I doubt it, I thought, cynically – just more of the old man – in my space, getting under my feet! ARRGHH!!

Tuesday 2nd April

Well, I didn't have time to dwell on Andrew's latest bombshell, since I had my new job to think about this morning.

I must say, I felt slightly irritated to be going off to work while everyone else is still on holiday. I decided to take the car as I'm still suffering from a swollen foot due to the venomous fish-stabbing incident. I hope my limp isn't too obvious – I don't want them to think I'm a liability before I've even started.

'Good luck Dora,' said Andrew, as I left the house. 'Break a leg!'

Pooch Parlour is a totally new direction for me as I've got no experience at all in this line of business, apart from the odd attempt at shampooing our own dogs, Fudge and Cocoa - and the cat occasionally. I've been quite excited about this job. I'll be meeting lots of new people and looking after their animals, plus it's practical so no boring office stuff, and it's part-time which gives me time to do other things – all great! It is slightly strange though, that no one else applied for it.

'Ah, Dora!' said Jack in a very jolly, loud voice, and bearing an uncanny resemblance to an English Bulldog. She handed me my brown poly-cotton outfit. 'Let's get started shall we! We've got a poodle called Queenie coming in ten minutes for a shampoo and set.'

I suppose for my first day it didn't go too badly really. I mean, Jack wouldn't have expected me to get everything right straight away, would she? Her other assistant, Bertie (a lanky girl with long tatty hair), said she thought that apart from misreading the soap instructions for the Hydrobath, I did OK, although Queenie's owner did look a bit surprised when I was still rinsing suds out of the dog's fur two hours later. The upside of this though, is that

Queenie fluffed up beautifully and looked a million dollars. Jack said she hoped Queenie didn't get an allergic reaction, because you only need '*one*' capful of liquid soap in the water tank - not a '*whole bottle*'. Oh well, we live and learn! I think they were quite pleased with my performance overall – we'll have to see how things pan out.

When I got home, Andrew hadn't thought about making anything for tea of course.

'I've been busy,' he said, affronted by my accusation of thoughtlessness.

'I've been doing research.'

'What research?' I asked.

'For my book.'

'Well, I suppose we should get used to starving to death, since that's what will happen when you become a writer instead of a reasonably well-paid lawyer,' I said crossly.

Honestly, if he's going to be at home he could at least think about preparing a meal - why is it that Andrew seems to be incapable of planning ahead, unless of course he's working out which pubs to visit on a night out with his mates, or which is the best hotel to stay in on a business trip – he seems perfectly able to plan those things well in advance. I looked in the kitchen food cupboard and fridge for inspiration, but realised that you can't actually produce a meal for six with a limp stalk of broccoli, some dried up 2-week old sausages, and one potato. It made me wonder what they'd all been living on while I was away on holiday.

'What's for tea Mum?' asked Luke.

'I'm not sure.'

'Can we have fish and chips again?'

'So,' asked Andrew at bedtime, - 'how did it go today?'

'Fine, I think. Jack and Bertie are nice. Are you serious about the writing thing, Andrew?'

'Of course!'

'Have you told Sharp and Prentice yet?'

'Yes.'

'What does Geoff say?' I asked.

'He thinks it's a great idea.'

'Mm,' I said, unimpressed. 'I hate to stick a pin in this plan of yours, Andrew, but what are we going to live on while you're doing this?'

'Don't worry about all that,' he said dismissively. 'I'll get a retainer and I'll go on that website as an advisor – you know, *Xpertatlaw.com*. It'll be fine. Anyway, I have to give a month's notice, so it won't happen overnight.'

I tossed and turned in the night, wondering whether, if I humour him, he might forget about it or change his mind. I do hope so – the whole thing has a ring of impending disappointment and failure about it and I do believe that my husband may be having a funny turn; not an epiphany, as he imagines, but a mad delusion. He may even be turning into one of those fantasists you hear about. I don't like it, not one little bit.

Wednesday 3rd April

'Let's go out for a nice walk,' I suggested to everyone at lunch time. 'We can take the dogs.'

'There's no such thing as a 'nice' walk,' said Flora sullenly. 'Going for a walk is SOOOOOOOO boring!'

'Yeah,' said Tom, - 'no one our age goes for walks – it's just lame!'

'I'm surprised you two aren't lame with lack of exercise,' said Andrew. 'If you don't use your muscles, they'll waste away and all you'll have left are two straws for legs.'

'Rubbish,' said Tom. 'Anyway – I get plenty of exercise doing games at school.'

'Yeah,' said Flora, - 'me too.'

I raised my eyebrows and shot Flora a look of baffled surprise. Flora's aversion to physical exercise is legendary and the litany of reasons to be excused stretches out into infinity.

'Well, you'll come, won't you?' I looked hopefully at Luke and Billy.

'Can we go to the new giant climbing net at the park – it's like a massive spider's web – it's really cool!'

'Yes, OK,' I said, not realising how much I would later regret saying those two little words.

Cocoa and Fudge heard the word 'park' and launched themselves at the back door, barking furiously.

It's a good twenty minutes to walk from our house down to Shillingsworth's only public park, and quite hard work with the dogs, as they're not good at being on leads and they pull a lot.

'We really should have persevered with the puppy training,' said Andrew, getting annoyed with them. The trouble is, they were banned from the first one I took them to, when we got them three years ago. The woman who ran the class said we weren't being consistent with their training at home so it was a waste of time. I think it was more to do with the fact that Fudge howled every time she gave an instruction, and Cocoa did a massive poo in her agility tunnel. Anyway, that woman wasn't practising what she preached at all. In her brochure, it says *'No Dog Too Tough to Train'*. It's very difficult to be consistent anyway – when you've got young children. You can't be watching them every minute of the day, can you? Of course, Luke and Billy didn't help matters by showing them how to do things like open the fridge door, and drop Flora's shoes in the pond. When we were told to leave Miss Stern's class, *Canine Training for All,* it was remarkably difficult to find another one with any spare places. Oddly, my friend Suzie's class where she took Ping-Pong (her Chihuahua), was supposed to have plenty but they told me they were full. I had my suspicions at the time.

Once we got to the park, Billy and Luke made straight for the new climbing web. Unfortunately, the dogs aren't very good at staying in the dogs' play area, and we often spend a lot of time removing them from the playground, the sandpit, the flowerbeds and the boating pond.

'This is why I prefer the common,' I said to Andrew, as we shouted at the dogs to get off the council's daffodil display. Then we heard Luke shouting for us.

'Billy's stuck in the net,' he said, pointing at the middle of it. Billy was wedged right in the middle of the spider's web, like a trapped moth he flapped his one good arm and legs, but to no useful effect.

'How did this happen?' I shouted up to Billy.

'Luke told me to,' said Billy, his face red with the exertion of trying to extricate himself.

'For God's sake, Luke!' said Andrew, - 'you know he's got a broken arm!'

Luke tried to look innocent – 'I didn't know he'd get stuck, Dad!'

This is the second time in the last six months that Billy has managed to wedge his slightly chubby self in a gap not quite big enough. Last time he nearly ended up in the A&E again, squeezing himself through the bathroom skylight and falling twenty feet with the window frame attached to him. Luckily Billy survived practically unscathed, but the cost of repairing the said skylight plus the conservatory below was not inconsiderable.

I must say, my climbing skills are rusty to say the least, and Andrew being quite a bit heavier than me, managed to make it twice as difficult; the ropes being jerked roughly away from me by the force of an unequal mass. By now a large crowd of onlookers and noisy children had gathered around the spectacle. The rope frame swayed back and forth, and Billy bobbed about like a sprat caught in a fishing net.

'We could get some vegetable oil and smear it on,' I suggested, - 'it's how you get a ring off if it's stuck on your finger.'

'Or,' said Andrew, clinging on to the ropes above Billy's legs. 'We could twist him round and round and sort of unscrew him – like a bottle top.'

'Get me out!' wailed Billy. We decided to go with Andrew's suggestion, since there was obviously no oil easily to hand and Billy was becoming distressed. Between us we managed to release him, although he lost his trousers in the process. The crowd applauded spontaneously and we all descended in an undignified scramble down to the ground. Billy's trousers were reapplied and he and Luke ran off to play football. The crowd dispersed and we got our breath back.

Then we remembered.

'The dogs – where are the dogs?' said Andrew, suddenly realising they'd been absent all through the commotion.

'They're a bloody nightmare,' grumbled Andrew, as we trudged everywhere looking for them. 'We should have just got the kids a hamster each, like I suggested.'

'Look, Andrew,' I said. 'I can see them – over there.' I pointed into the distance. Two brown dog-shaped objects were cavorting around in the allotments behind the duck pond. We could hear someone yelling at them quite a lot.

'We are really sorry,' I said when we finally got them on their leads.

'Well, that's all very well,' said the old man, whose vegetable plot had been trampled over, - 'but once you disturb an onion, that's it - they're stunted for life! They won't grow no more! And look at my leeks – all chewed up like that! Who'd want to eat 'em now! And just look what they've done to my prize parsnips – biggest ones I've ever grown – lovely they were, until your blasted dogs got hold of 'em!'

Fudge and Cocoa barked in agreement. The old man looked at them with pure loathing. 'If I had my way, those dogs would be cat food by tomorrow.' The word 'cat' prompted further fervent barking.

'I'd like to compensate you for your loss,' said Andrew, - 'and for the damage to your vegetable patch.'

'This,' said the old man, - 'is not just a vegetable patch! It's my life's work, this is! Vegetable patch indeed!'

'Well,' said Andrew, - 'whatever you want to call it – I'd like to pay for the damage.'

'I tell you what,' he said, - 'you look like a big strong chap. You can come and 'elp me sort all this out – my arthritis is playing up somethin' terrible at the moment.'

'Oh,' said Andrew, slightly taken aback, - 'I'm not very good at gardening.'

'No matter,' he said, - 'I'll tell you what to do – let's say Saturday morning – 8am sharp OK? Good. Don't be late.'

He hobbled off; his bandy legs, hunched shoulders and knobbly walking stick making it impossible for Andrew to refuse him.

Thursday 4th April

Today didn't go too well at Pooch Parlour. Bertie wasn't there, so it was a very busy day and I hardly had time to go for a wee, never mind eat any lunch.

'Is it often like this?' I asked Jack.

'Oh yes!' she said. 'We like a challenge – gets the blood pumping, Dora! It's good for you!'

Well, that's all very well, I thought, but she's been doing this for years. My dog trimming skills are still in their embryonic stage. If I go any faster, my current charge – a very fluffy Chow Chow - could end up minus his doo dahs if I'm not careful.

'Just go for it, Dora, you'll be fine!' shouted Jack, whilst wrestling an enormous St Bernard onto what she calls 'The Operating Table'. Her confidence in me, though, was seriously misplaced.

After an amateurish effort with the Chow Chow, resulting in a lop-sided look resembling a sort of wonky mullet for dogs, the owner paid the bill without batting an eye. When he turned to leave, I realised he was in possession of a long white stick. Jack commented later that in some instances having restricted peripheral vision can be a bonus. My next victim was a little West Highland terrier called Archie.

'Watch him,' said Jack, - 'he's a little nipper!'

As I've already intimated, my hairdressing skills have never been terribly good at the best of times, and Archie was a tricky customer. I admit I did have to resort to rather extreme measures to keep him under control. When I finally finished giving him an all-over trim, Jack came over to inspect my handiwork.

'Well, Dora, I've seen better. Never mind – practice makes perfect, eh!'

When the owner came back for him she didn't look too impressed and complained that Archie's cut was uneven and patchy.

'I'm very sorry,' I told her, - 'but he wouldn't keep still.'

'He keeps still for me,' she said.

'Well, he tried to bite me too.'

'He never bites me,' she said.

I was tempted to say, *'that's a shame'*.

Jack came to my rescue. 'Dora's new here,' she said.

'So I see!' said Archie's owner – a stout humourless woman with a round head and round glasses. She glared at me with her round eyes.

'We could give you a discount if you like,' offered Jack.

'Very well,' said the woman, - 'but I don't want *her* next time. My poor Archie looks all moth-eaten – he'll have to wear a coat until his fur grows back. And what's that grey stuff around his nose?' After I explained, she left with Archie in a bit of a temper.

'We have got proper muzzles for the lively ones, you know,' said Jack, - 'so no need to Gaffa-tape his mouth shut next time, OK?'

'OK,' I said, - 'sorry Jack.'

'Onwards and upwards eh!' said Jack. 'Mrs Peake's coming in a minute with her cat – that should be fairly straightforward.'

Well, the day didn't really improve much after this. Jack put me back on washing and shampooing again to keep me out of trouble. The trouble was, that Mrs Peake's cat Fluffy escaped before I could put her in the bath, and ran amok. But it was hardly my fault, since Mrs Peake refused to let me put a harness on her. Anyway, Jack is really regretting not replacing that broken cover on the ventilation shaft. And who knew a cat could leap so high! It's amazing what you can do with an industrial vacuum cleaner though – we managed to suck Fluffy out of there in no time! Mrs Peake certainly lived up to her name, though, when she returned an hour later to discover her Persian Blue was unrecognisable.

'What's happened to Fluffy?' she shrieked when she saw that her beloved cat looked like he'd been dipped in engine oil and set alight. 'What have you done to my poor pussy?'

Jack tried to mollify her. 'Mrs Peake, I'm terribly sorry but he ran away and got into a bit of bother – not to worry though, we'll sort it out in a jiffy, won't we Dora?'

'Oh yes, Mrs Peake, she'll be as right as rain, don't you worry!' Fluffy mewed pathetically and dug her claws into my arm.

'How about a nice cup of tea?' suggested Jack to Mrs Peake, gently steering her away from the sorry sight and into the waiting room.

When it was time to go home, Jack was very good about it all. 'Don't worry Dora, we all make mistakes – I'm sure you'll get the hang of it soon. See you next week!' she said, waving me off. I'm sure I heard a big sigh, though, as she closed the door.

'So,' said Andrew when I got home, - 'how was your day?'

'Well, I did a bit of a hatchet job on a Westie, but not before I bound and gagged him, I nearly lopped off a Chow Chow's testicles, and Fluffy the cat will be traumatised forever. How was yours?'

'Well, quite good really,' said Andrew smugly. 'Your mum came and took Billy and Luke to the cinema and Tom and Flora went into town. I've had a very relaxing day!'

How irritating, I thought. I mean, how come when he has the kids to look after, along comes a do-gooder to take them off his hands! I'll have to have a word with my mother. I mean, honestly! Talk about jammy! Andrew needs to be reminded about what it's really like to be a responsible hands-on dad – it's the only way he's going to change his mind about this sudden desire to work from home.

Friday 5th April

My friend Suzie rang me today, from her daughter's flat in London. Whenever I refer to her these days, I can't help but prefix 'Suzie' with 'poor'. So, anyway, *poor* Suzie has been in the worst sort of pickle you could imagine. Suffice to say that she should never have gone into business with a woman of dubious origins and even more dubious credentials. A woman so ferociously coiffed and lacquered that you could stub your toe on her, is surely not to be trusted.

'It's good news, Dora!' she said excitedly. 'The CPS has dropped all the charges against me!'

'Oh, thank God for that!' I said, delighted for her. 'So, what's happened?'

'Well, there was nothing directly linking me with employing illegal immigrants or with running a brothel,' she said, – 'so they had to let me go!'

'Well, that's a huge relief,' I said. 'When are you coming home?'

'Sunday.'

'OK – I think we should celebrate – is Warren coming too?

'No, he's gone to Dubai on another contract. To be honest, I'm glad. It's been a terrible strain. He hasn't really forgiven me yet for investing that money and losing it all.'

'Well, £70,000 is quite a lot of money,' I said, remembering how shocked I was when she first told me.

'Well, I know, but you'd think he would be happy I'm not going to prison, wouldn't you?'

'Andrew,' I said, when she'd rung off, - 'why didn't you tell me that Suzie's been let off? She just told me the police have dropped all the charges!'

'Two words, Dora – *client confidentiality,*' he said, stuffily. 'I am not at liberty to divulge these things without the client's consent - it's not official yet.'

'But I'm your wife!' I protested.

'Even more reason,' he said.

'But Suzie's my friend!'

'Even more of a reason,' he said. 'Look Dora, just be glad it's all over! Suzie can go back to normality, you can go back to not worrying about her, and I can go back to not being nagged every five minutes about what's happening with her case!'

'Was it that bad?' I asked.

'Yes,' he said, smiling.

'Thank you for helping her, Andrew,' I said, giving him a big hug.

'Just doing my job.'

'That's the thing, though – you are *so* good at it! Why do you want to stop? I just don't understand.'

'I just want a break from it, Dora – I don't know if I do want to give it up – it's just that I've been doing it a long time and I want to explore another interest – like you do sometimes – remember the pottery class?'

'Let's not!' I said, laughing. *What an unmitigated disaster that was! Sometimes I think I must have a blind spot where men are concerned. I was oblivious to that tutor's ulterior motives when he invited me to a private demo in his cubby hole, and I thought all that winking was just an unfortunate twitch.*

'By the way, Andrew, Suzie is coming home on Sunday so we'll have to tell your parents – they can't carry on staying in her house – they've already been there much longer than planned.'

'Oh God! I'd almost forgotten about that,' said Andrew, frowning.

'I'd better go over there now and talk to them.'

Poor old Andrew, I thought, watching him go off in his car – to be lumbered with slightly bonkers hippies for parents is one thing, but *homeless* slightly bonkers hippy parents is something else. Ever since they were evicted from Tepee Valley, we've been trying to think of what to do with them. Andrew said Uruguay might be a good place for nature-loving nomads, especially when they've just legalised cannabis, but Bob and Barbara couldn't be persuaded. Andrew brought up his idea only last week but didn't get the response he was hoping for.

'You'd like it, Dad - the President lives in a tiny house and gives away 90% of his income to poor people. He grows his own veg and washes his own socks.'

'We can't go there, we don't speak Uruguayan,' said Bob.

'That doesn't matter,' said Andrew, - 'no one does – they speak Spanish!'

'All right, clever Dick,' said Bob, getting irate.

'You could smoke as much weed as you liked, Dad – doesn't that appeal to you?'

Of course, Bob got cross with him and an argument ensued, as is often the case with those two when they get together.

Anyway, something will have to be done – I don't think Suzie will want their rusty old camper van, Mabel, parked in her drive when she gets back. Suzie's neighbours have already complained to the council about unsightly vehicles ruining the view, and suspicious goings-on at the house.

Saturday 6th April

We opened the curtains this morning to grey sky and drizzle.

'Not very good weather for gardening, is it? Don't forget your wellies and waterproof coat,' I said to Andrew.

'Hmph,' he said. 'Those dogs have got a lot to answer for. I was hoping to go with the boys to see Shillingsworth play Tuffington today.'

'Well, they'll probably lose again, so you won't be missing much.'

'That's not the point, Dora. Football is something the boys and I can do together – they'll be missing out!'

'I can take them,' I said.

'Oh, OK,' he said, resentfully.

'Go on or you'll be late,' I said.

'Bloody dogs,' said Andrew, banging the door on his way out.

'Well, you *are* to blame,' I told Fudge and Cocoa, who looked a bit startled. 'Poor Andrew is having to go and sort out your mess – and not for the first time.'

They looked innocent and wagged their tails. Any attention is better than none.

'Remember what you did last year?' I said to them. They looked dumbly at me.

'Well, I do!' I said. 'You got into Miss Pearly's greenhouse, didn't you! You ate all her tomatoes and knocked down her seed trays and then, as if that wasn't enough, you decided it would be fun to get a bucket stuck on your head, didn't you! I looked at Fudge. He wagged his tail eagerly because 'bucket' sounds a bit like 'biscuit', and he's ever hopeful where food is concerned. 'And then,' I said to him, - 'you couldn't see anything, so you panicked, didn't you!'

Miss Pearly was incandescent the day the dogs smashed eight panes of glass in her brand new bespoke cedarwood greenhouse, ruining her Surecrop strawberry plants, and mangling her Blushing Cherry tomatoes. And who could blame her! I was mortified. I couldn't look her in the eye at the Co-Op for months after that. Mind you, the dogs did suffer the consequences of consuming large quantities of squishy red fruit in one sitting, and had to stay outside for two days until they became socially acceptable again. And Fudge is now very wary of anything resembling a bucket.

Shillingsworth's football ground is mostly just that – a pitch. There is a small wooden hut for changing in, but that's it. After lunch, I dropped the boys off in the rain to go and watch their home town get thrashed by the Tuffington Wanderers, and decided to go and see my mother. She's been behaving slightly oddly recently, I think, although Andrew says I'm overreacting. My sister, Jess, agrees with me though, that we need to keep a sharp eye on her. I'm sure if Andrew's mother had suddenly taken up with a Worzel Gummidge character for a boyfriend, he would have something to say about it. Anyway, he thinks my mother should be allowed to date who she likes since Dad died four years ago, and it's none of our business. But even Billy thinks he's odd – only the other day he asked why Reggie had a mouse in his pocket and string round his trousers. And I'm not keen on his pesky Jack Russell (Tinker), either. 'Yap, yap, yap,' all the time – it would drive me mad living next door to that! In fact, it did used to drive Mum mad, but for some strange reason, she seems to have forgotten about it. He must have put some sort of spell on her.

When I got to Mum's house, I could hear the radio blaring away in the kitchen – I had to knock really hard to get her attention.

'Oh, sorry, Dora,' she said, opening the door. 'We've been listening to Desert Island Discs – it was Dame Edna – what a funny woman!'

'She's a he,' I said.

'Oh, poor soul,' said my mum, - 'I suppose they didn't do operations for that back then.'

Sometimes I wonder whether my mother might have a missing sprocket or two – well it would explain the dalliance with ragtag Reggie perhaps.

'Reggie, it's Dora!' said my Mum.

'Here again then,' I said, ungraciously.

Honestly, he seems to be here every time I visit – he might as well move in.

'I'll be on my way then, Ruth,' said Reggie, getting up to leave.

'Oh, you don't have to go, do you?' said Mum, - 'it's *Gardeners' Question Time* next – you love that programme!'

'S'all right – I'll listen to it at 'ome – I won't be able to hear it here over you two yacking anyways.'

'Bye, Reggie,' I said as he went off out through the back door. I looked at Mum expectantly.

'Oh, we've made a gap in the fence so Reggie can come in through the back door – makes things easier,' said Mum.

'What do you mean 'things'?' I said.

'Well, it just stops the neighbours gossiping,' said Mum. 'You know what people are like. Cup of tea, Dora?'

Andrew came home at tea time looking shattered. He kicked off his muddy boots and coat and flopped into his armchair by the TV.

'My back's killing me,' he said, wincing.

'Well, you're not used to hard labour, Andrew,' I said.

'Cyril made me dig his entire vegetable plot today – I mean, talk about slave driver!'

'You missed the match,' said Tom, rubbing it in.

'I'll run you a nice hot bath,' I said to him.

Later, I told him about Mum's arrangement with Reggie.

'Well,' he said, - 'we used to have gaps in the hedge at home – so all of us kids could play together. It was great – we could come and go as we pleased.'

'Well, that's what I mean! I'm not happy about it at all – Reggie can go in and out as if he owns the place – I don't know what Mum was thinking!'

'I think it's romantic,' piped up Flora, always ready to contradict my point of view. 'If they get married, I can be a bridesmaid, and the boys can all be page boys – it would be so cool!'

I pictured the scene and instantly repelled the ghastly image from my mind. 'Flora, your Nan would *never* marry someone called 'Bunion', so you can forget that idea.'

Sunday 7th April

After breakfast, Andrew said we'd better go and help Bob and Barbara pack up. I know from experience that Andrew's parents don't need any help with packing. What Andrew really meant was that we'd better go and check for any scenes of mass-destruction or stockpiles of useless items from scavenging in skips – Bob's favourite hobby. Last time we were there, there was a filthy old caravan parked in the drive, piles of rotting vegetables from the end-of-day 'bargain' hour at the market, and mountains of other people's garden refuse.

'It's good kindling,' said Bob, when we questioned him about the hedge-clippings.

'But Dad, you can't go around every week raiding other people's wheelie bins for sticks – not round here anyway,' Andrew told him sternly.

'I don't see why not!' Bob said.

'Well, you'll upset Suzie's neighbours,' Andrew responded, slightly exasperated.

'I think it's a bit late for that,' I whispered to Andrew when Bob wasn't looking.

The council had already been there with clipboards and cameras the week before.

'You'll have to move that eyesore,' Andrew told Bob at the time, pointing at the derelict caravan.

I managed to persuade Billy and Luke to come with us, to avoid any ructions. If I leave them home alone, I usually regret it. When we arrived at Suzie's, I was relieved to see that the caravan had gone. Unfortunately, though, there was a pile of rubble in the drive instead.

'Oh, for God's sake!' said Andrew, when he saw it. 'What's that doing there?' We parked on the road, since the drive was blocked, and went inside.

'Well,' said Bob, defending himself, 'I found the rocks in the garden not serving any useful purpose, so I thought people might like them for building walls or something. It's good to share things around, Andy. You know – what's one man's rubbish is another man's treasure!'

'Yes, Andy,' said Barbara, - 'your Dad's always thinking of others, bless him!'

Andrew rolled his eyes. 'But Dad, Suzie's back today and she can't get on to her own driveway.' But Bob wasn't listening and had already wandered off.

'We've put notes through people's doors to come and take the rocks if they want – I don't suppose they'll be there for long,' said Barbara. 'Your Dad wanted to make a flat area near the pond for us to do our Tai chi in the mornings.'

This was obviously a new thing, as I hadn't heard them mention it before.

'Tai chi?'

'Yes Dora, it balances your Yin and Yang ready for the day ahead. You should try it – it's very good for stress. By the way, I've made Suzie a present as a thank you – what do you think?' She held up a large cloth and some small matching squares.

*Oh Lord, I thought, that looks like the outrageously expensive wedding dress material Suzie's daughter, Violet, ordered. Barbara's chopped it up to make a table cloth and matching napkins! I'll have to hide it all as soon as they've gone - Suzie must **never** find out! Honestly, Andrew's parents seem to have no respect for other people's property! Andrew says it's since they started believing in Karl Marx.*

'Private property should be abolished,' ranted Bob one day when he was visiting us. This was after a spat with our neighbour when he 'borrowed' their whirligig washing post.

'They weren't using it for anything!' said Bob at the time.

'But Dad, you can't just go into someone's garden and take things!' Andrew had shouted at him. Bob's a very stubborn person though, and ploughs his own furrow regardless.

'Well, we'd better be off,' said Barbara, opening Mabel's creaking passenger door and climbing in.

'Well, it was nice seeing you,' said Andrew, looking a bit too pleased to see them go. 'Let us know where you are, won't you?'

'No worries,' said Bob, lighting up a joint for the trip.

'What are we going to do with all this?' I said to Andrew, as Mabel set off noisily down the road in a cloud of black smoke.

'Move it back,' he said, sighing heavily. 'The boys will help.'

'Not without a bribe,' I said.

So, most of the day was spent wheel-barrowing rocks backwards and forwards until we'd made a nice neat pile in the corner of the garden. I checked around Suzie's house for any obvious problems but it all seemed OK, apart from a pile of washing-up to do, and fridge clearing. It was a novelty, of course, for Bob and Barbara to have access to a fridge, and they seemed to have stuffed it with all sorts of odd things.

'Urrgh!' said Billy, when I showed him a pot of maggots. 'Why did Grandad have those in there?'

'To have on toast, of course,' said Andrew. Billy looked horrified.

'Dad's joking,' I said. 'They're for fishing.'

Discarding a giant bowl of fermenting nettle soup and some pigeon carcasses, I wondered how they would adapt to normal life again when they got old. I mean, you can't catch your own food when you're 96 and pushing a Zimmer frame around, can you? And who's going to spend hours boiling up woodland vegetation and bits of bark for you then?

Andrew complained about his back all the way home. 'My back's killing me!' he said, lying down as soon as we got in. He flopped onto the sofa and switched on the TV.

'What's wrong with Dad?' said Flora.

'He's allergic to exercise,' I said. 'As soon as he does any, his body reacts very badly and the defence mechanism kicks in, telling his brain he must lie down immediately and do nothing. He can move his eyes in order to watch the football match, which just happens to be starting right now, but moving anything else could prove fatal.'

'I heard that,' said Andrew from the lounge. 'I really am in pain, you know!'

Monday 8th April

Back to school – yippee!! As usual, we had the first-day-back morning mayhem - not helped by Andrew moaning about his back and getting in everyone's way, or by Tom and Luke falling out over who ate all the Chocosplits.

'You're such a greedy pig,' said Tom to Luke.

'It wasn't me, four-eyes!' said Luke.

'Shut up, fatso!' said Tom, poking Luke in the stomach.

Then Andrew joined in. 'Where's my coffee mug? Someone's used my mug!'

'Well, use another one then,' was my obvious answer.

'But I want *my* mug!' he said.

'Is this what my life has come to?' I asked myself. Honestly, it's like a madhouse here in the mornings – why can't my family behave in a civilised, sensible way? Why can't they be helpful and co-operative? I'm sure my friend Melanie's kids don't go on like this.

'Other people don't fight like you lot!' I said, - 'why can't you all be civilised? I bet Melanie's boys can have breakfast without starting World War Three!'

'What – James and Peter?' scoffed Tom.

'Yes,' I said, - 'they know how to behave nicely.'

'They are *soooo* boring,' said Luke. 'They make model aeroplanes and spend all day painting them.'

'That's very rude Luke!' I said. 'They are lovely boys, not doing anyone any harm – it would be nice if you were a bit more like that.'

'Yeah Luke!' said Tom, sniggering.

'I had a train set when I was your age,' said Andrew nostalgically. 'I used to spend hours in the attic playing with it.'

'That was in the old days Dad. Only saddos do that now. We've got X-Box!'

It's such a relief when they all finally leave the house in the mornings. I feel a great sense of achievement that they remain relatively unscathed, their uniforms intact (mostly), and they all have the correct implements, books, and government-vetted snacks on board.

I made myself a revivifying cup of tea and rang Suzie.

'How are you, Suzie? Glad to be home?'

'Dora, it's so wonderful to come home – I can't tell you what a worry it's all been. Your husband is a miracle worker! I can get on with my life now, but you know, I don't think I can have been in my right mind before – my kitchen cupboards are full of rotting vegetables which I don't remember buying. I don't even like turnips!'

'That was Andrew's parents, Suzie – I told you they were a bit eccentric.'

'Well, I suppose that accounts for the appalling smell coming from my dustbin.'

'I wouldn't look in there if I were you,' I advised her. 'I've seen the contents for myself and it's not a pretty sight.'

*Bob must have decided that burying body parts in the garden didn't work very well after Fudge and Cocoa dug them up again. I must say, though, that although I quite liked his squirrel and pigeon pie, I think I'd want a **bit** more culinary variety.*

'By the way, Dora, do you know what's happened to my rockery? It seems to have gone missing!'

'Ahhh, yes, I'm sorry about that, Suzie. I don't think Bob and Barbara realised that it was ornamental – I'm afraid they've changed the layout a bit.'

'A bit! It's completely flattened, Dora!'

I got off the phone before she could find anything else to complain about. It's good to see her back to her normal self though. I wish *my* only worry was the configuration of my rock garden. As it is, my head is spinning with all the worries I've got. Andrew with his mad scheme to put us all into penury, Flora with her flouncing about and stropping over nothing, Tom with his abysmal attempt to do revision for his GCSE's, Luke with his irrepressible attraction to mischief, and Billy who would follow a lemming over a cliff if someone told him it would be worth his while. Then there's my mother and her new-found beau …. I can't even think about that. And my job is definitely not as relaxing as I imagined it would be – I've had several quite disturbing dreams since I started working there, involving frenzied scissor-chopping and rapidly rising rivers of foam.

Jess rang me today, just to add to my list of worries.

'Oh, hello Dora, is everything OK?'

'Yes, mostly,' I lied. Well, Jess isn't particularly sympathetic to other people's problems.

'I hope you don't mind me calling, but Terry and I want to go away for a couple of days and we wondered if you could step in. It's only for two days…'

'Oh, yes, OK,' I said.

'Oh, that's great. Thanks - it's next week – Thursday and Friday. OK?'

'I think so,' I said. I was already regretting it as I put down the phone.

'What on earth did you say 'yes' for?' said Andrew as we were going to bed.

'Well, she caught me on the hop…'

'Honestly, Dora, last time you were left in charge of the bakery it was a disaster – I'm surprised she asked you!'

'Well that's not very supportive of you, Andrew! Anyway, you're exaggerating – it wasn't a total disaster!'

'OK, not total, just mostly …'

'Well, I tried my best, but Jess and Terry have been running Paradise Bakery for several years now – they can't just expect me to know what to do in every situation…'

Andrew said nothing and went back to reading his book.

It's true that last time I was left in charge things didn't go too well, but I'm sure I won't make the same mistakes twice. This time I'll be sure to remove things from the oven before they burn and cause the fire alarms to go off, and I'll definitely try not to drop any foreign objects into the dough.

Tuesday 9th April

Jack wasn't too pleased when I told her I would need Thursday off to help my sister out.

'You've only been here a week, Dora old girl, you can't just take orf when you feel like it, you know,' she said crossly.

The rest of the day didn't go too well after that. Queenie's owner came in complaining that her dog had developed a rash after her exposure to the soap overdose and that some of her fur had fallen off. It took Jack a while to talk the woman out of contacting Animal Welfare and I heard my name mentioned more than once from behind the office door.

'Don't worry,' said Bertie. 'It took me a while to get used to everything. When I first came here, I'd never even used a brush before.'

I looked at the long tatty trestles of hair hanging down her sloping shoulders and wondered how long it took dreadlocks to form by themselves.

'And,' she continued whilst out of earshot of Jack, - '*she's* not perfect, anyway! I saw her spray someone's dog with Febreeze once, 'cos she was too busy to wash it.'

The office door opened at this point and Queenie's owner marched past giving me a scornful glance.

'I suppose,' I said to Bertie as the woman went out, - 'Jack could dock my wages if she wanted to.'

Bertie gave me a funny look. 'We don't get paid, Dora, didn't you know? It's voluntary!'

'You're joking!' said Andrew later when I told him. 'Didn't you ask about pay when you were interviewed?'

'No,' I said sheepishly. 'It didn't come up.'

'No wonder no one else applied for it! Honestly, Dora!'

I don't know why it didn't occur to me to ask the obvious question, but it just didn't. It's all very well Andrew getting on his high horse, but he's far from perfect himself! However, I decided not to reel off all his faults at this particular moment – I was feeling rather weary and not in the mood for bickering.

So, it's back to square one again on the job hunting front. The truth is, my life is busy enough without the added encumbrance of having to fit in a job as well. Mind you, if Andrew is going to be at home soon, I'll need something to escape to – I can't possibly spend every waking hour in his company – he'll drive me mad, or we'll drive each other mad, if it's not too late already.

Wednesday 10th April

I hadn't seen Suzie for a while, so I decided to go and visit her this morning and take the dogs down to the common.

'It's so lovely to get back to normal life,' said Suzie, as she put Ping-Pong down to run off after Fudge and Cocoa.

'What are you going to do with the shop?' I ventured to ask. 'I mean, it's been closed now for weeks.'

'Well, Warren has had to take on responsibility for the lease, and the landlord has agreed that we can sub-let it, so we just need to find someone else to rent it. It'll need a bit of work though.'

That was certainly true – all those pink neon signs, mirror tiles and red fluffy wallpaper would have to go.

'Unless you want another massage business to take it on – then you wouldn't have to do anything.'

'There's no way,' said Suzie emphatically, - 'that I want another business like that in there – I only just escaped prison by the skin of my teeth! Violet still hasn't introduced me to her fiancé Oliver's parents yet – in case they saw it all in the papers!'

'Oh Suzie,' I said, - 'it was the local rag – no one outside Shillingsworth probably knew anything about it!'

'Well, my daughter is very highly strung – the slightest thing puts her on edge. Only yesterday I told her I couldn't find the material for her wedding dress – you know we had it sent over from France. Anyway, I couldn't find it anywhere and so now she's having a complete fit over it!'

'I thought Violet had changed her mind about that fabric?' I said.

'Yes, but we still need to send it back and re-order.'

Stupidly, I had hoped this problem would just sort of evaporate.

'Oh dear,' I said weakly. 'How's Warren?' I said, changing the subject quickly.

'Oh, Ok I suppose. He'll be in Dubai for six weeks and it's a relief not to have to see his disapproving expression any more. How about Andrew?'

'I think he's gone a bit funny – you know – a sort of mid-life crisis.'

Suzie looked intrigued and I explained his latest revelation. She was dutifully sympathetic.

'Men can be so thoughtless sometimes, can't they! Fancy thinking that he can just give up work like that.'

'Quite!' I said, though this was slightly tempered by the fact that I was about to give up my own job.

'But technically it's not a job, is it?' Suzie said, when I told her. 'Because you're not being paid, are you? Strictly speaking, it's charity work.'

I thought about this as we strolled along by the river, and suddenly a light went on in my head – one of those Eureka moments when you wonder why it didn't occur to you before. I decided to keep quiet about it for now though as I need to think it through properly.

Thursday 11th April

This morning Tom took so long in the shower I began to wonder if he'd gone back to sleep in there.

'For God's sake!' shouted Flora from outside the door. 'Some of us have a life to get on with!'

'It's usually you who takes ages', I was tempted to say, but didn't. I do try not to sink to their level.

'What's he doing in there?' said Luke, overfilling his bowl of cereal so that half of it went all over the table.

'He's got a GIANT zit on his head,' said Billy gleefully. 'I saw him jabbing it with scissors.'

'Yuck!' said Luke.

'Gross!' said Flora.

'Look you lot, you are not to say anything to him when he comes down. OK?'

Needless to say, I was wasting my breath. Tom finally appeared at the table with a large sticking plaster across his forehead and it only took a second or two.

'You look weird,' said Billy. Then everything erupted including Tom's boil which he'd over-stabbed, so it was bleeding profusely down his nose and into his cornflakes.

I made the others leave for school and found a bigger plaster.

'Just tell your friends you cut it on a cupboard door or something. They won't know,' I advised him. 'Or that the cat attacked you.'

That scenario was perfectly within the realms of possibility anyway. Scratch has always been a bit volatile and lacking in social graces, but recently he's been behaving in a particularly aggressive fashion. Ever since he started suffering from agoraphobia he's got much worse. That white cat, Clinton, from up the road is definitely to blame – coming into our garden as brazen as you like – I never thought Scratch would be afraid of anything. Maybe I should get him some professional help. We've tried just about everything else.

Anyway, I was just tidying up and putting the bread back in the breadbin when I suddenly remembered - *Oh help! I'm supposed to be looking after the bakery today!!*

By the time I got there, the delivery man had dumped a pallet-load of sugar right in front of the building, blocking the doorway.

'Honestly! What stupid twit did this!' I said loudly, when I saw it.

'Me,' said a man on a forklift behind me.

'Oh!' I said, - 'um ... sorry, but the thing is, I can't get in!'

'I'll have you know I've been doing this job for twenty years and I've won 'Best Employee' twice in a row!' He scowled down at me. 'Do you know that if there's no one to receive the delivery, we're supposed to take it away again? I've a good mind to do just that. You'll be charged for re-delivery as well.'

'Oh – well look, I'm really sorry – err, Wilf,' I said seeing his name badge. Please don't take it away again,' I said grovelling. 'I'm very grateful that you waited. Do you think you could just move that pallet a bit so I can get in? I'll make you a nice cup of tea.'

He cheered up then, particularly when I mentioned fresh muffins. I then had to listen to forty-five minutes of his current troubles, namely the unremitting road works on the M40, and the tragic demise of his pet cat from an anxiety attack. I was struggling to pay attention at this point.

'I'm sorry, Wilf, but I really need to get on,' I told him, showing him out.

Jess had left me a note as long as my arm. Typical of her! I looked at the list.

Dora

1. *Listen to answer phone messages.*
2. *Cut, shape and bake dough (50 baps and 65 tins). Like Terry showed you. Don't burn them.*

3. *Ice cake (in cupboard). They want yellow.*
4. *Make 25 gingerbread men (recipe on counter). No funny faces!*
5. *Make 20 cheese straws (recipe on counter)*
6. *Make 100 cupcakes – Katie will come in and do all the fancy icing as she's better at it than you.*
7. *Fill 30 lemon tarts (filling in fridge).*
8. *Order 10 pints of milk, 30 packs of butter and 10 pints of cream from Farmfresh Dairies for Monday.*
9. *Wash down kitchen including ovens and floor before you leave. Switch off lights and lock door when you leave.*

Well really! What a cheek! My sister seems to think I'm incapable of thinking for myself! And that bit about icing things – that was really unfair! I'm quite good at decorating – that's one of my skills, being a creative person. And, when am I supposed to find time for lunch? She's such a slave-driver! No wonder her poor husband Terry always looks so miserable.

Anyway, I dutifully went and listened to the messages. The first one was from Katie, saying she couldn't come in to help, as her septic toe had flared up again. The next message was from Jess saying that Terry was suffering a bit from last night's take-away because he shouldn't really eat curry as it doesn't suit him and she *had* told him not to…anyway, could I please throw away the rest of it which he'd left in the fridge, even though she'd expressly asked him *not* to put it in there. She signed off saying '*don't burn the bread, Dora*'. My sister really can be very irritating.

The next five messages were people ordering things which I wrote down with difficulty, as I'd forgotten my glasses in my rush to leave the house.

By the time I'd put all the sugar away in the store room, it was lunch time. Honestly, I don't know how I was supposed to get through all that work without Jess and Terry's assistant, Katie to help.

By the end of the day, I was cream-crackered! Jess would be pleased though, as I did manage to bake all the bread without burning it even slightly this time. The only thing that went a bit wrong was that I knocked Wilf's half-drunk mug of tea all over the counter and it was quite difficult to read Jess's recipe sheets even after I'd dried them out on the oven top. I could really have done with my glasses too because Jess's writing is quite hard to read at the best of times. Anyway, I was very glad to finally lock up and go home for tea.

'How'd it go?' asked Andrew when I got in. 'Any fires, floods, mass poisonings?'

'No – everything's fine,' I said, giving him a scornful look - 'how about you?'

'Just another boring day at the office. Do you know, Dora, I can feel the heavy burden of responsibility slowly lifting from my shoulders at the thought of a new direction – a light twinkling at the end of a long dark tunnel….'

'Scratch has pooed on the sofa!' said Billy, putting a stop to Andrew's soliloquy.

'Scratch needs to see a psychologist,' I told Andrew later on as we got ready for bed.

'What! Don't be ridiculous, Dora!' He said, predictably.

'He's not himself,' I said. 'He's refusing to go out and now he's started a poo protest – he's obviously depressed! And have you noticed how fat he's getting? He's probably got an eating disorder or something.'

Andrew sighed heavily. 'Sometimes, Dora,' he said, 'I think I'm caught up in some sort of mad dream that I can't wake up from.'

Friday 12th April

Wilf was there again this morning when I got to the bakery, with another delivery. I offered him a cup of tea again, as he looked so miserable.

'Me and the Mrs, we're missing our cat something terrible,' he told me.

'Oh dear!' I said, glancing at the clock and wondering how on earth I was going to get through Jess's list by the end of the day. 'I'll tell you something,' he said, jabbing a finger in the air. 'If I find out who was responsible for poor Fluffy's untimely end, I'll swing for 'em!'

'Fluffy?' I said, suddenly feeling slightly nauseous.

'Yes – my daughter Hillary's choice, not mine. I wanted something more heroic - you know, like Horatio, or Wellington. Anyway, doesn't matter now, does it, 'cos he's been taken from us in an act of unspeakable callousness!' Tears welled up in his eyes.

'I'm sorry to hear that,' I said, trying to be sympathetic. 'Perhaps you should think about getting another cat...'

'What! Certainly not! We can't replace him just like that! My wife can't even bear to empty the cat litter tray at the moment!'

Luckily for me, the phone rang. 'Sorry, Wilf but I've got to go - my sister is here tomorrow though. I'm sure she'd love to hear all about it.'

There was no time to waste - I had so much to do! Anyway, I thought I did pretty well in the end without Katie to help. I had to guess a bit with the recipes Jess left because of the tea spillage, but I'm a resourceful person and I think I managed to work it all out eventually. I must say, I thought Jess's lemon filling smelt a bit funny though, and it had lumps in it which is a bit unusual. Oh well, it's not for me to worry I suppose – she has her own way of doing things. I thought my cheese straws came out well though, and my gingerbread men were almost perfect, except that fifteen of them had cracked and lost their arms and legs. Nothing that couldn't be fixed with a bit of glue to stick them back together though, and once they were decorated you couldn't see the joins at all. I did have a bit of fun decorating them, despite being told not to by Jess. Well, I couldn't help it! She probably won't notice anyway, being so busy all the time. The last hour was spent icing the cake and the buns. The thing was, though, that I couldn't find yellow colouring anywhere. I searched high and low for it. I mean, I do think that if you're going to be icing lots of cakes, you'd have the right ingredients to hand, wouldn't you? I eventually found a little bottle of it in completely the wrong place. Honestly! Who puts food colouring in the cutlery drawer! Anyway, it's a good job I found it, because I was just about to give up and do green instead – there was plenty of that, of course, due to the Kermit cake order last month.

I think that the contents might be a bit past the sell-by date though, because the finished effect was more beige than yellow, so I stuck some Maltesers on it to jazz it up a bit.

Saturday 13th April

Jess really has a knack of ringing at the most awkward times. I was just trying to tempt Scratch into his travel cage with some giblets so I could take him to Dr Megg - the cat psychotherapist - when she rang up. She was in such a flap over something, but I really couldn't spare the time. She was saying something about someone called Sue, but I didn't have time for a long chat.

'I'll call you this afternoon, Jess,' I said. She was still gabbling away when I had to put the phone down. Honestly, doesn't she think about anyone else but herself?

It turned out, that Dr Megg lived about half an hour away in a small farm cottage and it took me a while to find her. Inside there were cats everywhere. Scratch instantly hid at the back of his cage, ears back and tail like a bottle brush.

'I need to see him alone,' she said, indicating I should wait in another room.

'Oh, right,' I said.

I did as instructed, and waited for what felt like an eon in the ante-room which smelt of rotting cat food and rising damp. Eventually she opened the door.

'I'm going to have to see him again,' she said. 'He has a severe inferiority complex, probably relating to his home environment.' She peered sternly at me over her glasses.

'What do you mean?' I asked.

'Well, he's feeling very insecure - he's not being given the sort of attention he needs. You're plainly giving him food instead of affection as he's so obviously obese. And, I would say his name doesn't help either – it makes him feel disrespected – he feels he's not taken seriously enough, so basically he has very low self-esteem.'

'Really?' I said, amazed at her powers of deduction.

'I'm more of a Cat Whisperer than a therapist,' she said. 'I can hear their thoughts.' She smiled a cat-like smile and it suddenly dawned on me how like a cat she was – she even had pointy ears and whiskers.

'That'll be £65 please, Mrs Loveday,' she said, extending a paw. 'Shall we say the same time next week?'

As I put Scratch in the car, I'm sure I heard her meowing.

When I got home, everyone had gone out except Andrew.

'Jess has been on the phone again,' he said. 'She says she needs to speak to you urgently.'

'Oh, that sounds ominous,' I said. 'Didn't she say why?'

'Well, she mentioned a few things…' Andrew hesitated, - 'something about an old people's home threatening to sue the Bakery for trying to poison some old ladies with lemon tarts that tasted of Chicken Korma. Then there were the gingerbread transsexuals that didn't go down too well at the Freemason's charity coffee morning today. In fact, apparently, Mr Cratchit, the Master of Ceremonies' denture snapped in two when he bit into one of them – he's very unhappy about it.'

'That must have been the glue,' I said, biting my lip.

'Glue!' exclaimed Andrew.

'Yes, I used some glue to stick the broken ones back together…'

'What sort of glue?' asked Andrew, appalled.

'Well I could only find some Araldite – I thought it would be OK.'

'Good Grief Dora! That stuff sets like a rock! And it's toxic!'

'Whoops,' I said, - 'I only used a tiny bit…'

'You'll have to go over and see Jess, Dora,' said Andrew in his bossy lawyer's voice. 'There were some other things she needs to talk to you about anyway.'

'Oh dear! I've made a bit of a mess of things this time …'

'I suspect that is an understatement,' said Andrew most unhelpfully.

I grabbed a sandwich quickly, got in the car and drove reluctantly to the Bakery where Jess was waiting to boil me in oil.

'What were you thinking of!' she said, holding up my ginger person with pink knickers and sporting a large moustache. 'And,' she said angrily, - 'what possessed you to use glue on them? Are you completely mad?'

'Sorry, Jess. I just thought it'd be fun to do something different for a change, and I'm sorry but it didn't occur to me about the glue being harmful – I really did only use a little bit.'

She scowled at me and carried on ranting. 'All the cupcakes you made have been sent back because apparently they're so full of salt they're inedible – didn't you read the recipe properly? It's teaspoons of salt, not tablespoons! And the cheese straws are like cheese rods – unbreakable! Goodness knows what you did to that recipe! The only saving grace is that the bread delivery went smoothly.'

I felt myself shrinking like a woolly hat in the hot-wash.

'And to top it all, I thought I asked you to throw that curry away, Dora! I can't believe you used it for the tarts! Didn't you see my lemon filling in the fridge? In this bowl!' She held up a glass bowl and waved it in my face. 'Didn't you think it was a bit odd to find lemon filling in an aluminium container with a cardboard lid saying, 'Aloo Palace'? Honestly Dora, didn't you have your glasses on?'

'Jess, anyone could've made that mistake,' said Terry, coming to my rescue. 'I mean, they do look similar…' She glowered at him and he decided not to make any further suggestions for his own safety.

'Well, I did have to do everything without Katie here to help me,' I said. 'I was on my own and there was such a lot to do.'

'And please tell me what happened with this?' Jess said, pointing at the dung-coloured cake which overnight seemed to have developed some rather interesting dark green veins. 'What did you use to colour the icing?' she asked.

I explained how I couldn't find the usual one and how I'd come across an old one in the drawer. Jess was silent for a minute or two.

'You mean this?' she said, going to the drawer and getting it out.

'Yes, that's it,' I said, - 'the label's come off but it looked OK to use.'

Jess looked at me with astonishment. 'This,' she said, 'is Katy's ointment for her septic toe.'

'Oh.'

'Now I'm going to have to chuck the whole thing out and start again.'

'Can't you just scrape it off?' I dared to suggest.

'No,' said Jess. 'I've had enough complaints already – I don't need another one saying my cakes taste of TCP. Anyway, you also took the liberty of covering it in Maltesers. The customer who ordered this cake is lactose intolerant Dora.'

'Oh, I'm really sorry Jess,' I said. 'What can I do to help rectify things?'

'Nothing,' she said. 'Oh, and by the way, thanks a bunch for telling whinging Wilf that he can come and have a cup of tea and a chat in the mornings! I haven't got time to listen to his hard-luck tales! I've got a business to run!'

I decided to go out with the dogs on my own to the park when I got back from seeing Jess. I needed to unwind and de-stress. She can be so critical sometimes – I don't know how Terry puts up with her. She's really upset me this time though – and well, I know things went a bit pear-shaped, but what about thanking me for stepping in and helping her out at the last minute! She's so ungrateful at times. It's not the end of the world, is it, if one or two old ladies got a bit of a surprise, and a few stuffy old blokes didn't like my creative biscuits, or that I accidentally doused the cake in TCP – I didn't actually poison anyone, did I? I mean, nobody died, did they?

Sunday 14th April

'I'm going to have a nice quiet day today,' announced Andrew when he woke up this morning.

'Really!' I said. *There's no such thing in our house, so I wasn't sure what secret plan he had to guarantee such a thing.*

'I'm going to get on with my novel – I've already planned out the main characters and the plot.'

'What's it called, Andrew?' I asked him.

'Well, I'm toying with *Coldfinger*, *Die Another Way*, or possibly something simple like *Stabbed*.'

'I see,' I said. 'Well, you can always change it later I suppose…'

'I don't know, Dora - a bit of support would be good instead of pouring cold water on my ideas!' he said, getting cross.

'Sorry, Andrew. You mustn't be so sensitive though – I mean you have to get used to the odd bit of criticism you know. Anyway, I'm sure it'll be very good once you get going,' I said, suddenly remembering that I need Andrew on-side when I tell him about my secret moneymaking scheme. I've decided to put it past my friend Melanie first though.

After breakfast Tom said he was going to the cinema and Flora said she was going out with her boyfriend Matthew.

'What about your revision?' Andrew said to them both.

'It's cool Dad, don't stress,' said Tom.

'Yeah,' said Flora, - 'we are doing *loads* of revising.'

'I'm very interested to know,' said Andrew, - 'when it takes place, because you both seem to have a lot of other things going on.'

'Chill, Dad,' said Flora, - 'we've got it covered.'

'Well,' said Andrew, as they sauntered off up the road, - 'I suppose we can't tie them to their desks, can we?'

The trouble is, there's no sense of urgency with any of my children. They just don't seem to see the necessity of putting effort into something until it's too late and then there'll be tears and they'll only have themselves to blame.

'We've got to get them to take these exams more seriously, Dora,' Andrew said, - 'or they'll never leave home! Imagine that!'

I'd rather not. A ghastly image filled my mind: What an awful thought – four feckless failures draining us of all our hard-earned money! Like hungry vultures waiting for us to fall off our perches, fighting over a few pathetic scraps…

'Maybe we should give them an incentive, Andrew. We could say to them that if they do well in the exams, we'll pay for a new laptop or something….'

'I'm not sure I agree with that, Dora – it's bribery.'

'I know.'

'I think we should just tell them that if they don't do well, they will have to get a job and move out.'

'Andrew! You can't do that, that's worse than bribery, that's blackmail! Anyway, that's an awful way to treat your own flesh and blood. I can't believe you're even thinking it!'

'Life isn't a bed of roses, Dora. They need to learn some harsh truths – they can't expect to be supported for ever!'

Sometimes I'm not sure I like my husband very much. I do wonder if he even thinks about the things he says or considers the consequences. He's so uncompromising! I daren't tell him about the Cat Whisperer – he'll think I'm wasting our money and that I've definitely lost my marbles.

'I'm going into the study now to write,' he announced, and put up the 'Do Not Disturb' sign on the door.

'What's he doing in there?' asked Luke.

'Daddy has decided to write a novel,' I told him. Luke looked perplexed.

'Will it be like my Spider-Man books?' asked Billy with more enthusiasm.

'I don't think so – it's more of a murder mystery.'

'Is he going to be famous?'

'No, Billy,' I said with certainty, - 'I'm afraid not.'

'Oh,' said Billy, disappointed.

'Why is he doing it then?'

'Well, that's a good question. Sometimes grown-ups need to have a hobby – something fun to do that isn't work.'

'Like making Lego cars and Plasticine animals?' suggested Billy.

'Why can't he play football or play on X-Box?' asked Luke. 'Writing's for geeks. It's so boring!'

'Don't be rude, Luke. Everyone has different interests. Anyway, you won't always be obsessed with football and X-Box – you'll grow out of those things eventually.'

Luke looked horrified. 'No way!' he said. 'Come on Billy, let's go outside.' They both went off into the garden to destroy more shrubs with their football and annoy the neighbours with lots of shouting. After a few minutes Andrew emerged from his study looking cross.

'How can I be expected to write with that racket going on! It's like a madhouse here – I can't think properly!'

I rang Melanie and suggested we all meet up in the park. Her two boys (James and Peter) are about the same age as Billy and

Luke. We left Andrew on his own, and quite frankly I was glad to – the miserable old killjoy! I hope his book isn't as joyless as he is, or it will definitely be a massive flop.

It was great to catch up with Melanie again – it's been quite a while since we came back from our holiday together. My boys were a bit luke-warm about meeting up with James and Peter though.

'They're so boring,' moaned Luke as we walked along the road to the park.

'It's only for an hour or two!' I said. 'It won't kill you.'

'But Peter says football is for morons.'

Reflecting on the obvious irony of Luke's comment, I wondered whether it would be worth giving him a lecture on empathy, but changed my mind when Billy piped up saying: 'He likes stick insects though. Peter's got loads!'

Luke went quiet for a bit. 'OK, but stick insects are even more boring than model planes and stuff.'

'Well, I don't care what you say, Luke! Peter likes them! I'm not playing with you now!' Billy said crossly.

Luke scowled, kicked the football down the road and ran after it.

'Don't worry about what Luke said,' I told Billy. 'He'll soon learn to be more tolerant, or no one will want to play with him.'

Melanie and I walked round the perimeter of the park so I could walk the dogs – I wasn't taking any risks after our last fiasco, and kept them on their leads.

'Don't get stuck in that net again!' I shouted to Billy as we left the boys to play.

'Is Andrew serious about this writing business?' asked Melanie.

'For now,' I said. 'To be honest though, I think it's just a phase - it'll probably wear off – like the cycling, which only lasted a couple of months.'

'Oh well, at least he can go back to Sharp & Prentice later on,' said Melanie.

'Thank goodness! I don't want to be totally cynical about it but I'm not sure he has much of a clue about being a writer – he's never tried anything like this before.'

'Mid-life crisis?' Melanie suggested.

'I hate to say it but I'm afraid I think it could be.'

'What about you?' she asked. 'How's the pet grooming going?'

'It's not,' I said, to her surprise. 'I've given it up.'

'Oh, that was quick!' Melanie said. 'What happened?'

'Quite a lot actually, but I won't go into it all now.' I decided not to give her all the gory details – I mean she probably thinks I'm pretty inept already, especially after our disastrous holiday together. It wasn't *all* my fault though! How am I supposed to know that there's more than one Rabbit Island in the Eastern Hemisphere? And that the one we should have gone to (the one that was featured on 'Wish You Were Here' with Judith Chalmers), was a far cry from where we actually ended up. Anyway, suffice to say, things went downhill from the first day we got there. Luckily, Melanie is a trooper and she made the best of it, which is why I like her.

'The job turned out to be voluntary.' I told her.

'No!' she exclaimed. 'That's terrible! Fancy not telling you!'

'Anyway,' I said, - 'I've got an idea that I want to tell you about.'

'Ooh, intriguing,' she said. 'I'm all ears.'

'Well, you know Suzie has an empty shop to let out?' Melanie nodded. 'Well, I was thinking about turning it into a charity shop.'

'Really?' said Melanie, - 'what sort of charity?'

'I haven't quite decided, but it could kill two birds with one stone so to speak. Suzie needs to let out the shop and I need a job.'

'Well, it sounds like a good idea,' said Melanie, - 'but how can you make any money doing that?'

'You can be a charity and still earn a salary, Melanie – I've looked into it.

'Brilliant!' she said. 'Have you told Suzie yet?'

'No – I wanted to see what you thought about it.'

'Well, you've got Andrew and Geoff to do all the legal stuff. You just need to decide what to sell and who it's for! How about *The Knackered Mother's Benevolent Fund*?'

'Or,' I said, laughing, - 'how about this - *Mothers Under Financial Stress!*'

'Mmm,' said Melanie. 'I'm not sure you'd want *that* acronym…'

'Oh,' I said. 'I see what you mean! I'd get lots of visitors though, wouldn't I!'

'Not the sort you want!' laughed Melanie. 'Anyway, Dora, Suzie would have a fit!'

'Now let's be serious,' I said after a bit.

'Well, I don't see what's wrong with helping mothers in distress,' said Melanie.

'I know, but there's already one of those in Shillingsworth. I need to think of something different.'

'It'll probably just come to you in a flash,' said Melanie, - 'like a bolt from the blue!'

When I got back two hours later, Andrew was still ensconced in the study. I made him a cup of tea and took it in to him.

'How are you getting on?' I asked.

Andrew looked up from a blank piece of paper and sighed. 'I can't seem to get going – it's much harder than you think!' he said. 'I've gone through half a pad of paper – look!' He pointed despondently at the waste paper basket which was overflowing with screwed up scrawlings.

Later on, when we were going to bed, I told him about my idea. He was a bit sceptical about it.

'It's quite hard work running a shop, Dora – I'm not sure you'd cope. It's a big responsibility.'

'Well, I think I'd manage, Andrew – it can't be that difficult.'

I went to sleep dreaming about my new enterprise. This could be it, I thought. This could be the answer to all our worries!

Monday 15th April

I was just sitting down with a nice cup of tea, having waved everyone off to school, when the doorbell rang. It was Suzie, looking a bit cheesed off.

'Dora, I need your advice,' she said.

'Really?' I replied, somewhat surprised.

'Yes! Violet has suddenly decided she wants to get married on the top of Ben Nevis! It's ridiculous, Dora! I can't believe she's serious!'

'Oh dear!' I said. 'She's probably been watching that TV programme where people get married in unusual places. Did you see the one where this couple were underwater, Suzie? It was amazing! They were in the Bahamas - the water was beautiful and they were surrounded by all kinds of tropical fish! It looked fabulously romantic…'

'Well I don't think the icy peak of Ben Nevis is at all romantic - it'll probably be covered in snow with a howling wind blowing. It's insane!'

'Why has she decided to do that?'

'Because her fiancé, Oliver, is a mountaineer in his spare time – it was his idea.'

'But it's so far away!'

'I know – and neither of them is even Scottish – I don't know what's come over them. Mind you, before this they were threatening to get married on the Hitchin Flyover where Oliver works! How utterly dreary is that! They couldn't have come up with a more ghastly location if they'd tried!' She got out her hanky and dabbed her eyes.

'Oh dear,' was all I could manage.

'Dora, I don't know what to do to persuade her against it – she just won't listen.'

'What about all the guests?'

'Well, they'll have to wait at the bottom in the car park – we can't expect Grandma to clamber up a mountain with her failing eyesight and chronic angina. And then there's Uncle Charlie – he's in a wheelchair, for God's sake, so that's a non-starter.'

'It's amazing what they can do now for people,' I started to say, but Suzie gave me a withering look.

'Violet says that the guests will be able to watch the service on a video link by the public loos,' said Suzie, sniffing into her hanky.

'She won't be wearing a dress for this then?' I said, suddenly realising there was an up-side to Violet's mad scheme.

'No. She and Oliver are going to wear matching orange survival jumpsuits from Cragscramblers.com. They'll look like they've just escaped from Guantanamo Bay! She's refusing to have a bouquet as well – she says she's going to carry a Venom Ice Hammer and a bar of Kendal Mint Cake. It's awful Dora – I just can't believe it!'

'Who's going to marry them up there?'

'Oliver's uncle – he's a vicar and an outdoor fanatic like Oliver.' She sniffed into her hanky again. 'Violet says she wants the reception to be at somewhere called the Nevis Bunkhouse – I mean it sounds like a wooden shed, Dora!'

'It might be quite nice Suzie.'

'I doubt it. When I rang them up they said they could only cater for twenty people at a time and asked me whether we wanted ham or cheese and pickle sandwiches with our beer.' Suzie's eyes filled with tears.

'Where are they going on their honeymoon?' I asked, refilling her cup with more tea.

'Somewhere called the Muckle Hell Crags in the North Sea.'

'Is that an actual place?'

'Yes, Dora, I've seen the pictures. It's nothing but gannets and rocks.'

'It's a far cry from her original plan to have the wedding at a posh hotel in the Chilterns isn't it, and the honeymoon in Mauritius!'

'She says it's all my fault, Dora! Because there's no money left for a proper wedding, they've decided to do something cheap and crazy instead. She says she won't have it anywhere near Shillingsworth because of what she calls my 'tarnished reputation', and she thinks that Trudy Stoker from the Citizen will do another article and stir things up. Oh Dora, I feel terrible…' Suzie blew her nose loudly and wiped away a tear.

'Oh dear Suzie, but it's not all bad is it? I mean it's not as if she's going off with Oliver and not inviting anyone – it'll still be a wedding even if it's a bit, well…. odd…'

'How will I explain it to my friends, Dora? It's so embarrassing!'

'Well, I'm your friend, and it doesn't bother me, does it!' I said.

'I know, but Justine and Bunny will think it's terrible,' wailed Suzie. 'They would never allow their daughters to get hitched on a mountain top, or on any other rough sort of terrain for that matter…'

I pictured Suzie's designer friends tottering up a rocky track in their Jimmy Choos with their ridiculous chain-laden shiny handbags, worrying about the effects of the Scottish weather on their dermatologically challenged skin. I smiled at the thought of it.

'Dora,' said Suzie irritably, - 'what am I going to do?'

'Suzie, it doesn't matter what they think – if it's what Violet wants then that's all that matters, isn't it?'

'That's easy for you to say, Dora – you don't care about appearances.'

I did have to bite my tongue at this point. I know she's a bit right, but I'm not a complete slob! I do have some standards!

Suzie looked at me and realised she'd overstepped the mark.

'Sorry, Dora, I'm just a bit overwrought.'

'That's OK, Suzie. Look, I think you just have to go with it – it's probably not going to be as bad as you think – I mean Scotland is lovely in the summer, isn't it?'

'Oh I suppose so,' said Suzie. 'At least I won't have to organise anything since Violet seems to have done it all already.'

'On a completely different note, Suzie,' I said, - 'what do you think about me taking on your shop?'

'Really? Oh Dora, that would be marvellous!' Suzie cheered up a lot then and forgot all about Violet for the time being.

Tuesday 16th April

I decided to visit my mother today since it's over a week since I saw her last, and who knows what might have happened in that time. I've been quite worried about her – I don't think old people are very rational sometimes, and my mother has taken to doing some odd things lately. The blue dye incident is just one example. She's still got blue ears and a streaky blue neck. 'It's just a bit of fun!' she'd said when she dyed her hair for Flora's party. Well that's all well and good, but when she goes out people stare – *a lot!*

When Jess rang up again today, she told me that our mother has decided to invite Aunt Alice to stay for a few days. This news worries me hugely – Aunt Alice (my mother's sister) is a total nightmare. She has to be the most tactless and objectionable woman alive. She upsets everyone. In fact, I thought my mother had sworn she'd never have her over again after the last horrendous experience.

'Why is she doing that?' I asked Jess, amazed.

'Who knows!' said Jess, - 'why don't you go over there and try and find out.'

'Yes, I think I will,' I said. 'How are things at the bakery?' I asked nervously.

'Apart from all the people who want to sue me, Dora, it's fine thanks,' she said sarcastically. 'By the way, why did you order 30 pints of cream? I don't know what I'm going to do with it all!'

I hot-footed it over to my mother's house straight after breakfast to see what she was up to.

Mum, are you in?' I shouted through the letterbox. I could hear the radio playing loud music in the kitchen. Eventually she came and opened the door.

'Couldn't you hear me, Mum?'

'No, sorry! I was listening to Joe Loss. Oh, it takes me back, Dora, to when your Dad and I used to go to the Shillingsworth Palladium and dance the night away.'

'No Reggie, then,' I said, noticing he wasn't here for a change.

'No, he's gone to see his mother.'

'He has a mother!' I said, surprised.

'Yes, Dora. She's 98. She's in one of those nursing homes by the park.'

I must say, I hadn't thought about Reggie having any relatives – it seemed so unlikely that he could possibly be related to anyone. Mind you, thinking about it, no one would believe that Alice was my mother's sister.

'Jess told me you've invited Aunt Alice to stay.'

My mother looked a bit embarrassed. 'Yes, I have, Dora, and I know what you're going to say.'

'Well, it's just a bit strange, you know – when the last visit was such a disaster.'

Alice has always been a difficult person, to put it mildly. She upsets people all the time and pretends she has no idea she's done anything wrong. Last time she came, she told my mother that she should have married that 'other nice chap called Allan' instead of my Dad because 'he was better looking' and then her daughters would have been 'more attractive to look at'. She told Jess that her cakes weren't as good as Grandma's and that perhaps she should just stick to supplying nursing homes and school canteens because 'geriatrics and children don't really notice what they're eating, do they?' Honestly, she has the social skills of a rhinoceros on roller-skates.

'I know she's a pain, but she *is* my sister and she's my only relative apart from you lot.'

'I know, Mum, but she always says such awful things to us.'

'Well, we'll have to try to ignore it,' said my mother. I rolled my eyes.

'You look just like Flora,' she said, noticing.

'Well, I just think it will end in tears! When is she coming?'

'On Sunday.'

'Oh, as soon as that!' My heart sank. It will involve unprecedented manoeuvring skills and superhuman strategies of coercion and duplicity to persuade my kids to entertain her for even one second.

'Yes, I thought we could come over and visit on Sunday afternoon.'

Later, with trepidation, I told the family over dinner about Alice's impending visit. Andrew didn't mince his words, as usual.

'I thought that vicious old bag was banished from your mother's house forever!'

'Andrew!' I said, - 'you don't have to be quite so rude about her!'

'But she is, though!' said Flora. 'She asked if Gaz had mental health issues and when I said he didn't, she said there was no excuse for him looking like one of those ASBO people and I should be more selective.'

I looked at Andrew, who was trying not to laugh.

'It's not funny, Dad! She's a witch!'

'Yeah,' said Tom, - 'she told me that I was too thick to do exams and I should just go down to the job centre instead.'

'Well, that's not exactly right, Tom – what she actually said was that you reminded her of Grandad Jarvis and might be more suited to manual work than academic studies.'

'That's the same thing,' said Tom.

I couldn't be bothered to argue. 'Tom, you'll just have to ignore it.'

'Can Luke and me put a spider in her tea like last time?' asked Billy.

'No!' I said.

'I didn't know you did that!' said Andrew. 'I thought it was divine intervention!'

'What's that?' asked Billy.

'It's when the hand of God reaches down to change the course of nature.'

'So, you thought God put the spider in Aunt Alice's tea, Dad?' said Luke.

'Not really, no – it's just something that people say…'

'So, if it happened again, we could just say that God did it,' said Billy.

'No! NO spiders! OK, Billy!' Andrew said, eyeballing him.

'OK,' said Billy, obviously disappointed.

'We will put up with her visit as best we can and there will be no shenanigans,' I said, looking at Luke and Billy in turn.

After the meal, the kids all left the kitchen and I asked Andrew how things were going at work.

'To be honest, I'm glad I'm escaping soon. I can't wait for a change of scene,' he said smiling. I tried to smile back.

'Did I tell you about Violet?' I said. 'She's decided she wants to get married on the top of Ben Nevis.'

'What a great idea!' said Andrew, - 'we should have done something like that. Think how much cheaper it would have been, and we wouldn't have had to waste money on all those people we never see any more.'

Well, I suppose he has a point, but does my husband have no sense of occasion? I mean, honestly! I hope he doesn't go on like this if Flora ever gets married, poor girl.

'Where's Scratch?' he suddenly asked. 'I haven't seen him for ages.'

'Come to mention it, neither have I,' I said. 'Maybe he's finally gone outside. Dr Megg must have had an effect on him.'

'Dr who?'

'Oh,' I said, remembering I hadn't told him yet. 'Um, Dr Megg the pet psychotherapist – she saw him the other day and….'

'Do you mean you spent money on one of those quacks, Dora?'

'Well, yes Andrew – actually she's not a quack - she calls herself a Cat Whisperer.' I covered my ears in anticipation of his response.

Andrew's eyes expanded like saucers. 'Dora! Those people are nuts!'

'Well, she said that Scratch had an inferiority complex and emotional issues – I think she's right, I don't care what you say.' I covered my ears again.

'Give me strength!' said Andrew, - 'I think you're the one who needs to see a shrink!'

Wednesday 17ᵗʰ April

'You could be a charity shop for helping all the ill hedgehogs,' suggested Billy this morning when I told him about my plan.

'Don't be silly, Billy,' said Flora, - 'you can't have a whole shop just for a few hedgehogs!'

'OK! And stick insects as well then!'

'What's the point in that,' said Luke, - 'they only live for a year!'

Billy looked upset. 'There's no need to be so unkind,' I scowled at Luke.

'Well, it's true though!' said Luke.

'I think you should have a shop for helping old people,' said Flora, - 'then you could help people like Grandma and Grandpa so they're not homeless any more.'

'Well, that's a possibility, although I'm not sure Barbara and Bob see themselves as being homeless exactly – more as free spirits.' I said.

'I know,' said Luke, - 'you could help kids that get expelled from school.'

'Really?' I said, somewhat surprised at Luke's offering. 'What made you think of that then Luke?'

'Well, Archie Cavendish got expelled last week for stealing everyone's bus money and Mr Strickland said that he needed special help in the assembly yesterday.'

'Special help!' guffawed Tom. 'I've never heard it called that before!'

'How about a charity for Mad Wives and injured Cat Whisperers,' Andrew added on his way out to work. He grabbed his briefcase and the car keys and yanked the back door open, letting the dogs in. They instantly jumped up on him with their muddy paws.

'Get down!' he yelled at them. 'Blasted dogs!' he said trying to brush the dirt off his suit trousers.

'Why is Dad all grumpy?' asked Tom when he'd gone.

'Yeah, and what's a Cat Whisperer Mum?' said Luke.

I must say, I do feel a bit deflated after this morning. Andrew is not being particularly helpful at the moment. He's so obsessed with his writing plans that he's ignoring everything else. I think we need to have a conversation about work/life balance. After all, when I'm running my shop, he won't be able to lock himself away in the study in the evenings – I'll need him to help much more. Anyway, so far, I haven't seen much evidence of any writing except lots of discarded bits of paper. Maybe that's the real reason he's being so grumpy – maybe he's got Writer's Block! Yes, that's probably it! Perhaps I should try and help him with that. There must be techniques you can use. I'll give it some serious consideration.

I decided I'd better do some housework – goodness knows how long it's been since I did any. I got the vacuum cleaner out of the cupboard with every intention of using it when I heard a funny squeaking noise. At first, I thought it was a mouse. *Where is Scratch when you need him, I thought.* I turned on the cupboard light and got the surprise of my life! I couldn't believe my eyes! There was Scratch curled up in an old Sainsbury's shopping basket surrounded by lots of little wriggling balls of fluff!

'I don't believe it!' said Andrew, when he came home from work.

'Yeah, Dad – isn't it amazing!' said Flora.

Andrew didn't look too impressed. 'How on earth did that happen? I mean, how come we didn't know Scratch was a girl?'

'Well, we certainly know now, don't we! And we also know why he (I mean she) has been acting so strangely recently,' I said.

'And why she got so fat!' said Andrew. 'The other thing we know is that Dr Megg is a swindling charlatan! You should demand your money back, Dora!'

'You children need to be careful not to disturb her too much.' I told them. 'They've only just been born, so Scratch needs time to rest. Eight kittens are a lot for one cat.'

'Eight!' exclaimed Andrew. 'We need to start advertising them straight away,' he said, looking worried.

'Why can't we keep them?' asked Billy.

'Yes please! Can't we keep them?' joined in Luke.

'We're not keeping them,' said Andrew sternly. 'We've got enough animals in the house already!'

The children weren't going to give up that easily though.

'Dad, that's not fair!' said Flora.

'Come on Dad, it won't make that much difference,' said Tom.

'Yeah, Dad, don't you want us to be happy?' Flora said, looking at him all teary-eyed.

'What do you mean *'it won't make much difference'*?' said Andrew, ignoring Flora's pleading expression. 'Are you kidding, Tom! That's eight times more food, vets' bills and flea spray – tons more cat hair on all my chairs and trousers, never mind half the mouse population of the surrounding area ending up under our sofa.'

They all looked very disappointed and slouched downhearted out of the kitchen. Billy's parting words were; 'you're the meanest Dad ever!'

When we went to look at Scratch later, we realised there were actually nine all together.

'Good grief,' said Andrew, bending down to get a closer look. 'Dora, four of them are white – they've got to be Clinton's offspring.'

'Yes, that's what I thought. The others are all tabby like Scratch – oh, and one ginger! They're very sweet aren't they, Andrew?' I said, hoping he might relent a little.

'If Flora has one, the boys will all want one each too. It's better if we just get rid of them all as soon as possible.'

'Andrew, I think we should continue this conversation somewhere away from the cupboard.'

Andrew sighed. 'They can't understand us, Dora, they're cats!'

'Well I think they know more than you think they do, Andrew.'

'That's the trouble with this family,' he said, - 'you're all soft in the head.'

Honestly, I do wonder sometimes how I managed to marry someone like Andrew. He calls it 'being realistic' but he can be so mean-spirited at times.

Later, when he was settling down in bed with his new book *Kill or be Killed*, I said to him, 'you know Andrew, you could be a bit less hard-hearted.'

'What's that supposed to mean!' he said.

'Well, you can be very cynical sometimes, and insensitive.'

'I'm just being realistic,' he said. 'It's better than being a complete pushover like you, Dora – you're far too soft on those kids. They walk all over you!'

'No they don't!'

'Yes, Dora, they do!'

'OK, maybe they do – a bit. But I can't be someone I'm not, can I?'

'No, Dora, but that's why you need me to be tough – I refuse to bend – they can beg all they like, but I won't give in. They have to learn they can't just have whatever they want – that's not real life, Dora.'

Thursday 18th April

Breakfast was very subdued this morning. The boys were quiet for once – no fighting and no insults – it felt odd.

'Sorry kids,' I said, - 'but Dad's right about the kittens. We can't keep them – it's not practical.'

They left the house looking as if they were going to a funeral.

I decided to go into the garden and tidy up a bit. Mind you, I'm not sure you could really call it a garden. Most of the grass has been flattened into a bald mud patch by endless football playing and the dogs have dug up any remaining plants that might have survived being peed on frequently, so the surrounding hedge is about all that's left of any real plant-life. However, the hedge did need trimming, so I got out the shears and started chopping. I hadn't been out there for long when our neighbour, Mona, spotted me.

Mona Knightly and her new boyfriend Roger are a funny pair. Mona's husband Derek left her last year for reasons unspecified, but Andrew and I have our suspicions. We used to hear them arguing in the evenings. Well, it's difficult to ignore when you can hear what's actually being said, isn't it! It made quite interesting entertainment when there wasn't much on the telly. Anyway, the upshot was, that Mona liked to go out late at night to some place called *Party in the Woods* – whatever that is! I mean, it's a weird name for a nightclub, isn't it! I'm sure there's nothing called that in Shillingsworth. I've asked around and people just give me funny looks. Anyway, Mona was always on about going to this place, which to be honest sounded a bit boring really. We used to hear Derek complaining that there were only a handful of people there, that it was too dark to see even with his glasses on, and that it was cold and damp underfoot and he was sure that it didn't help his chilblains. We also heard him shouting very loudly one night that he didn't much fancy some stranger gawping at his 'technical expertise'. I don't quite understand why he would be worried about a few dance moves, but there's no telling with some people, is there? Anyway, Andrew and I did get a bit fed up with listening to them and it was a relief when Derek finally left. His parting words were unforgettable though: "Mona, now you've gone too far – going to *parties in the woods* is one thing, but webcams on YouTube is a step too far. I'm off and good riddance!"

'Well,' said Andrew that night, - 'who'd have thought it! You never know what's going on in your own street, do you!'

'Well, I feel a bit sorry for her,' I'd said, - 'she just wants to enjoy herself and he's being so boring! I mean, he could have made a bit of an effort and risen to the occasion!'

Andrew burst out laughing and didn't stop for ages.

'Well, I didn't think it was *that* funny.'

'Dora, I think I need to explain something to you,' Andrew had said in his irritatingly patronising voice he usually reserves for the children.

After Derek left it was peaceful for a while but now we've got Roger and it's all started up again. Mind you, this time they argue about how many hits they should be getting. I said to Andrew that I didn't think it was a very healthy relationship. Then I saw Mona hanging some very peculiar things out on her washing line. Billy saw them too and asked why she had swimming hats with holes for eyes.

'Cooeeeee…,' said Mona, as I was just getting into my stride with the hedge-cutting.

'Oh, hello Mona. How are you?'

71

'Having a ball!' she said. 'I've never been happier, Dora. Being with Roger has turned me into a new woman! How about you?'

'Well,' I said, trying to think of something exciting to say. Mona didn't want to hear about me though.

'You should come out with me one night, Dora,' she said, - 'you'd love it! We have such a fun time, me and my friends. You could do with a change of scene, couldn't you? You're looking so worn out these days - I know just the thing that would cheer you up! My Roger loves to meet new people – he finds it *so* stimulating! Perhaps Andrew would like to join us in some adult fun too – it's a shame to keep him all to yourself, Dora!'

She leaned over the fence, revealing a large floppy cleavage stuffed into a shocking pink plunge bra which in turn was busting out of the top of a tight purple satin blouse.

'Just call me if you fancy it!' she said, and waddled off up the path to her back door, her mini skirt riding up to show her black suspender belt half-buried inside her fleshy thighs. She tossed back her synthetic black curly hair, waved and smiled – her blood red lipstick like a large wonky chilli-pepper plastered across her moon-shaped face.

'Why is the hedge only half done?' asked Andrew when he came home.

'I lost momentum,' I told him. 'I'll tell you later,' I said, indicating Billy by moving my eyes sideways.

'Have you got something in your eye, Dora?' said Andrew, not really paying attention.

'I'd like to hear about everyone's day,' Andrew announced, when we sat down. 'Flora, let's start with you. What did you do today?'

'It was totally boring, Dad – there's nothing to talk about.'

'Oh, well, what about your friends – you saw them, didn't you?'

'Yes, I suppose so – they're all being totally boring as well.'

'OK, what about you Tom - anything?'

'Um, well, Mr Prosser confiscated my phone in PE – it's so unfair, Dad! I can't get it back until tomorrow.'

'Why did he do that then, Tom?'

'Dunno.'

'Cos, he was watching YouTube videos,' snitched Luke.

'Shut up Fat Face!' said Tom.

'OK, OK, that's enough!' said Andrew. 'I'll try Billy instead. 'Billy, what did you do today?'

Billy thought for a while. 'Well, we learnt about ants.'

'What did you learn about ants then, Billy?'

'They bite you.'

'Yes, and what else?'

'I can't remember,' said Billy.

'Surely you can remember something!' said Andrew, getting slightly exasperated.

Billy thought a bit more. 'Annabelle Stamper tied Harry Pratt to the bicycle racks with her skipping rope and they didn't find him till break time and she had to go to the Headmaster's office and then she had to go in the corner for the rest of the day.' Billy took a breath. 'And then when it was time to go home, she had to say sorry to Harry in front of her mum and in front of his mum and then she was crying and said it was all Harry's fault because he called her a bum hole!'

'I see,' said Andrew. 'You've certainly remembered some things very well.'

Billy looked pleased with himself.

'Luke, please tell me *you* did something constructive today – I'm beginning to wonder whether anyone learns anything in school these days!'

'Well, Dad, Mrs Vickers said I did well in my biology test and she was going to give me ten out of ten …'

'Brilliant,' said Andrew, all too soon.

'But then she said that it was 'remarkably similar to Joseph Champion's', and when she asked me to spell *photosynthesis* and I couldn't, she changed her mind and said I could only have two out of ten.'

Andrew's slightly saggy face sagged slightly more, with a look of despondent resignation.

'Does anybody have anything positive to add to this conversation?'

There was silence around the table.

'Well,' I said, thinking to lighten things up a bit, - 'I've been invited for a night out with Mona from next door.'

'OMG Mum!' said Flora. 'She's hysterical! Is it a nightclub?'

'I've no idea. Anyway, I won't be going.'

'Why not?' said Andrew, smiling an evil smile. 'You might enjoy yourself.'

'You're invited as well,' I said, which shut him up.

Once all the kids had left the kitchen, I told Andrew about Mona's invitation in greater detail.

'Good grief!' he said, - 'I hope you turned it down!'

'I said I'd be too busy, but that you might be able to go.'

'You didn't!' said Andrew, looking mortified. 'Dora, you didn't!'

I smiled at him. 'No, I didn't, but it's good fun winding you up!'

'Phew,' he said. 'You had me going then.'

Friday 19th April

I'd arranged with Jess and Mum to go to the garden centre today – mainly because I'm the only one with a car big enough to transport all their plants and bags of compost. This time we had an extra passenger in the shape of Reggie, who wanted to bring Tinker, his Jack Russell.

'Tinker don't like bein' left all on 'is own,' said Reggie when I turned up to take them all out.

'Well he'll have to be on his own in the car when we get there, Reggie – they won't want him running around in the shop.'

'Oooh, this is such fun - I love a trip to the garden centre,' said my mother. 'It feels as if Spring is definitely here now, doesn't it, girls?' She clambered into the back seat with Reggie and Tinker who'd already started barking.

'Can't you shut that dog up?' said Jess, who is much more outspoken than me, but I was thinking the same thing.

'Tink's just happy, aren't you, boy? Ehh?'

Jess caught my eye and I knew this trip was definitely *not* going to be 'fun'. By the time we got there, my ears were ringing and I was quite relieved to leave the pesky dog in the car.

'Leave a window open, Dora,' commanded Jess bossily.

Honestly! I've got two dogs of my own – I don't need my childless, pet-less sister telling me what to do! She can be so annoying sometimes! It's as if she thinks I'm completely incapable!

'I'll get one of them trollies Ruth,' said Reggie. 'I'll be back in a mo'.'

'Isn't he a sweetie?' said my mother. 'He's so thoughtful.'

'He's just getting a trolley because he wants one,' said Jess uncharitably.

Reggie re-appeared with a trolley full of compost and grit bags.

'Have you noticed,' I said to Jess, - 'that he keeps fiddling with something in his pocket?'

'Oh, yes, you're right! What's he doing?'

'Well, he's either playing with his money, or something else…'

'That's disgusting! What *does* our mother see in him!'

'Want a nut?' Reggie asked, offering us a tatty paper bag from his other pocket.

'No thanks,' we both said.

76

'No worries – one for me,' he said, popping a hazelnut into his mouth, - 'and one for little Johnny,' he said, stuffing one into his other trouser pocket.

'Dora, I must get one of these,' said my mother, pointing out a large sky-blue urn. We loaded it onto the trolley and Jess got another one for all the plants. Just as we approached the till, we heard an almighty commotion coming from the café.

'There's a dog in the Deli,' said the girl at the till. 'Apparently, he's eaten half a salami, a tray of pigs in blankets, and a haggis. No one can catch him, the little bugger!'

'What's she sayin'?' Reggie asked, a bit hard of hearing.

'There's a dog causing havoc in the food department, Reggie,' I said.

'Some people just don't know how to control their animals,' said Jess haughtily.

We finally got out to the car with everything and I opened the boot to load it all in.

'Dora, you left your car door open!' said Mum. 'Tinker's not here!'

'Oh cripes!' I said, panicking.

'No prizes for guessing where Tinker is, then,' said Jess.

'Come on, Reggie,' I said. 'We'd better go and face the music.'

'This dog is a menace!' said the Manager, crossly. 'He's caused total chaos in the kitchen and upset my customers.'

'We're very sorry,' I said. Tinker had finally been caught and was sitting happily munching on a large chorizo. He'd been tied to a shopping trolley with a piece of gardening twine.

'I'm afraid you'll have to pay for all the damage,' he said, - 'and the food he stole,' he said, indicating Tinker's half-eaten sausage.

Reggie didn't look quite so happy about this.

'Don't you 'ave no insurance?'

'Not for damage done by wild animals on the rampage!' he said.

'My Tink's no wild animal, 'e's just havin' a bit of fun!' said Reggie.

'A BIT OF FUN!' the Manager exclaimed, getting red in the face. 'Just look at the mess!'

I cast my eyes around the kitchen and it was a sorry sight. Three trays of vol-au-vents were scattered across the floor, and olives and cherry tomatoes were rolling around in copious amounts of vinaigrette – lettuce and rocket leaves floated across the surface like boats on the Riviera.

'He's completely ruined my display of artisan cheeses and Mediterranean salads,' said the chef, joining in. 'We've got Ainsley Harriott coming in this weekend for a TV promotion! It'll take me ages to re-create the display – and now I'll have to use grapes instead of olives, which just isn't the same thing at all!'

His eye started to twitch at this point.

'And not only that, but he ran round all the tables and stole several slices of Battenberg straight off my customers' plates,' said the Manager.

'I'd better take you back to the car,' said Reggie, untying Tinker and escaping the heat of the kitchen.

'What took you so long?' said Jess irritably, when I finally returned to the car.

'He wouldn't let me leave until I agreed to pay for the damage.'

'How much, Dora?' asked my Mum.

'Three hundred quid.'

'That's extortion!'

'Well, Tinker did steal a whole ham apparently, on top of everything else, and it wasn't possible to retrieve it after it had been dragged round the car park twice through all the puddles.'

The only compensation for this calamitous outing was the fact that Tinker did not bark once all the way home. In fact, it was quite peaceful until we got home to Mum's. We'd only just offloaded everything when Reggie suddenly shouted, 'Oh No!'

'What is it, Reggie?' said Mum.

'It's little Johnny – he's escaped from my trousers, Ruth!'

'Oh dear!' said my mother.

'Well, put him back!' said Jess. 'Honestly Mother – tell him!'

'What are you going on about, Jess?' said Mum.

'He must have escaped when I went to the gents,' said Reggie sadly. 'I didn't notice till just now.'

Jess pulled a disgusted face, and was just about to make a complete fool of herself, when Reggie asked if we could nip out again to the pet shop and buy a replacement.

'I've always had a wee mouse for a pet since I was a boy,' he explained.

Saturday 20th April

'You know,' said Andrew this morning, - 'we haven't heard anything from my parents since they left.'

'Well, it's only two weeks ago.'

'I know, but they said they'd be in touch.'

'They'll get in touch when they remember – you know what they're like, Andrew – I wouldn't worry.'

'I hope you're right.'

'What are your plans today, Andrew?' I asked him, knowing the likely answer.

'I need to get to grips with my writing, Dora – I'm not getting very far with it.'

'Do you think you could spend some quality time with the children first?' I suggested.

'Doing what exactly?'

'Well, maybe go to the park, or what about the cinema? I don't know – I just think you should spend a bit of time with them. We could all go out – how about the bowling place?'

'Oh, all right,' said Andrew reluctantly.

'Great! Let's have tea out as well for a change.'

'You mean, spend the *whole* day with them, Dora?' Andrew exclaimed. 'Are you serious?'

'Of course! Don't be such a damp squib! It'll be fine once they're out.' I knew this was an unlikely scenario, but my philosophy is "try, try, and try again". Andrew is the opposite.

'Last time we had a family outing, it was terrible,' he said. 'Don't you remember?'

'Well, yes of course, but that doesn't mean the same thing will happen again.' I crossed my fingers behind my back.

'Dora, you are ever the optimist!'

Well, someone has to be, don't they? I mean, if Andrew got his way we'd never go anywhere together. I know it's difficult with four of them, but it's not impossible.

'Last time,' said Andrew, - 'Flora was a nightmare, Luke and Billy wouldn't stop fighting, and Tom said that if he didn't die of boredom first, he'd throw himself in front of a bus.'

'Well, perhaps going to a museum was a bit challenging for them,' I said. 'What about my bowling suggestion? That would probably go down better don't you think?'

'What about just staying at home and avoiding all the hassle?' said Andrew.

I gave him a hard stare.

'Well, don't say I didn't warn you,' he said, reluctantly agreeing.

'Yeah, bowling!' said Luke, when we told them.

'Cool!' said Billy.

'OK, I s'pose,' said Tom.

'Do I *have* to come?' said Flora.

'Yes, Flora, it'll be good fun!' I said.

She scowled and curled her lip. 'But you said I had to do more revising,' she said, suddenly thinking of a get-out.

'You can do it tomorrow.'

'Well, can Gaz come then?'

Gaz has recently been reinstated as Flora's boyfriend following the demise of Matthew, after she saw him canoodling with Scarlett Fuller behind the school refectory. Gaz has little to recommend him, not least his name, but we don't have much influence over Flora and must grin and bear it – hopefully she'll come to her senses eventually.

'Mega Bowling' was as expected – noisy and overcrowded. But apart from Andrew being a little too competitive, and Billy getting his thumb stuck in a bowling ball, it mostly went quite well. Even Flora enjoyed herself. We did have to explain to Gaz that you have to *roll* the ball, not *throw* it down the alley.

Afterwards, we went to 'Chicken Licken' for tea where the kids all ate enough grease and sugar to put Billy Bunter to shame.

'Can I have another Double Sundae Scoop with extra cream and chocolate sprinkles, please?' asked Luke, after scoffing the first one in seconds.

'No,' said Andrew. 'You'll be sick!'

'I'm never sick!' said Luke.

'You can have mine,' said Flora, - 'I'm full.'

'Well, Gaz,' said Andrew, as we all got up to go, - 'did you have a good time?' Gaz looked at Andrew with an expression of bafflement. Flora saved him from further humiliation – 'of course he did, Dad!'

'That wasn't so bad, was it?' I said to Andrew when we went to bed.

'Well, it did go better than I expected, Dora, I'll give you that. Gaz was as chatty as ever, wasn't he!' Andrew said sarcastically. 'Do you think there's any brain activity at all? You know - the lights are on but no one's there!'

'I've seen him talking to Flora, so he obviously hasn't completely lost the power of speech – it's just reserved exclusively for her, I suppose! Old people are aliens, Andrew – teenagers can't be seen communicating with us – it's not cool.'

'I'm not old Dora!'

'Oh, you are, Andrew! You're practically embalmed!'

'I'll show you,' said Andrew, laughing. 'Come here and I'll prove it to you!'

Sunday 21st April

Well, suffice to say that Andrew's enthusiasm did not match his physical condition (currently not in the best of nick) and this morning he woke up complaining that he's done his back in again.

'Dora it's because of Cyril's allotment - I haven't recovered from all that digging he made me do. It's got nothing to do with last night,' he said, obstinately.

Honestly, I just despair. It's so typical of Andrew to overstrain himself in an effort to prove someone wrong. I've told him before, it isn't necessary to attempt all the positions in the Kama Sutra that we haven't done yet – particularly no.71.

This was all I needed with my mother arriving in the afternoon and Aunt Alice in tow. Actually, it's usually the other way round. Alice is always the one in front, marching ahead with everyone else trying to keep up.

Andrew retreated into the study to work on his book, while I rushed around trying to make the house look vaguely presentable.

'Why are you bothering, Mum?' said Flora, - 'Nan won't notice if the place is untidy.'

'It's not your Nan I'm worried about,' I said.

Last time Alice came here she offered to pay for a cleaning service to come in for a week to do a 'deep clean'. Not only that, but she asked if I had any old newspapers, and when I found her one, she promptly laid it down on a chair and sat on it. "I can't abide foreign hairs on my clothes", she'd said by way of explanation. Scratch gave her a look of utter contempt, proving that despite what Andrew says, that cat understands more than we think.

Anyway, I went through the house like a Whirling Dervish, issuing instructions to the children, the dogs, and even the cat. By the time we sat down for lunch, I was shattered.

'How's the book going?' I asked Andrew.

'Well, I've done a synopsis,' he said.

'Can we see it?' I asked.

'No, it's not fully formed yet, Dora – it needs fine-tuning before I show anyone.'

'Oh, I was hoping I could help a bit – you know give you some inspiration. We could all give you some ideas, couldn't we, kids? It'd be fun!'

'Mmm,' said Andrew, - 'I'm not sure - it could have the opposite effect – it could stifle my creativity…'

'Oh, come on Dad, tell us what it's about. What's it called?' asked Flora.

'Well it's only a working title, but it's currently called 'Fifty Blades'.

'Isn't there something else called that?' said Flora.

'No, not exactly,' I said, trying not to laugh too much. 'Andrew, you don't want to be associated with something like that, do you? I mean your book has nothing to do with …' I looked at Billy, - 'that sort of thing.'

'It's called being savvy,' said Andrew. 'See – I knew you would stick a pin in my balloon!'

'What's the story?' asked Tom.

'It's about a woman who was murdered by her husband,' said Andrew, looking at me, - 'but no one can find enough evidence to prosecute him.'

'How did she die?' asked Billy, wide-eyed.

'Well, there's a hint in the title…' said Andrew.

'I'm not sure this is suitable for Billy's ears,' I said. 'He's only six, remember!'

'Well, I haven't decided yet anyway.'

'He could poison her with cyanide and then chop her up, then he could put all the pieces in hydrofluoric acid, and then he could bury any left-over bits in someone else's garden.' Luke suggested.

'What on earth have you been watching, Luke!' I said, horrified.

'Why doesn't he just divorce her if he doesn't like her?' Tom said.

'Maybe he can't afford to because she's got all the money,' I said.

'Or maybe she's blackmailing him – he's got a terrible secret that he's trying to hide.'

'Yeah,' said Luke, - 'maybe he did something really terrible like set his parents on fire, or drowned them in the sea, or electrocuted them to death and made it look like an accident…'

'This conversation is getting far too gruesome – that's enough,' I told them. 'It's not quite what I had in mind when I suggested we could help Dad with his book. Anyway, your Nan will be here soon with Aunt Alice.'

'Best behaviour please!' I said to the children, as I heard Mum's car pull up outside the house.

'Do we *have* to stay downstairs,' complained Tom.

'Yes, you do – for at least for half an hour. Or you'll lose your internet access.'

'It's so unfair!' whinged Flora.

'It's pure blackmail,' said Tom.

'Ah, Alice!' How lovely to see you!' said Andrew, grinning wildly. 'Let me take this from you,' he said, removing her immaculate white mohair coat.

'Sorry we're a bit late,' said Mum, - 'someone blocked me in.'

'That would never have happened in Chelsea Gardens,' said Aunt Alice, referring to her own place of residence. She closely inspected the chair which Andrew offered her, before sitting down.

'Have you been decorating, Andrew?' she asked, noticing a torn piece of wallpaper dangling down by the sofa.

'Oh no!' I said, - 'that was the cat.'

Aunt Alice stiffened. 'I can't abide the creatures,' she said. 'They're nothing but a nuisance, tearing and scratching at things and then leaving their dead animals and fur all over the place. I'd *never* have a cat!'

'Tea, Aunt Alice?' Flora intervened, offering her a teacup and a plate of biscuits.

'Thank you, Flora. Perhaps Aunt Alice would like a tray?' I suggested.

'I'm not in a nursing home yet, Dora!' said Alice, crossly. Some of my relatives might prefer it if I was though!' she said, looking at us in turn.

'Goodness, Alice,' said Andrew, - 'what a marvellous dress you're wearing – is it Viyella?' I looked at him with raised eyebrows. (Well, he was going a bit overboard with the distraction technique.)

'Oh, you mean this?' she said. 'It's quite old – I wouldn't wear my best dress here, what with all the animals and children...'

'Quite right, Alice. You wouldn't want them ruining your things – they're almost feral you know! We have barely managed to tame them...,' he smiled a toothy grin at Alice, who wasn't sure what to make of Andrew, so she turned her attention on me just as I bit into a Ginger Cream.

'Dora dear, don't you need to watch your figure? You know what they say - "a moment on the lips, a lifetime on the hips"!'

'Too late for that,' I said, ignoring her.

'Is Flora going to a funeral?' Alice asked, as Flora tried to escape into the kitchen.

'No, Alice, she just likes dressing like that – it's called 'Gothic' – it's very popular with young people,' said my mother.

'Goodness, Ruth! It's positively morbid! If I looked like that all day, I think I'd be feeling suicidal!'

'That's the idea,' said Andrew. 'They enjoy being as miserable as possible – you know what that's like, don't you, Alice? I mean, you remember what it's like to be a teenager, don't you?' he added quickly.

'In my day, there was none of that nonsense was there, Ruth? We just got on with life – we had fun!'

'Really?' said Andrew. Alice gave him a funny look.

'Aunt Alice,' said Billy, - 'can I show you my stick insects? I've got twelve!'

'Perhaps later,' I said, seeing the look of disgust on Alice's face. 'I'm sure Aunt Alice would love to see them after she's had her tea,' Andrew said.

Alice cast around looking for another victim. 'Tom dear, you've grown quite a bit since I saw you last. Mind you, you don't want to get as big as your father – it's very difficult to find clothes to fit properly,' she said, eying up Andrew's midriff (his jumper was stretched across his expanding belly like a skin on a drum).

'What's that on your head, Tom?' she said, noticing the bloodied carnage in the middle of his forehead.

'It's a massive zit!' said Luke, laughing.

'Shut up, you four-eyed squirt!' said Tom, thumping him. Luke retaliated by thumping him back.

'Stop it, boys!' shouted Andrew.

'Well, *really*!' said Aunt Alice, - 'I've never witnessed such appalling behaviour! You boys are a disgrace! If I were your mother,' she said, looking straight at me, - 'I wouldn't tolerate it!'

'Go upstairs!' I told them, - 'Now!'

'Well, boys will be boys,' said my mother. 'My two were always fighting.'

'That doesn't surprise me one bit!' said Alice, narrowing her eyes at Andrew.

When she finally decided she'd had enough of us, she said to my mother, 'come on Ruth, we'd better be going – I must admit, I do find visiting people quite tiring.'

'I'll get your coat,' said Andrew, jumping up and rushing off to get it.

When he didn't come back, I went to look for him. 'Andrew, where are you?' I called out.

'Dora - upstairs – quick!' he said in an urgent whisper.

'What on earth's the matter?' I said, opening the door to our bedroom.

Andrew was pointing at Aunt Alice's coat which he'd laid on the bed earlier.

'Urrgh!' I said, clapping my hand to my mouth. 'What sort of animal is it?'

'She's eaten half of it, so it's hard to tell,' said Andrew.

I looked at the disembowelled entrails splattered across Alice's beautiful snow-white coat; the blood oozing from the pile of body parts was rapidly creeping across the entire garment.

'Quick, Andrew, get it off our bed before it stains the quilt! Shove it in the bath. We'll have to try and wash the blood off.'

We gathered up the remains and put them in a carrier bag. The coat was well and truly soaked through, and even after five minutes of rapid water pressure, the stains refused to budge.

'Quick, spray it with bleach, Andrew!' I told him.

'What's taking so long, Dora?' shouted my mother from downstairs.

Unfortunately, the bleach had a very strange reaction with the fabric and the coat was now covered in large ugly orange patches.

'What are we going to do!' said Andrew.

'Sun damage?' I suggested, in desperation.

'How do you explain the fact that it's soaking wet, Dora? Anyway, there hasn't been any sun today.'

'No, Ok, well …. I know – I accidentally spilt some perfume on it and tried to wash it off.'

'That's more plausible,' said Andrew.

'Or,' I said, suddenly considering Aunt Alice's imminent scandalized reaction, - 'how about - *Andrew* accidentally spilt aftershave on it and tried to wash it off....'

'I prefer the perfume version,' said Andrew.

'Just coming,' I called down.

'You've been ages!' said Mum.

'Aaarrgh!' shrieked Alice on seeing her decimated pride and joy.

I told my white lie, which went down like a lead balloon.

'I've had that coat since 1952,' she said. 'I got it for my 21st birthday – it cost me two weeks' wages! And now it's COMPLETELY RUINED!'

'I'm sure we can sort it out, Alice,' said my mother, trying to calm her down.

'I'm not staying a minute longer in this house!' said Alice. 'I need to go and lie down. Come on, Ruth, we're leaving.'

'Dad, what did you mean by "there goes our inheritance"?' Luke asked, later on, when we sat down for dinner.

Monday 22nd April

I feel quite exhausted today, and Andrew's no help moaning about his bad back. The dogs are in the doghouse too. In our rush to try and save Aunt Alice's coat from looking like a mauled rabbit, we'd forgotten about the carrier bag of offal, which was discovered by the dogs as we waved the seriously disgruntled

Aunt Alice off down the road. They'd emptied the contents all over the bathroom floor and proceeded to eat them. Flora found them mid-chomp whilst the kittens sat observing them with great interest. Unfortunately, Flora made the perfectly reasonable assumption that the dogs were eating one of the kittens, and the blood-curdling scream that followed was loud enough to be heard half way down the street. When we got upstairs, Flora was hysterical, the dogs were cowering under our bed and the kittens had made a hasty retreat back to the safety of the airing cupboard.

'It's not one of the kittens!' Andrew shouted over the hysterics. 'Look! It's got wings, Flora! Calm down.'

By the time we'd managed to get Flora to stop hyperventilating and cleaned up the carcass for the second time, I would have reached for the Valium if I'd possessed any. Andrew and I made do with a large gin instead.

This morning Fudge and Cocoa were still in shock, having been screamed at with the velocity of a rocket launcher, and the kittens refused to be coaxed from their basket.

'Don't worry, Flora,' said Andrew – 'I'm sure they'll get over it! And it was an easy mistake to make.'

Flora went off to school still a bit tearful. 'Not a word!' I said to the boys, fixing them with an extra stern glare. It would be just like them to say something to upset her again. As it was, Luke had already worked out what sort of bird had been mutilated by the colour of its feet, and Billy had asked if you can get pigeon-flavoured cat food. Tom had laughed at this, but actually he had a point – as Andrew said; 'No, Billy, you can't, but it's a bloody good idea! Someone should market that! Anything that reduces the town's pigeon population is a great idea in my opinion!'

After they'd all gone out, I took the dogs for a walk – they needed a calm and familiar activity to help them forget the traumatic experience from yesterday – and to be honest, so did I. I don't just mean Flora's hysterics either. Aunt Alice really gets under my skin – everyone's skin. It's no wonder she's been single all these years. I wondered how my mother was coping and whether she'd introduced her to the hapless Reggie! The thought of that suddenly made me feel a bit sorry for him – she'd make mincemeat of him, that's for sure. I resisted the temptation to go over there, though - one large dose of Alice is quite enough in the space of twenty-four hours. Anyway, taking the dogs out is great for mulling things over – I really wanted to focus on the shop idea. The trouble is, I needed some inspiration. I decided to walk over to Suzie's house.

'You have to think about your strengths and skills,' said Suzie. 'What are you good at?'

I tried really hard to think about this. 'I'm not sure,' I said lamely.

Suzie got out a pen and paper. 'Right,' she said, - 'let's make a list.' I groaned inwardly, but let her do it anyway – it's one of her favourite things.

'**_STRENGTHS AND WEAKNESSES_**' she wrote at the top.

'Do we have to have the second bit?' I asked. She ignored me and carried on. So, while the dogs played outside in the garden, we drank two pots of tea and compiled a list of the good, the bad, and the downright ugly. It was as I expected - heavily weighted on the negative side.

'Don't worry, Dora,' said Suzie brightly, - 'lots of people are only good at one or two things!'

I looked at the list.

Skills

Looking after children

Looking after dogs

Looking after cats

Looking after old people

Not Good At

Organisation

Being efficient

Maths

Delegating

Negotiating

Strengths

Friendly

Willing to help people

Creative

Weaknesses

Push-over/doormat (Suzie's description)

Too accommodating

Gullible

Not giving enough time for YOU or YOUR FRIENDS
Not much confidence

'Well,' I said, when she'd finished compiling this piece of distinctly unhelpful information, - 'no wonder I haven't got much confidence! I mean, just look at all the negatives! Anyway, how's this helping me to decide what to do!'

'Dora – look at the positives - you can get help with the other stuff.'

What do you mean by 'doormat', anyway?' I said to her – 'that's a bit unfair!'

'OK, sorry Dora,' she said, - 'but your kids do run rings around you.'

'I'm not sure how helpful this exercise has been,' I said despondently, just as the phone rang. Suzie went to answer it.

'That was my mother,' she said, when she came back. 'She wants me to have her cat while she goes in for her hip operation – it's a nuisance actually, because Ping-Pong hates cats.'

'Why doesn't she put it into a cattery?'

'She says she can't afford it.'

'Isn't there some sort of refuge – you know - a charity of some kind?'

'Dora, you're a genius! Think about it! What a perfect solution that would be! That's your charity right there!'

'Is it?' I said, dubiously.

'Yes, Dora! Just think of all those poor old people with pets, who have to go into hospital or whatever – you could find temporary homes for them. The charity would pay people to look after them!'

'I'm not sure …. It sounds a bit complicated, Suzie. I mean, how do I find all the people to do it?'

'I'll help you, Dora! It's just what I need to give myself something to focus on. It'll take my mind off Violet's wedding as well.'

Suzie seemed quite fired up about the idea. I tried to look enthusiastic, but it was all a bit sudden. 'OK, Suzie,' I said, - 'but let me talk to Andrew about it first.'

Tuesday 23rd April

I woke up feeling much more energized today. Suzie's idea has grown on me. I didn't have a chance to talk to Andrew last night though - he said he needed to concentrate on the synopsis for his book. I decided to be brave and visit my mother and Aunt Alice. I tried to persuade Jess to come too, but she said she was far too busy dealing with the nursing home complaint.

'They might sue me, Dora – it's all very stressful. One of the old ladies claimed that the tart she ate gave her the Norovirus! It's rubbish of course, but all the same, I could do without the hassle. It's very bad for business. Anyway, I saw Aunt Alice last night and that was enough – do you know what she said to me! She told me that she thought I ought to stop dying my hair at my age because Terry probably wouldn't notice due to his lack of observational skills.'

'Why did she say that!'

'Because, when she showed us the sad remains of her best coat which you apparently managed to ruin, Terry said he thought it looked OK and that splodgy patterns were on trend right now. Anyway, I've got to go, Dora – I have to speak to the insurance company about Mr Cratchit's broken denture.' She hung up.

When I got to my mother's house, they were just coming out of the front door. My mother was looking distinctly frazzled.

'Ah, Dora!' she said, looking pleased to see me. 'We're just going for a walk by the river. Would you like to come with us?'

'Yes – I would have brought the dogs if I'd known. You should have rung me.'

'Well, I for one am glad you didn't', said Aunt Alice. 'They nearly knocked me off my feet yesterday – you should be able to control them a lot better, Dora.' My mother and I exchanged knowing glances.

'Did you ever have any pets?' I asked her.

'We had rabbits, Dora – a much more sensible choice in my opinion.'

We walked in silence for a bit until we got to the common. It was a nice day for a walk and quite a few people were out enjoying the sunshine. Dog walkers were out in force, giving plenty of encouragement to Alice for more moaning, and it wasn't long before she piped up within earshot of the owner of a large black Labrador.

'Just look at that!' she said loudly, - 'it must cost a fortune to feed. Mind you, it's quite fat, isn't it, Ruth! It probably doesn't get enough exercise – some of these dog owners are very lazy.' I smiled at the man with the dog and hoped he hadn't heard her.

We walked on towards the river, my mother trailing behind, further and further.

'Keep up, Ruth!' shouted Alice.

'Don't forget, Alice, Mum broke her leg in January – it's still healing and she can't walk very fast,' I said.

'That was weeks ago,' retorted Alice, unsympathetically. 'She's always been a dawdler, Dora. I, on the other hand, have always kept myself very fit – plenty of exercise and fresh air, whereas your mother preferred to be cooped up inside. No wonder she looks so pallid. Come along, Ruth – I haven't got all day – I need to be off by twelve o'clock.'

'Oh,' I said, - 'going so soon, Alice?'

'Yes, I'm afraid so – I've got the Parish Council AGM this evening and goodness knows what they'll agree to if I'm not there to stop them.'

While we waited for my mother to catch up, a very peculiar looking dog came bounding towards us.

'Ooh, look,' said my mother, - 'it's one of those bald dogs from Peru or somewhere ….'

'Well, I've never seen anything so ugly!' said Alice. 'Who on earth would keep such a monstrous looking animal!'

As it got closer, I realised with horror that I recognised it despite the bright pink sheepskin jacket it was encased in. It was

Queenie – or what was left of her. I looked around for her owner, but she wasn't in plain sight, thank goodness. Queenie decided to follow us.

'Shoo,' I said. 'Go away!'

'She's just being friendly,' said Mum. 'Perhaps we should try to find the owner…'

'No!' I said, rather abruptly. My mother gave me a funny look.

'Um, what I mean is – she'll probably go and find her owner if we just ignore her.'

'It doesn't look as if that's going to happen,' said Alice, two minutes later, as Queenie trotted persistently beside us. 'It's going to follow us home at this rate. If we could walk a bit faster, it might help,' said Alice, scowling at the dog and then my mother.

'I'll try running in the other direction,' I said, getting slightly anxious. This did not have the desired effect as far as I was concerned, and Queenie turned instantly and ran after me.

'Go away Queenie!' I shouted at her when I was sure my mother and Aunt Alice couldn't hear me. The dog just looked at me with its steely black eyes and refused to budge. I ran all the way back to the gate with my heart pounding, shutting it just as the dog lurched towards it.

Phew! Thank goodness for that, I thought. Queenie narrowed her eyes at me from the other side of the fence. I made my escape down the road as quickly as I could.

'Whatever happened to you?' said my mother when I caught up with them twenty minutes later, having skulked round the perimeter of the common and down the other side. 'We were just thinking about going home. My leg is giving up on me.'

'That dog came straight back, Dora,' said Alice. 'And then her owner came and found her. It's a terrible thing you know – what happened to her dog. It's not naturally hairless at all. The lady who owns her said she was a show dog before – you'd never know now, would you! Apparently, some complete moron at a second-rate pet parlour covered her in neat bleach or something and burnt all her fur off! What a dreadful thing to do! Honestly, some places will employ anybody these days,' said my aunt. 'There's no proper vetting – it was probably some illiterate ex-convict from Albania or somewhere – you can't trust anyone these days.'

'It might have been an honest mistake,' I said. 'You've only heard one side of the story after all …'

'Pahh!' said Aunt Alice. 'Dora, you've got your head in the clouds as usual! Anyway, she said she was going to demand compensation and go to the papers with her story. She said her dog Queenie was traumatised by the whole thing – apparently her fur may never grow back! I told her I knew how she felt since I'd had a similar experience recently with my lovely fur coat.'

'Dora, are you all right? You look a bit pale,' said my mother.

Wednesday 24th April

As I've said before, there are times when I seriously wonder how I could have married such an unsympathetic man as my husband. Last night I tried to ask his advice about the fact that at any minute I might be lambasted in the local papers by that Rottweiler, Trudy Stoker, in one of her awful articles which she has the audacity to call 'investigative journalism', but is in fact, sensationalist tosh.

'Don't worry, Dora,' said Andrew, when I told him how upset I was. 'It was an accident, so all you have to do is plead ignorance – that's not difficult for you Dora, is it! Mind you, you might have to defer your shop plans for a bit. Get it? DE-FUR!'

'That's not funny, Andrew!' I said, crossly.

'I thought it was quite good!' he said, laughing at his own pathetic joke.

He's right, though. How can I possibly think about starting a charity to help animals and their owners with this hanging over my head? Just to add to my stress levels, we got a postcard from Barbara this morning. On the one hand, it was a relief to know they are still alive and well, but on the other hand, their latest news was cause for more concern, as usual.

'Why can't they just be like normal people!' shouted Andrew, when he saw the card. 'It's ridiculous! I'm going to work!' he said, throwing the card down on the kitchen table. I picked it up and read it out:

Dear Andy and Dora,

Your father thinks he has found the elixir of life in the form of a special plant extract which can only be grown in a small forest area of Colombia. We've met a wonderful man called Pablo Narco who says he can help us

cultivate and sell it. We've sold Mabel and will be flying out to Bogotá on
Saturday.

Love, B&B XX

'What's the matter with Dad?' asked Luke.

'He doesn't like Grandma and Grandpa's latest plans,' I said.

'Why?' asked Billy.

'Well, it's a bit crazy.'

'Is the plant like the weeds they smoke sometimes?'

'Well, it probably has medical properties…'

'Are they ill?' asked Billy, looking concerned.

'Not in the way you think,' I said.

'They're bonkers, aren't they!' said Tom.

'Well, they're eccentric,' I said, - 'which is slightly different.'

'Yeah, like I said – they're bonkers.'

Poor Andrew. I'm still cross with him for his unsupportive attitude to my perfectly legitimate anxiety over Queenie, but all the same, I do feel sorry for him. I mean, his parents really take the biscuit. Don't they realise they cause us more worry than the kids!

Today's the day I decided to put an ad in the paper to sell the kittens. I didn't tell the kids for obvious reasons. Secretly though, I've decided to keep the ginger one. I won't tell Andrew either – he'll only make a huge fuss about all the extra cost.

Thursday 25th April

Flora had a complete meltdown this morning because she's lost her phone, yet again. Of course, it was everyone else's fault but hers. Andrew tried to give her a spare phone until hers is found. She looked at it with disdain.

'I'm not using that ancient thing!'

'But Flora, it's just for emergencies.'

'I'd rather die than be seen with *that!*'

'Don't be so ridiculous, Flora! It's only three years old. There's nothing wrong with it!'

'Why don't you use it, then!'

'Flora, there's no need to be rude!' I said to her.

'Mum – it's an old people's phone – literally no one would have one like that! It's out of the ark!'

'It'll only be for a short time,' said Andrew.

'Do you want me to lose *all* my friends, Dad! I'll be a laughing stock! You just don't understand!'

'Flora, you're being dramatic!' I said.

By now the boys were sniggering and Andrew was rolling his eyes and puffing out his cheeks. This was all too much for Flora.

'I HATE ALL OF YOU!' she screamed, and banged out of the house. She forgot her school bag and had to return for it, banging the door even louder on her second exit.

'What's an arc?' asked Billy.

'It's a football move,' said Luke.

'No Luke, you pillock, she means the arc Noah put the animals in to stop them drowning!' said Tom.

Billy looked perplexed. 'Is it as old as that then?'

'The phone isn't actually out of the ark – they didn't have phones then, Billy,' said Andrew.

'Why did Flora say that, then?'

'It's just a saying, Billy – like 'as old as the hills' or 'you can't teach an old dog new tricks'.'

Billy looked even more confused. 'But my friend Sam Watson from school taught his dog, Spike to play dead the other day, and he's 14 – that's old for a dog, isn't it?'

'OK, maybe that wasn't a very good example,' said Andrew. 'How about erm… 'Time waits for no man'.'

'What does that mean?' asked Billy.

'That you can't stop time,' butted in Tom.

'Yes, you can, because my watch stopped last week and it still says 5 o'clock.'

'But Billy, it's not 5 o'clock, is it! It's 8.30 and … good grief, I'll be late for work,' said Andrew. 'I need to get going.'

After everyone had gone, I rang my mother.

'How are you, Dora?' she asked. 'I was worried about you yesterday – you looked terribly pale. You're not ill, are you?'

'No, Mum, I'm fine. What about you?'

'Well, I must say, I do feel a bit exhausted – I'm glad she didn't stay any longer.'

'Did you introduce her to Reggie?' I asked.

'Yes, but it was very brief.'

'Oh really?'

'Yes – I'd rather not talk about it,' she said.

'Right, OK. Well, at least you've done your duty and put up with her – it'll be her turn to invite you next time.'

'Oh, I couldn't possibly go and stay with her,' said my mum. 'It's all chintz and china cabinets. She can't cook and her spare bed is like sleeping on a rock. She's got cream carpets everywhere and doilies under *everything*. I mean, honestly – you can't move without her thrusting a napkin at you. She's obsessed with cleaning and tidying – I can't bear it. I'd rather be at your house, Dora!'

'Oh ... thanks!' I said, not exactly sure what she meant by that.

'By the way, Mum,' I said, trying to sound casual, - 'you know that woman with the bald dog at the common yesterday?'

'Yes....'

'Do you think she was serious about taking legal action?'

'Oooh yes, I'm sure. She was ever so cross, Dora. She said the woman who treated her dog should be locked up! Why do you ask?'

'Oh, nothing really – I was just wondering.'

'Of course – you worked in that Pooch Parlour place for a while didn't you, Dora?' My mother said suddenly.

'Well yes, but I don't remember her,' I lied.

'Good job, Dora! She's got the bit between her teeth, that woman. She'll be like a terrier! Ooh, that reminds me – Tinker was quite unwell after our trip out that day, you know. He was terribly sick all over my nice Ikea rug.'

I must say, after talking to my mother on the phone, I felt pretty queasy myself. I rang Suzie for some moral support.

'Look, Dora, you can't let a little thing like that get in the way of your plans!' she said. 'It wasn't your fault anyway – they should've trained you properly. If anyone's to blame, it's the owners.'

I imagined poor Jack being cuffed and shoved into the back of a police van. I felt terrible.

'Suzie, I couldn't let that happen – it wouldn't be fair. It was just an unfortunate accident.'

'It'll probably die down,' said Suzie. 'Anyway, it costs a lot of money to sue someone – she's just blowing off steam. She could buy ten Queenies for the cost of a lawyer. I should know!'

'I hope you're right, Suzie!'

'I'm sure,' she said. 'Now Dora, we need to get things moving with the shop, don't you think? We should go down there and see what needs doing.'

'Yes, OK.'

'How about tomorrow?'

Suzie's right – I've been mulling it over too long – I just need to get on with it now.

Friday 26th April

I tried to talk to Andrew again last night about Queenie, but he was in a silly mood and just told me not to 'tear my hair out' over it! Honestly, he thinks he's being funny.

I met Suzie outside the shop mid-morning and we went in to check out the space.

'Well,' said Suzie, 'I don't think it'll take long to get it looking like a normal shop again – it's mostly a cover-up job. We can paint over the red wallpaper.'

'What about the penis-shaped counter and naked women?' I asked her, pointing at the interior doors.

'Well, we'll have to cover those up too – it'll be fine,' said Suzie confidently. 'It does feel a bit weird coming back here though. The sooner we change it the better. Have you decided on the name of your charity, Dora?'

'Well, I've got a rough idea. What do you think about 'Animals in Need of Shelter'?'

'Too long, Dora – and I don't think AINOS is a very good acronym to have, really.'

'Mm, OK, what about 'Animal Respite Service'?'

'Worse,' said Suzie.

'I don't think I'm very good at this,' I said.

'What about 'Pets' Haven'?' said Suzie. 'It's nice and simple.'

'Let's go with that then,' I said. 'You can't do anything rude with that, can you?'

Later, when the kids got home from school, I told them about the advert in the paper. My news was met with sighs of disappointment of course.

'Well, we'll have to keep them for a few weeks still, because they can't leave their mother yet anyway,' I said, which mollified them temporarily.

'How are things going with your book?' I ventured to ask Andrew after tea.

'Not bad, Dora. I think I'm ready to start writing. I've done quite a bit of research now. I must say, I'm getting the bit between my teeth now that I've only got one week left at work!'

'Is it only a week?' I said, slightly shocked at how quickly the time has gone.

'Yes, Dora! Just think how wonderful it will be! I'll be able to help more with things here, especially if you're going to be setting up the shop. It's exciting times, Dora, don't you think?'

'Well, yes – if you put it that way, Andrew. I certainly could do with some more help at home.'

'Exactly! So, don't look so worried, Dora – I can't wait!' Andrew went off at this point to watch the news and put his feet up, while I cleaned up in the kitchen, filled the dishwasher and washed up. I can't help thinking that the chance of Andrew suddenly being more useful around the house is as likely as a meteorite landing on his head.

In the evening, various people came to see the kittens. Our first visitor was a mother with her little girl. I quickly put the ginger one (which I've secretly named Rufus), in the bathroom, while they looked at the others.

Unable to choose between a white one and a tabby, they said they'd reserve two and went away very happy. Then the doorbell went again while I was still upstairs and Flora answered it – luckily! I leaned over the bannister and with horror realised I recognized them. Andrew came up to look for me.

'Dora, there's a couple here to see the kittens – where are you?'

'In the bathroom,' I hissed.

'Well, don't be long.'

I opened the door a crack – 'Andrew, I can't come out – you'll have to deal with them.'

'Why?'

'It's Mr and Mrs Peake – you know – their cat Fluffy was the one that died…' I shut the door quickly and locked it.

'What darling little creatures,' Mrs Peake said, when she saw them. 'It's so hard to choose isn't it, Wilf?'

'Yes dear, it is. What about a white one – I've always fancied a white cat.'

'Mm, I don't know, dear – it's a shame there isn't a ginger one,' said Mrs Peake. 'I've always liked ginger cats.'

'Oh,' said Andrew, - 'there is a ginger one, but I don't know where he's got to – I'll see if I can find him.'

My heart sank – I should have told Andrew! Then Rufus started meowing loudly.

'Shush,' I said, picking him up and stroking him so he'd purr instead. He was having none of it though, and leapt out of my arms and scampered up the shower curtain. I tried to get him down but he clawed my arm – I squawked in surprise and accidentally pulled the rail off the wall which came clattering down into the bath, along with a piece of the wall.

'Blast!' I said

'There's a lot of noise coming from somewhere!' said Mrs Peake. 'Is someone in trouble?'

'What's going on, Dora? Open the door!' said Andrew.

'It's OK, Andrew – nothing to worry about. OUCH!' I said, as Rufus landed on my shoulder and stuck his claws into me again.

Then he started scrabbling at the door and meowing again, so out of desperation I tried singing to cover up the noise.

'Are you sure she's all right?' asked Wilf.

'Oh yes, don't worry – this is normal,' said Andrew.

'The ginger one's taken,' I shouted from behind the door.

'Oh, I'm sorry,' Andrew said to them both, 'I didn't know.'

They seemed to take an eon to choose, and in the end they couldn't decide and finally made their way back down the stairs.

'Shame we didn't meet your wife,' said Wilf.

'Yes, I'm sorry,' I heard Andrew say, - 'but she's not very well, I'm afraid.'

'Oh, I'm sorry to hear that,' replied Wilf, - 'my sister has a mental illness – it's a terrible thing.'

'Yes,' I heard Andrew say, as they went out of the house - 'she's OK if she takes her medication regularly. Well, see you again – bye for now.'

Saturday 27th April

I suppose it was my own stupid fault, but honestly – who would've guessed that Mr and Mrs Peake would turn up at our house! I'm now sporting two large plasters on two of my fingers, and having to put up with a throbbing pain in my shoulder.

'So, who's reserved the ginger one then?' asked Andrew last night as we went to bed.

'Suzie,' I said, hoping that would suffice.

'But Ping-Pong hates cats!' said Andrew.

Oh, damn it, I thought, typical that he should remember that -especially when he can't remember other far more important things, like our Wedding Anniversary, for instance!

'I think it's a present for Violet,' I said, compounding the lie. He seemed happy with this and moved on to complaining about the shredded shower curtain and the hole in the bathroom wall.

Flora's phone is still missing which is causing a fair amount of stress. I wouldn't be surprised if it's in her room somewhere – the 'room of doom' as we've labelled it. I mean, honestly, you can hardly get the door open for all her stuff lying everywhere. The cupboards and drawers must be completely empty. Anyway, she swears she's looked everywhere and that it's not in her room.

'I'm off out with Gaz,' she announced around lunch time today.

'But what about revising?' said Andrew, - 'your exams are next week!'

She ignored him and left the house.

'I can't get through to her at all!' complained Andrew.

'Well, we'll just have to hope she's more prepared than we think she is. What are you planning today, Andrew?'

'I said I'd take Luke and Billy swimming after lunch.'

'Oh,' I said, somewhat surprised.

'Well, I did take on board what you said about spending more time with them, Dora – I'm not completely thoughtless. Do you want to come with us?'

'No, it's OK – I've got plenty to do here,' I said.

I used to quite like swimming, but my recent experience at our local pool has left me with a strong aversion to it. After the extremely traumatic near-drowning of Billy, followed by an unfortunate and completely unplanned indecent exposure incident, I think I've developed pool-phobia. I don't think the lifeguard is going to forget the sight of a large pair of unfettered flapping breasts lurching towards him in a hurry, is he? The fact that some unknown person uploaded the whole thing onto YouTube is another reason to avoid our local pool – I mean, they might still be there just waiting for the next opportunity. You just don't know who's in our midst, do you? As we tell Flora every so often, 'stranger danger' is a fact of life. Mind you, you couldn't get more strange than her current boyfriend Gaz - I mean, how do you eat anything with what looks like a curtain hook through your tongue? It must be impossible to eat spaghetti, for instance, mustn't it? At least he's had his

'PEAS' tattoo covered up after a number of people pointed out the spelling error. I'm not sure I like what he's had done instead, but Flora insists that 'loads of people have butterflies with giant skull faces' and it's not 'weird or stupid' as Tom suggested. I don't know — I sometimes feel like I'm turning into my mother at times like this — I just can't understand them at all.

'Didn't you want to go swimming with Dad?' I asked Tom when he came into the kitchen looking for more food.

'No way!' said Tom, looking completely affronted by the idea. 'He's *so* embarrassing!'

'Don't be silly, Tom.'

'He is though, Mum — last time I went, he tried to dive off the diving board — you should have seen him!'

I tried to imagine Andrew diving, but I couldn't because I don't think I've ever seen him doing that.

'He did a massive belly-flop, Mum, and *everyone* was looking. The lifeguard told him off for splashing too much.'

'I wish I'd seen that!' I said.

Some more people came to look at the kittens this afternoon, so now we only have three left to find homes for. After that, I actually enjoyed some peace and quiet for once.

According to Andrew, the swimming outing was a great success, but Billy and Luke had a different take on it, and couldn't wait to tell me.

'Mum,' said Billy, as soon as they got through the door, - 'Dad got stuck in the water shoot!'

'Only temporarily,' said Andrew, trying to play it down.

'It was *so* funny, Mum!' said Luke. 'They had to send for someone to rescue him – over the loudspeaker!'

'Don't exaggerate, Luke!' said Andrew. 'It was totally unnecessary for anyone to help me – I was just resting for a minute.'

'What – half way along the shoot?' said Luke, laughing. 'It was at the bendy bit – you know – where the shoot goes round the corner.'

'What were you doing on the children's slide anyway, Andrew?' I asked him.

'He said he could go down faster than anyone else,' said Luke, - 'with his special technique.'

'I'm surprised they let you on there anyway,' I said.

'He wasn't supposed to be,' said Luke. 'When the lady got him out, she told him he was a 'very naughty boy' and that the Fireman Sam Shoot was for kids twelve years and under, not for great big oafs like our Dad!'

Andrew looked suitably embarrassed.

Later, Billy told me how they got him out and I nearly died laughing. It was lucky for him that they'd recently installed the ceiling hoist for disabled swimmers! I mean, how else would they have got him out? He might have been in there for days! Now there's a thought.

Sunday 28th April

Andrew is still smarting after last night. He had a bit of a sense of humour failure when Tom said he should have stuck to improving his diving style.

Today he's hiding in the study with only his book for company. He didn't even want the dogs in there.

'They fidget and snort too much,' he said. 'I need to concentrate.'

I decided it would be a good idea to leave him alone for a while anyway. I suspect he's feeling a bit worried about turning fifty soon. That's the real reason he got stuck in the water shoot. He's just like an overgrown child sometimes.

I went outside to hang out some washing and then regretted it, seeing Mona out there doing the same thing.

'Just hanging out some smalls,' she said, waddling down the garden path. 'They'll be dry in no time in this breeze,' she said, pegging out some underwear that looked like shoelaces held together with rivets. 'Have you thought any more about coming out with us one evening, Dora?'

'Oh yes, well it's a bit tricky with the kids and everything – I'm not sure I can, at the moment.'

Suddenly there was an almighty commotion coming from my house – the kids were shouting, the dogs were going mad and then Scratch shot out into the garden, hotly pursued by Tinker yapping like crazy. Over the fence they went into Mona's garden, with Tinker snapping inches from Scratch's tail. She shot up the washing pole and onto the whirligig which began to spin round uncontrollably. Tinker scrabbled at the bottom of the pole, barking for England.

'Oh, I'm sorry, Mona!' I said. 'I didn't know my mother was coming and I had no idea they were bringing Tinker!' My mother came hobbling out across the grass shouting for Tinker, but as usual he ignored her completely. The whirligig flew round and round with Scratch clinging on for dear life, her fur all on-end like a giant powder puff.

'Oh no!' shouted Mona, running to retrieve her undergarments, which were flying off in all directions, and being propelled across the garden with the speed of a pinwheel in a gale, over the fence into the neighbour's back yard, and beyond. Mona finally got hold of Tinker and thrust him into my mother's arms. Scratch saw her opportunity to escape and tore back into the house.

'Sorry, Mona!' I said – 'Tinker's terrible if he sees a cat.'

'Well, he should be tied up!' she said crossly. 'just look at my smalls – they're everywhere! I'll have to wash them all again! That's if I can find them!' She stalked off to look for it all.

'Oh dear!' said my mother. 'Sorry, Dora.'

'Why didn't you tell me you were coming?' I said. I could have made sure the cats were all upstairs.'

'Well, we were on our way to Beds Galore, and we thought we'd stop by,' said Mum. 'Tinker ran into the house before we could stop him.'

'Oh well, you did me a favour actually,' I said. 'Mona wants me to go on a night out with her and her friends.'

'That's nice, Dora – you should go out. It would do you good!'

'They're a bit weird Mum. I'd rather not.'

'What do you mean 'weird', Dora?'

'Well, they're swingers, Mum.'

'Good grief, that's not back in fashion, is it? I mean, swinging was old fashioned when I was young – it was a forties thing.'

'I think that's a different kind of swinging, Mum.'

'Oh well, I don't know what you mean then.'

'It's, um well, like an orgy I suppose.'

My mother's eyebrows shot up to join her hairline and her eyes threatened to pop right out of her head.

'Never!'

'Yes, Mum – and even worse, it's al fresco.'

'What – in this weather?'

'Unbelievable, isn't it!'

'Good Lord!' said my Mum. She was a bit speechless for a while.

We tied Tinker to a radiator pipe to prevent further mayhem and I made us all some tea.

'So why are you going to Beds Galore?' I asked them both.

'Reggie's bed is completely shot,' said my mother. 'The mattress is lumpy and the base has collapsed.'

'I don't think it's that bad!' said Reggie. 'I've had that bed for forty years – I'm used to it.'

'I see,' I said, not really seeing at all. I mean, why does my mother care what Reggie is sleeping on?

Monday 29th April

I rang Jess last night because the bed thing was playing on my mind. Jess agreed it was quite worrying.

'How does Mum know Reggie needs a new bed?' asked Jess.

'I don't know.'

'Why didn't you ask her, Dora?'

'Well, it didn't seem appropriate – you know, in front of Reggie.'

'For goodness' sake, Dora! You should have just come out with it!'

'Well, you ask her then!' I said, getting cross.

When I asked Andrew what he thought about it, he just laughed and said Beds Galore was full of cheap, second rate furniture that wouldn't withstand much action and what was my mother thinking of! I mean, really! I can't get Andrew to take my worries seriously at all these days. At least Jess is with me on this one.

Today I got to grips with the shop, and I ordered the new sign for the front which is coming on Wednesday. It felt really good to put things in motion at last. I went with Suzie to buy some paint and some fabric to dress the window.

'I never did find that fabric, Dora,' she said when we were browsing in the haberdashery department.

'Oh,' I said. *Now was my opportunity to come clean, I thought. It had been weighing on my mind a great deal – it would be one less thing to be worrying about.*

I took a deep breath. 'I think Barbara might have accidentally used it for something when they were staying in the house.'

'*Accidentally*! How can you *accidentally* use something that plainly isn't yours to use!' said Suzie.

'Um, well they are a bit odd like that.'

'You're telling me, Dora – people are still knocking on my door asking if I've got any leftover rocks or vegetables for sale.'

'How much was it again, Suzie?'

'£800 quid, plus postage.'

I gulped. 'I could pay you back in instalments, Suzie – when the shop is up and running.'

'OK, thanks, Dora – although, it's not your debt is it! Barbara's the one who should be paying for it.'

'I know, but they've gone to South America to live in the jungle and we may never see them again. Anyway, they don't have any money – theirs is a hand-to-mouth existence I'm afraid.'

'I know how that feels,' said Suzie.

'Really?' I said, incredulously. Suzie has always had more than enough money. She's never really had to work, and I don't ever remember her being short of anything.

'Oh yes – well, since the salon went down the pan, Warren has been very strict with my expenditure. Do you know Dora, I'm only allowed to have my hair done once a fortnight now, and he's banned me from buying any more shoes or handbags for the next six months. It's so mean of him, Dora!'

'Oh, well it's not *that* awful, Suzie – I mean, I hardly ever go to the hairdressers and I've managed with the same shoes and bags for five years now…'

'Exactly!' said Suzie. 'I don't know how you put up with it! I would die of shame if it was me! Andrew really ought to be more attentive.'

'Well we can't afford things like that on Andrew's salary with all the children to feed as well, and it's only going to get worse now he's taking a break from work to write his novel. I don't know how we're going to manage…' Suddenly I felt very sorry for myself and began to cry.

'Oh Dora, I'm sorry. Look, don't worry,' she said, putting a comforting arm round my shoulders and offering me a lavender scented floral hanky. 'You can have some of my old stuff if you like – I mean, I've got loads more than I need anyway. I was only going to put it here in the shop,' she said smiling, pleased with herself at her own benevolence.

Tuesday 30th April

Jess rang me this morning in a flap because Katy is ill and she needed someone to do the deliveries.

'You'll be able to manage that won't you, Dora? It's just a matter of driving round and dropping off a few orders this morning – please Dora, I'm desperate!'

'Ok,' I said, even though I swore I wouldn't help her any more after the last disaster. 'I'll be there in twenty minutes.'

I should have emptied my car of all the recycling, spare coats, dog blankets and general rubbish before I went, but there was no time.

'For God's sake, Dora!' said Jess, when I arrived at the bakery. 'Your car is a total health hazard,' she said, eying up the biscuit crumbs, discarded drink bottles and empty crisp packets littering the floor.

'Well, you didn't give me much notice, did you!'

'Well, I can't put my muffins in there! You'll have to take Terry's van,' she said.

We loaded up Paradise Bakery's smart new van with the orders and she gave me a list of the addresses.

'You can't go wrong, Dora – the order numbers are next to each address – see?'

'OK, Jess. Don't worry!' I said, seeing the expression on her face.

'I can't help it,' she said. 'I'm still being harassed by Sunset Villas. Those old biddies at the nursing home are nothing if not persistent.'

Well, anyway, it was a piece of cake driving round and delivering – quite relaxing really. I don't know why she makes such a fuss about everything.

When I got back into my own car afterwards, I did realise it was in quite a bad state – compared to the beautifully clean and gleaming new van with its fresh new interior and pristine seats.

Jess was right about my car – how did it get into this condition so quickly? I only cleaned it recently.

'It's six months ago, actually, Dora,' said Andrew at tea time.

'Really?'

'Yes.'

'Oh, well anyway, it took me all this afternoon to clean it. You children,' I said, eyeing them all in turn, - 'need to stop treating it like a rubbish bin. Honestly, you wouldn't believe what I found in there! For instance, Billy, please stop putting half-eaten sweets in the door pockets, and Luke – I found six letters from school about homework detentions screwed up and shoved under the seats. Tom – ditto. And all of you – please refrain from throwing crisp packets and drink cans onto the floor, and shredding up paper all over the place – it looks like it's been snowing in there! Honestly kids, it looks like a compost receptacle and smells like one too. I even found a piece of toast with jam on it in the glove compartment! And Flora – I don't know how I'm going to get all that nail polish off the front seat, short of re-upholstering it.'

'Well, you spilled coffee all over the floor last week!' she retorted.

'That was because the cup-holder broke, not because I couldn't be bothered to put a lid on something!'

'Well, it wasn't my fault – you were in a hurry and made me get out of the car before I'd finished doing my nails…'

Andrew butted in before this argument escalated any further.

'Well, never mind – these things happen. Let's just try as a family not to trash Mum's car, OK?'

When the kids had all left the kitchen, I couldn't help but challenge Andrew over what he'd said to them. I mean, if it was his car, he'd have gone ballistic.

'*These things happen!*' I parodied. 'I can't believe you said that! If Flora had spilt black nail polish all over your cream leather seats, you'd probably have strung her up!'

'Yes, I know, but your car is old and pretty bashed-up already, so it doesn't matter that much, does it? Anyway, I'm going to try and have a calmer, more relaxed approach to life, Dora. Since I've started writing my book, I've realised how stressful my job is – I definitely need to relax more and not take things too seriously. I need to try not to get worked up over things. You should try to be more laid back as well – it's better for our health.'

'Oh,' I said, - 'well, that'll be interesting – especially if it's along the same lines as helping more around the house…'

'Yes, Dora, you're going to see a new more relaxed husband,' he said, picking up his newspaper and wandering off. Five minutes later he was stomping round the house looking for his glasses and shouting that he couldn't find them.

'They're on your head,' said Tom.

* * *

MAY

Wednesday 1st May

I went to meet Suzie once all the children had gone to school, to try and get more done at the shop.

'Look at all this stuff!' said Suzie, pointing at the piles of bin-bags by the doorway. 'Isn't it amazing! You only put the ad in the window on Monday. What a fantastic response!'

We put it all into the back room to sort out and soon realised this wasn't going to be quite as straightforward as we first thought.

'What sort of person sends dirty knickers to a charity shop!' said Suzie, holding up a large pair of smelly grey pants.'

'Urggh,' I said. 'We'd better put gloves on for this job.'

'And look at this, Dora,' said Suzie, pointing at a pair of rock-hard cheesy football socks.

'We'd better make a throw-away pile,' I suggested.

'There's going to be a lot of washing and drying to do, Dora. We haven't allowed for that in our calculations have we!'

'No,' I said, looking at a growing mountain of whiffy old clothes, most of which had seen better days.

'I think we should be ruthless,' said Suzie. 'No one's going to buy half this stuff, are they?'

By the time we'd gone through it all, only about a quarter of it was any good for selling.

'Oh my God, Dora! Look at this!' Suzie uncovered a floppy blow-up doll complete with hair and make-up but no clothes.

'Urgh! Don't touch it, Suzie – you don't know where that's been!'

'We'd better load up your car with all the stuff we don't want, and get it to the tip,' said Suzie.

'*My* car?' I said.

'Well yes, Dora. We can't use mine – it's not big enough.'

She was right of course, but I couldn't help thinking that mainly there was no way on God's earth that she was going to allow any of it anywhere near her immaculate, unpolluted, Mini Convertible. We shoved it all into my car – half the bags split open when we moved them, spilling the contents out onto the floor. I must say, I hadn't reckoned on this – having to sift through loads of dirty old stuff not even fit for a jumble sale. Some of it was shocking. I mean, the pants and socks were bad enough, but there was a lot of useless junk as well. I mean, who on earth was going to want broken crockery with Spaghetti Bolognese still stuck to it? Or a cage, complete with wood shavings and hamster poo? There were some truly hideous ornaments as well, which I can't imagine *anyone* giving house-room to.

'Good God,' said Suzie, when she saw a particularly grotesque clay monkey-head on a spike with its mouth open and a candle stuck between its teeth.

'What on earth is it?' she said.

'I don't know, but it's horrible!' I said, throwing it into the boot of my car, along with some extremely vulgar pink plastic lampshades, a broken commode, and the semi-deflated blow-up doll.

I went off to the tip, leaving Suzie to get on with the painting. When I got back, our new sign had arrived.

'It's fab, isn't it!' said Suzie.

'PETS' HAVEN'! - it feels like it's actually happening now!' I said, pleased as punch.

'Very nice,' said Melanie, who'd decided to pop in to see how we were getting on. 'You've done a great cover-up job – you'd never know it used to be a knocking shop, would you!'

We had a really fun afternoon in the shop, making it look nice and having a laugh. Suddenly I felt so much better about everything. Even the thought of the furless Queenie and her litigious owner didn't seem quite so overwhelming. Unfortunately, my good spirits only lasted until I got home.

'Mummy, Mrs Pincher says you should be listening to me reading EVERY day, and she wants to see you tomorrow morning,' said Billy as soon as I walked through the door.

'Mum, I need French food for my French class party next Tuesday,' said Luke. 'I told Monsieur Bonheur that I'd bring croissants for everyone.'

'Can I have five pounds, please – I owe Findlay Dent because I accidentally cut his tie in half,' said Tom, nonchalantly.

'Mum, Aunty Jess rang up,' said Flora, - 'something about a mouse, and someone having a heart attack and can you ring her back.'

Thursday 2nd May

Well, honestly! I don't know how Jess can blame me over a mouse getting into her muffins. It's not my fault! I mean, it must have got there when she was packing them up – it's the only explanation in my view. The dinner lady at the nursing home got a bit of a surprise when she opened the cake box – apparently it leapt out, flew through the air and landed in the big vat of pea and ham soup she was cooking at the time. The manager told Jess that the poor woman got such a shock, she had to take the rest of the day off.

'It was a white mouse, Dora!' said Jess, when I spoke to her on the phone. 'How many wild white mice have you seen at large? Don't you see – it must have been Reggie's mouse! He must have been in your car all along since he went missing that day.'

'No, Jess, that's not possible – we'd have seen him,' I said. 'And he'd be dead by now, stuck in the car all that time.'

'Nonsense,' said Jess emphatically. 'There was enough old food in your car to keep him alive for a year at least!'

'Well, how did he get into your van then?'

'I don't know. Maybe he escaped in your handbag or your coat pocket? He's used to being in a pocket, isn't he!'

'Well, it all sounds a bit improbable to me,' I said.

'I'm telling you, Dora – it *was* him!'

You can't win with Jess – once she gets a bee in her bonnet, that's it. I could curse Reggie though. I mean, if she's right, it's his fault, not mine.

'Maybe Reggie could identify it,' I said.

'Are you serious, Dora? It's pea green and suffering from a bad case of Rigor mortis, and anyway it's been disposed of - along with 65 of my chocolate-chip muffins which I won't get paid for! I've only just managed to placate Sunset Villas over the lemon tart fiasco, and now I've got another fight on my hands with Twilight Mansions. It beggars belief Dora!'

'Well, I don't see how you can blame me, Jess.'

'Well I can, and I do!' she said, putting the phone down.

At the shop, Suzie was already sifting through more stuff when I arrived.

'Dora – I've brought you some things I don't want. Why don't you swap your old bag for one of mine,' she said eyeing up my battered and scuffed old brown leather handbag.

'Well, I suppose it wouldn't do any harm to get rid of this old thing – thank you, Suzie,' I said graciously. I tipped out all the contents of my bag onto the table, and then wished I hadn't.

Suzie pulled a disgusted face. 'Dora, how can you have *that* much stuff in there – don't you ever clear it out?'

'Well, occasionally,' I said, embarrassed at the sight of all the sweet wrappings, screwed up tissues and shopping receipts. 'It's a hangover from having small children, Suzie – you never know when you might need something in an emergency.'

'Mmm, well, Dora – I'm not sure when you would need this, or this!' she said, pointing at a whoopee cushion and a packet of slug pellets. 'There's so much stuff here, Dora, your bag must weigh a ton!'

'Well, I know. I just haven't got round to sorting it out. There's a story behind all these things, Suzie,' I said, seeing her looking disapprovingly at my collection of seemingly random items.

'I'd like to know the story behind this!' she said, holding up one of the willy-shaped nutcrackers.

'Oh yes, that was a present for someone,' I said, - 'my old boss - remember JR's Bits & Bobs? Anyway, I got the sack before I could give it to him.'

'I'm not surprised,' said Suzie. 'Why have you got two phones, Dora?'

'Oh no! That must be Flora's phone! Oh dear! I must have picked it up thinking it was mine. It's been missing for a week!'

When I gathered up the rubbish to throw it away, I also noticed some tell-tale teeth marks on a Garibaldi biscuit which had been lurking at the bottom of my bag for goodness knows how long. Oh well, even if Jess is right about Reggie's mouse stowing away undetected all that time, it's still pretty unfair to lay the blame at my door. Anyway, I feel sorry for the poor mouse – I mean what an awful way to go! There he was, thinking he'd died and already gone to heaven, feasting on an endless supply of delicious cakes, when some daft old bat screams like a banshee, making him jump out of his skin, propelling him through the air and straight into her witch's cauldron of boiling green foam. I suppose I ought to let Reggie know, but then Jess would know that I know, and I don't particularly want Jess knowing that I know, so I think I'll just let this one go. I'm in enough trouble as it is. Flora will be particularly unforgiving when she finds out I've had her phone all this time.

Friday 3ʳᵈ May

'I need to take your car today,' said Andrew this morning.

'Oh, why?' I said, slightly annoyed at this last-minute request. 'I was going to load it up with stuff from the shop later.'

'I need it to take out a load of people from the office – it's my last day at work and we're having a meal out afterwards.'

'Oh, OK. So, I'll have yours then.'

'Yes, if you need a car, but please don't put any charity bags in it, will you? Or let the kids eat in there or have drinks, and don't let Cocoa and Fudge in it either.' He gave me a stern look.

'I'm surprised you want to use my car,' I said.

'Well, you did clean it out the other day, didn't you? So, it can't be too bad, can it? Anyway, I've got six people to transport so it'll save on taxis.'

'He's so typical,' I moaned to Melanie later that morning when we were in the shop. 'Why are men so obsessed with their cars?'

'Oh, I know!' said Melanie. 'It's a pity they don't feel that way about the house they live in.'

'Well, I've got some more stuff to take to the tip, and I need to collect dog and cat food from the pet shop, so that's two rules broken already!' I said.

'You'd better cover everything in plastic just in case,' said Melanie, - 'or your life won't be worth living!'

On the way to the pet shop I stopped off at my mother's house for a cup of tea.

'I'm in Jess's bad books again, Mum,' I told her.

'I know,' said my mother. 'Jess told me yesterday when she brought Reggie's mother's cake round. She's going to be 99 years old tomorrow! We're going over to the nursing home for afternoon tea. Actually, Dora, we could do with a lift – my car needs to go into the garage on Monday morning.'

'Oh, OK. Have you told Reggie about the mouse?'

'No – I think it's best forgotten.'

'How can Jess blame me for Reggie's mouse contaminating her cakes – it's ridiculous Mum!'

'I know, but you know what she's like, Dora. And she's under a lot of stress at the moment what with one thing and another…'

My mother didn't elaborate, but she was obviously referring to the curried tarts and Mr Cratchit's dental disaster.

I changed the subject. 'How is Reggie?' I asked. 'Got a new bed yet?'

'Ooh yes he has and it's a million times better than the terrible old thing he had before. It's lovely and firm and you can't feel the springs when you lie on it – much better for us old folks with dodgy backs. It's got a built-in overhead light and side tables to put your things on and it's fully adjustable so you can move it up and down. We've had great fun with it!' said Mum.

I really don't know what to make of this. I think my mother might be losing her mind, as I've suspected all along. I mean, doesn't she realise that people her age, are supposed to be swaddled in a woolly blanket in front of the TV in the evening, settling down to watch a nice natural history programme or something, with a cup of hot sweet tea and a chocolate digestive!

I thought you'd cleaned your car out,' said Andrew, crossly when he came in late this evening.

'I did,' I said.

'So why did Geoff find a pair of grubby old pants and some stiff sweaty socks on the back seat?'

'Oh, they must have fallen out of one of the bags – sorry!'

'And when I opened the boot to put my colleague Shama's briefcase in there, it was really embarrassing – I mean who drives around with a life-size blow-up doll in their car? Or a filthy old toilet bowl?'

'It's a commode,' I said.

'Well, whatever – it almost put me off my dinner, and God knows what Shama must think!'

'Sorry, Andrew, but I forgot that stuff was in there – I meant to off-load it at the tip.'

Actually, I don't care what Shama thinks – in fact, I hope it does put her off Andrew. She's been sniffing round him ever since she joined the practice. Mind you, Andrew's kidding himself if he thinks a young girl as pretty as she is, would really be interested in a portly, middle-aged man like him with four kids and a dodgy bank balance.

Saturday 4th May

'So, where was it?' demanded Flora this morning when I handed over her phone.

'You've got it back now - it doesn't matter where it was, does it?' I said.

'Yes, it does.'

'Well, it was on the table.'

'But I looked there three times!'

'Well, it was in a bag.'

'What bag?'

'I saw it in Mum's bag,' said Billy, dobbing me in – 'when I was looking for my jelly beans.'

'I can't believe you had it all along!' shouted Flora.

This was followed by more shouting, stomping and door-banging.

I gave Billy a lecture about going near people's private property.

'You can't just look in other people's bags, Billy.'

'Why not?'

'Because that's their personal stuff - it's bad manners to look without permission.'

'But you had Flora's phone,' said Billy. 'And they were *my* sweets.'

'Yes, Billy, I know, but I put the sweets in my bag because you left them on the back seat of my car where they could have spilled out onto the floor.'

'Well, you should have asked my permission to take my sweets, since they were *my* sweets…'

'OK Billy – sometimes there are extenuating circumstances.'

He looked bemused. 'What's exterminating stances?'

'*Extenuating circumstances* means that sometimes it's not wrong to do something if there's a good reason, therefore I can break my own rule if I want to.'

Billy didn't look impressed.

'I'm your mother, Billy – just accept it.'

Andrew was in a good mood this morning, since today marks the first day of his sabbatical. He was singing *I Did It My Way* in the shower at the top of his voice, much to Flora's disgust, and then he was being far too jovial in the kitchen at breakfast time.

'Andrew, you're scaring everyone,' I told him.

'Don't be ridiculous,' he said. 'Am I not allowed to be happy?'

'Well, it's just that we're not used to it,' I said.

'Yeah, Dad – it's not normal,' said Tom.

'Have you been smoking Grandpa Loveday's weed?' said Luke.

'No, I haven't – I've just been released from the shackles of my stressful and often pointless day-job! I'm free for a whole six months!'

'That's not fair!' said Luke. 'Can't we have six months off school as well?'

'No – you've all got exams to pass, whereas I did mine years ago. Then I went to university, then I got a job, followed by more jobs, followed by even more jobs, so now I deserve a rest. You lot haven't even begun to know what hard work is!'

'Well, I still don't think it's fair,' said Luke.

'I tell you what, we'll all go out this evening for dinner to celebrate – what do you all think?'

'OK, but it has to be 'Chicken Licken',' said Luke.

'OK, done!' said Andrew.

'Do we have to go there?' I said to Andrew when the boys had all gone off to play outside.

'Well, they like it there – it's their favourite place.'

'I suppose so. It would be quite nice if we went out together without the children for a change, Andrew.'

'OK, I'll book something for next weekend, Dora – what do you fancy?'

'Oh, I don't know ... there's a new Italian place that's supposed to be good – Suzie told me about it – it's called

'Lorenzo's'. I might have the shop open by then too, so it could be a double celebration!'

'Good plan,' said Andrew, and he went off whistling happily to himself.

After lunch, I went off in my car to collect Jess, Mum and Reggie, plus the birthday cake.

'You'll have to have it on your knee, Jess,' I said, when she opened the boot, saw the revolting commode and shrieked with disgust.

'It's stuff people have given me for the shop and I haven't had a chance to get rid of it yet,' I explained.

'What sort of people would give you stuff like *that!*' said Jess, getting into the front seat with her cake box.

'I left you some things of my mother's outside the shop last week, Dora – did you get 'em?' said Reggie, half overhearing our conversation. 'There was a bag of some old clothes of Ma's and an old chair with a bucket thing – a commode, I think it's called. They're handy things, they are, when old folks can't get up the stairs no more…'

I looked at Jess who was pulling a disgusted face. 'But Reggie, it's broken and stained!' I said.

'Well this is nice,' said my mother, in an effort to change the subject. 'All of us together.'

'Mm,' said Jess, looking at me. 'So, where are we going exactly?'

'It's called 'Sunset Villas',' Mum said, - 'just by the park.'

'I don't believe it!' hissed Jess. 'Out of all the nursing homes in town, it has to be that one!'

'Is something the matter?' asked Mum.

'No, everything's fine,' said Jess, gritting her teeth.

When we got there, we told Mum and Reggie to go on ahead.

'For goodness' sake!' said Jess. 'I can't go in there – they'll recognise me!'

'I know – I've got some old clothes from the shop in the boot. I'm sure there's an old scarf and coat you could put on so they don't realize it's you.'

'I could just pretend I'm ill,' said Jess.

'No – Mum will suspect something's up, Jess. Anyway, Mum said the old lady's looking forward to meeting us.'

'Oh, for goodness' sake! All right then.'

I opened a bag of old clothes and sifted through it. I pulled out a yellow and black woollen scarf and a tatty green raincoat with a stain on the collar.

'Ergh – they're really whiffy, Dora!' She put them on anyway and went into the foyer holding her nose.

'Why are you dressed like that?' said my mother loudly, when she saw Jess. 'And why have you got a scarf round your head? You look as if you're about to head into a snowstorm – I can hardly see your face!'

'I was cold, Mum,' said Jess. 'I might be coming down with something.'

The receptionist gave us a funny look. 'Are you here for Ruby Bunion's birthday party?' she asked. 'It's in the social room – that way,' she said, pointing.

Ruby was in the centre of the room surrounded by staff, other residents, and a big bunch of helium balloons with 99 written on them all. We went over to present her with her cake and introduce ourselves.

'Oooh, what a lovely cake,' she said, lifting the lid.

'Happy birthday, Ma,' said Reggie.

'Thanks, son,' she said, looking adoringly at him as only a mother could.

After this we had to endure an hour of 1940's war-time songs Karaoke-style. When our mother got up to sing *Keep the Home Fires Burning* in an out-of-tune warble which even Reggie seemed to find disturbing, we decided it was time to go.

'I'm getting broiled,' complained Jess, - 'and this coat smells of wee. I can't stand any more of this appalling singing either. Can't we go now?'

Suddenly, Ruby piped up - 'that woman's wearing my scarf and coat, Reggie! I thought I recognised them. You've stolen my clothes!' she said, pointing an accusing bony finger at Jess.

'Don't be silly, Ruby,' said my mother.

'I'm not!' said the old lady, sticking to her guns. 'I'd recognize that coat anywhere.' Then she spotted something else.

'I thought I said I didn't want no more cakes from *that* bakery! I've already been poisoned once!' She was pointing at the cake box which said Paradise Bakery in large pink writing.

'I'm sorry,' said one of the nurses to my Mum, but we'll have to remove this cake and dispose of it. We've had enough trouble as it is with that company. We can't take any more risks.'

'I've only just got better from that Norovirus,' said Ruby. 'It nearly finished me off, it did!'

'It wasn't Noro,' said the nurse.

'Well, whatever it was, I was sick as a dog – them tarts were lethal – someone was trying to kill me and no mistake!'

'No one was trying to kill you, Ruby, you just had an upset tummy,' said the nurse, trying to calm her down, - 'curry doesn't suit you, that's all.'

'They were, I tell you. And now look – that's the one who brought me this cake and she's stolen my clothes an' all!' The old lady began to hyperventilate. 'Someone bring me my inhaler – quick, before I expire!' she said, falling back into her chair. She scowled at Jess and then she pointed her finger at Reggie. 'You want me dead now, don't you, Reggie Bunion! I see what you're all up to. Well, you won't get nothing from me when I die, Reggie, my son! I'll see to that!'

'Ma, no one's trying to get rid of you – we just came to see you on your birthday…' said Reggie.

'Well, you can bugger off,' she said.

'We'd better just go,' I said.

When we got back from 'Chicken Licken', later on in the evening, I told Andrew about it.

'What a waste of a good cake,' said Andrew.

'It was awful,' I said. 'Ruby accused us of trying to do away with her!'

'She's probably senile, Dora – old ladies get like that.'

'Reggie was a bit upset by it – he told her she was a daft old bat. Then the nurses said if we didn't leave they'd call security.'

'Oh well, she'll have forgotten all about it by tomorrow and Reggie will be the apple of her eye again – just you wait and see!'

'I hope I don't get like that!' I said.

Andrew didn't answer. Sometimes I wonder whether he listens to half of what I say to him.

Sunday 5th May

Andrew took the boys to watch Shillingsworth football team play at home this morning, despite the fact that it was pouring with rain. Flora was supposed to be revising but when I put an ear to her door, I could hear some tinny-sounding music and Flora having a very long phone conversation – probably with Gaz. I know it was long, because I listened eight times during the course of the morning. Mind you, I have no idea what they were talking about – it sounded like inane nonsense to me – something about 'moshing in pits' and 'walls of death'. When I asked Tom about it later he told me it means loads of rock fans crashing into each other at high speed who are probably on speed, or something like it. I mean, really? I think I ought to speak to Andrew about it – Flora might be getting into something we don't like – it's a dangerous world out there. Look at Bob and

Barbara, for heaven's sake! We haven't heard a peep out of them since they left the country. Anything could have happened to them.

I rang my mother to see how Reggie was.

'He's a bit upset,' said Mum.

'Well, I thought he might be.'

'Not about Ruby, Dora. He says she's always like that.'

'Oh, what then?'

'He's upset because you were taking the things he gave you to the tip instead of putting them in the shop. Jess told him.'

'I see. Why did she say that!' (*trust my sister to let the cat out of the bag*)

'Reggie told her she shouldn't be wearing his mother's old coat because she might stretch it, and then you wouldn't be able to sell it in the shop. Jess got cross and told him the stuff was only fit for the tip, and 'who would want a manky, old-lady's mac that smelt of widdle anyway'.'

'Well, I'm sorry but I have to agree with Jess, Mum – none of it was good enough for the shop.'

'Well, he says he wants it returned – Ruby told him to get it back.'

'For goodness' sake! What's he going to do with it? I'm beginning to think this shop is more trouble than it's worth,' I said, sighing.

There was a knock at the door, so I rang off, and went to see who it was.

'Any jobs you need doing? said a small boy scout, - 'we're collecting for the elderly.'

I was tempted to give him Reggie's old rubbish and send him round there with it.

'OK,' I said, - 'what have you been doing for other people so far?'

'Cleaning cars, gardening, dog walking - and some people just give us money!' he said, looking at me hopefully. Then I had a bright idea. I gave him and his two friends a roll of black bin bags and asked them to collect old clothes, bric-a-brac, and anything that people didn't want, for Pets' Haven. They looked a bit dubious about it at first but when I said they could have £20 plus a bag of sweets each, their enthusiasm renewed itself and off they went.

I busied myself in the kitchen, making Sunday Lunch and the family favourite, apple crumble, for pudding.

'Dora, that was fantastic,' said Andrew, after the meal, patting his stomach with happy appreciation.

'Can I go to Oscar Barker's house now?' asked Billy.

'Who's Oscar?' I said.

'He's my friend from down the road – you know, the house with the giant unicorn in the front garden.'

'OK, but be back in time for tea.'

'Aren't they a bit mad, those people?' said Andrew, when he'd gone.

'He's an artist, Andrew, and his wife teaches yoga – that hardly makes them 'mad'.'

'I know, but isn't it the Barkers who home-school all their children?'

'Yes.'

'That's mad in my book. Who on earth in their right mind would want six children at home 24/7?'

'Well, some children just aren't suited for mainstream education, Andrew. Maybe we should consider it for Luke and Billy – I mean, they don't seem to find school very stimulating, do they?'

'Stimulating! They don't go to school to be stimulated, Dora – it's *supposed* to be tortuous and dull! It teaches them about the real world! I haven't got time for all this airy-fairy nonsense about being a free spirit instead of having a proper job. What is it Gideon Barker does again? - messing about with plaster and bashing rocks, isn't it? Well, that's just living in cloud cuckoo land as far as I'm concerned.'

'He's a sculptor Andrew.'

'Well, whatever – that unicorn thing looks as if the local Kindergarten made it.'

'Honestly, Andrew! Don't be such a philistine. Not everyone is academic like you – some of us have different skills.'

'It's a matter of application, Dora – anyone can faff around being arty-farty if they want. I'm talking about the harsh reality of life.'

'Well, what about you then, Andrew? I mean you're doing this writing thing – isn't that farting about then?'

'That's different – I've only got 6 months to focus on it and then I'll have to go back to the real world of work.'

'I still don't understand what we're going to live on during this time, Andrew.'

'I told you, Dora – it's fine. I'm doing a bit of work part-time for Sharp and Prentice, and I've got a retainer. Xpertatlaw.com has put me on their list of on-line advisors, so I'll be getting paid for each consultation. Anyway, you'll have your shop up and running soon, won't you? That'll bring in some income. It looks like you've got some donations right now,' said Andrew, pointing at the street outside our front window.

My boy scouts had been doing a brilliant job collecting for me – the front lawn was covered in black bin bags and boxes full of stuff.

'It'll have to come in to the house,' I said to Andrew. 'If it rains again it'll all get soaked.'

At tea time, Billy announced that he wasn't going to school the next day.

'You are!' said Andrew.

'Oscar says school is for losers.'

'Does he!' I said.

'He says it's better to learn stuff at home because then you get loads more time to play.'

'Well, I'm sorry to tell you, Billy, but there's no way we're home-schooling any of you.'

'But Dad,' said Luke, - 'we wouldn't have to do exams!'

'I wish I didn't have to!' said Tom.

'Me too,' said Flora.

Billy scowled and stabbed a fish-finger with his fork. 'It's not fair! Oscar's Dad lets him stay at home! School stinks!'

Monday 6th May

We will have testing times ahead and I must say I am not looking forward to it at all. Tom has three exams this week and Flora's start in one weeks' time. Having nagged for England, Andrew and I have decided there's no point now as it's too late if they haven't got the message. Anyway, there's no point making ourselves ill over it. One good thing is that Billy will finally get his plaster taken off tomorrow, so at least there'll be fewer breakages and less spilled food on the floor.

Andrew has already buried himself in his novel. He let me see his opening paragraph last night. I thought it needed a bit of work still, but instead, decided to say it was wonderful - he's still a bit tetchy after we all laughed at his dodgy ideas for the title.

He read it out:

Chapter 1 (Darkness Falls)

Outside, the frosty, dank, chill of the night closed in like a heavy, impenetrable black shroud, sweeping away the last paltry fragments of the flickering, fast- dissolving Autumn twilight. A man, barely visible within the creeping shadows of the half-rotten abandoned buildings lining the slimy crumbling walls of the canal, ran swiftly, soundlessly – briefly he stopped to take a breath, his expelled air forming a small plume of white, ghostly vapour above his perfectly smooth, shaved head, and then, in a moment he was gone.

No one saw the knife, spinning, slicing through the air - a silver streak of light, its serrated edge glinting viciously in the moonlight, arching its way across the foreboding, murky canal to its deep, watery grave beneath the swirling, foul-smelling scum on the other side. No one saw the sickening, blood-spattered clothes, still dripping, still warm against his own clammy, pasty, pock marked, skin. No one saw his hard, pitiless face – his eyes, emotionless, black as two pieces of round, shiny coal, his features set like granite stone against the merciless, punishing cold night air. No one saw him run like the wind – like a speeding bullet, across the rickety, worn-out bridge, across the gritty, cold, flattened waste-ground of the deserted carpark beyond, down to the grim, featureless housing estate which crawled - like an ever-mushrooming viper's nest along the outer edges of the bleak, desolate, forgotten town of **Blackridge.**

Andrew looked very pleased with his efforts.

'It's great Andrew,' I said, - 'very atmospheric! (*I decided to keep shtum about the flowery language.*) Where's Blackridge then?'

'It's made up – it's not a real place Dora.'

'Thank goodness for that!'

'Well, I've got lots to do,' I said, looking at all the stuff the boy scouts had brought me. It took me all morning to take all of it down to the shop and sort it out. Melanie came along to help and we got loads done. 'I think I'll be ready to open soon Melanie.'

'You'd better set a date – tell the papers Dora!' she said. 'We need to write a press release.'

'OK – yes you're right,' I said, - 'it's just that I'm not keen on Trudy Stoker who usually reports on these things. You can't trust her Melanie.'

'I know, but it's only a press release for a shop – I mean, what can she do with that?'

Melanie and I went to the coffee shop afterwards since we felt we'd earned it.

'I've been exercising muscles I didn't know existed!' said Melanie, flexing her biceps. We took our cups to a seat by the window where we could look out and see the world go by.

'How's Andrew's book going?' Melanie asked.

'Well, he's just started it. Whether he'll have enough staying power I don't know – he can be quite impatient, so we'll see.'

'Well, Geoff will miss him at the office - he'll have to find another lunch companion now, and the rest of them are pretty dull, apart from Shama of course!'

'Yes – I'm not sorry he won't be spending time with her! Honestly, she's like a man-magnet with her long sleek body, beautiful black shiny hair and thrusting breasts. Why does she have to be so out there with them? She doesn't seem to know how to be subtle.'

'I know Dora. I don't know how they get any work done around there.'

'Well Andrew must get some work done I suppose – he's sorted out the lease on the shop and got my charity set up, so it's all good to go! I'm getting quite excited about it. Suzie says she's setting up an interview on our local radio station (Fun-time FM), on Thursday morning with Cheeky Chas, the 'DJ with the cliché', as Andrew calls him. To be honest, I'm not particularly looking forward to that – I'll probably make a complete hash of it.'

'You'll be fine Dora. I tell you what, we'll have a practice tomorrow. I'll make up some questions and you can answer them – you won't feel so nervous about it then.'

'Oh, thanks Melanie – I'm not very good at public speaking. I asked Suzie to do it but she didn't want to do it either!'

'You'll be fine,' said Melanie. 'It's just a matter of being prepared. Don't worry Dora – you just have to be yourself.'

When I told Andrew later, he said I could always imagine I was someone else – like actors do. He said it works for his barrister friends.

'But Melanie said I should just be myself,' I protested.

Andrew just looked at me and said I should strongly consider *his* suggestion.

Tuesday 7th May

The kittens are getting everywhere now and causing havoc. This morning I found one of them in the recycling box with all the yogurt cartons. It's a good job I saw him there just in time, before I put him out for the bin men! The other day, Billy found four of them in his bed, and yesterday, Andrew stopped two of them getting through a gap behind the bath where they could have fallen down under the floorboards. It's quite a worry.

Perhaps we should have kept the old playpen – it would have been perfect for corralling cats.

After the usual morning routine of complete chaos and lots of shouting – the three older children finally left the house and I left Andrew and Billy sleeping. I went off to see Melanie and to go through some preparation for the radio interview.

'So, Dora,' she began. Once we'd each got a mug of coffee, - 'what gave you the idea to start your charity, Pets' Haven?'

I was silent for a while. 'Um, well, I don't know really – I think my friend Suzie told me to do it ….'

'No Dora, you can't say that,' said Melanie straight away. 'You need to say something inspiring – you could tell a story about an animal you looked after, or an old person you met who needed help…' She looked at me and waited.

'Oh, OK – well…oh, I know! I helped Suzie out when she went to prison and I looked after her dog Ping-Pong for her.'

'Melanie sighed. 'You can't say that either Dora.'

'No – I suppose not.'

'Look, just say something along the lines of – you've always loved animals and think it's important they stay with their owners – that when someone goes into hospital for a short time, you want to make sure they are looked after and can go back to the owner. You need to make it clear it's for poor people who can't afford kennels too, or you'll be inundated.'

'This isn't easy, is it?' I said.

'Well, let's try another question,' said Melanie. 'How will the animals be cared for?'

'I don't quite know yet – my husband is getting nervous – he thinks we'll end up with them all at our house!'

'OK…how about using the questions to your advantage Dora?'

'How do you mean?'

'Well you could say that you've got some lovely people lined up to board the animals, all vetted and fully insured, blah, blah, but you are looking for lots more like them.'

'Oh, I see.'

'You need to use the interview to get publicity for the charity Dora, and to try and get more donations and more people to look after the animals – it's a fantastic opportunity to get everyone's attention.'

'Yes, you're right but it all seems quite complicated Melanie – I think I'll get in a terrible muddle.'

'No, you won't – I'm sure you'll be fine. You just need to think about the best way to promote it.'

'What sort of experience do you have with animals Dora?' asked Melanie, resuming.

'Um…. I've got some of my own at home, and I worked in a pet parlour for a bit, but that didn't go too well…'

'Dora, you've got to be positive about everything – you can't sound so negative!'

'But it didn't go too well.'

'I know, but maybe you should just say you've worked with animals professionally.'

'Ooh, that sounds good doesn't it!'

'Yes Dora – you have to put a positive spin on everything. It's a game Dora. Marketing is just about perception. Like …. I don't know…. take those disgusting jam things you put in the toaster. What were they called – Tarty Goppers or something? Anyway, they were advertised relentlessly on TV and everyone was brainwashed into saying they were delicious. The fact that they actually tasted like an old gym shoe was irrelevant – everyone was duped into buying them.'

'That's conning people.'

'Well, not really. You're just presenting your product in the best light.'

'I'm not very good with these things Melanie. Last time I spoke to a media person, I accidentally told them about a disaster at Jess and Terry's bakery and I got into terrible hot water over it.'

Melanie looked sympathetic, but I could also see that she secretly had grave concerns about my ability to pull this off.

'Perhaps Andrew could help?' she suggested, confirming my suspicion.

Wednesday 8th May

I don't think Tom's English exam went too well yesterday. We tried to ask him about it after tea last night, but his response wasn't reassuring. Flora didn't help by telling him that it's - *Julius Caesar*', not 'Julius Seizure' - and that Caesar didn't say 'Eat you

Brutus'! 'It's '*Et tu*' she said, - and it's '*Ides* of March', not 'tides'. You're such an idiot Tom!'

Well, it's not Tom's strongest subject, so there's no point in worrying about it is there? I'm sure he'll do better in the other exams – that's what I told him anyway. Of course, Andrew overreacted as usual.

'What sort of stupid teacher didn't notice you getting something like that wrong!' he sounded off, - 'I mean, what are they teaching these days! They all seem to be imbeciles! No one's getting a decent education any more!'

'Look, it doesn't matter Andrew. Tom's skills lie elsewhere,' I said, coming to his rescue. At this point Tom shouted at Andrew, telling him he was a 'pompous old twat' and went upstairs where he refused to come out of his room for the rest of the evening.

'Great!' I said. 'Now look what you've done!'

'Well, I'm sorry Dora, but I sent my kids to school in the vain hope they might receive a decent education. Now I'm beginning to wonder if Gideon Barker hasn't got the right idea after all!'

Honestly, Andrew seems to have no thought about the consequences of his actions! I sometimes wonder if some bits of his brain didn't cease to develop past the age of sixteen himself! The last thing I want right now is Tom being upset – exam time is stressful enough.

'You'll have to find a way to make it up to him,' I said at bed time. 'You can't go around upsetting them at the moment – anyway, I thought you were supposed to be advocating calmness and a stress-free life now you've stopped working at the office! You need to practice what you preach Andrew!'

I decided to get the girls over for lunch today and thrash a few ideas out. I reluctantly invited Jess over as well, being a bit of an expert at these kinds of things, although I knew she'd be hideously bossy.

'Now,' she said, taking charge of the proceedings, - 'Dora needs help and I should know because I'm her sister.'

'Thanks Jess, but I'm not completely helpless!' I said, already regretting my decision to include her. Anyway, the others all nodded in agreement.

'I think she needs a press secretary,' said Jess. 'Now I can't do it because I'm far too busy with my own business.' She looked at the others.

'Melanie's good – she used to be in marketing, didn't you?' I said to her.

'Right that's sorted then,' said Jess, not waiting for Melanie to agree.

'So, what that means Dora, is that you don't speak to the press or any other media people without them going through Melanie first – OK?' Jess looked at me the same way my old teacher used to.

'Yes Miss,' I said.

'Well Dora, it's for your own good – remember the 'dishcloth' incident?' she said, lowering her voice when she said 'dishcloth'.

'How could I forget,' I said.

The others looked puzzled, then Melanie remembered. 'Oh yes! I know Dora's cooking can be a bit unusual, but I've never heard of a cloth cake! That was *so* funny,' she said, hooting with laughter.

'Well, I didn't think so,' said Jess, peevishly, - 'and neither did some of my customers!'

Melanie shut up and looked sheepish. 'Sorry,' she said, half-rolling her eyes in my direction. I smiled weakly.

'Now,' resumed Jess, - 'we need to write a press release and give Dora practice for the radio broadcast. I've been on the radio myself several times – it's an acquired skill.'

'I was on it once,' said Suzie, - 'for my beauty salon. It was quite a scary experience. They asked me why we'd decided to provide treatments for men as well as women.'

'Oh, I remember,' I said. 'You said men enjoyed the treatments as much as the girls…'

Melanie snorted, spilling some of her tea.

Well, that's just the kind of thing Dora would say!' said Jess haughtily. 'It won't help your cause if you don't take this seriously,' said Jess, getting tetchy. 'You don't want people thinking your charity is a joke – no one will take you seriously! Now, I'm going to ask you some questions as if you're on the radio.'

'I tried that already, with Melanie,' I said.

'Well, you can't have enough practice in my opinion.'

'OK,' I said, obediently.

'Right Dora,' said Jess, - 'tell me the idea behind Pets' Haven.'

'Well, it's for people who have to go into hospital or are ill for a short time maybe, who don't have anyone to care for their animals. The idea is to give short-term respite while the owner can't look after them.'

'I see,' said Jess. 'There are hundreds of people in that situation though aren't there, so how will you decide which ones are deserving and which ones can afford to pay for a kennel or a cattery?'

'Umm, well, I could ask them how much they earn…'

Jess looked at me sternly. 'You can't do that!'

'Well, I don't know – I haven't figured that bit out yet…'

'Well you need to, or every Tom, Dick and Harry will be knocking at your door Dora! You'll be overwhelmed with requests!'

I suddenly felt a bit ill.

'Well let's put that on the back-burner for now,' said Melanie, seeing my expression. 'We'll come up with something, don't worry.'

'Mmm,' said Jess, not impressed. 'OK, what about caring for the animals Dora. What plans do you have for that?' She looked at me intently.

'Well – I'm getting lots of lovely people on board right now,' I said, remembering what Melanie had said. Melanie nodded at me encouragingly. 'We would welcome anyone who would like to be involved to come forward and contact us – we're looking for animal-lovers of course, with a kind and compassionate attitude and would love to hear from you if you're interested…'

'Say where they can contact you,' butted in Jess.

'Yes, I was just about to…'

'Is it paid, or voluntary?' barked Jess.

'It will be paid work and we'll be checking everyone properly. It's very important that everyone is fully vetted and their homes checked for suitability. It's a very responsible job and we will be making sure these animals get the best possible care.' I looked at Melanie for confirmation.

'Good,' said Jess, sounding like a teacher again.

The next hour was spent writing the press release. By the time everyone left, I felt as if I'd been interrogated by the Gestapo. Honestly, Jess was worse than I'd imagined she'd be. The others gave me the raised-eyebrows/wide-eyed look, as they left.

'Thanks for coming,' I said. 'Thanks for all your help!'

'Of course, the truth is that it was mostly Jess speaking and the others hadn't really got much of a word in. Typical of Jess of course. Oh well, she did have some useful things to say – I just wish she said them in a more people-friendly way.

'I'm really worried about tomorrow,' I confessed to Andrew, later on.

'Well, just think before you speak,' he said, - 'and I'm sure you'll be fine – remember what I said about acting? Pretend to be someone else - maybe you could imagine you're Jess…'

'Speaking of Jess, she asked me how I was going to decide who gets help and who doesn't – she's got a point, Andrew – I don't actually know how to get around that…'

'Well, since we don't have time to work that out literally the night before,' he said, somewhat sarcastically, - 'I think the best thing is avoidance – just say that each case will be considered on merit and that the aim is to help people and animals who are most deserving.'

'Yes – that sounds OK, doesn't it! You're very good at these things, Andrew. You could have been a politician!'

'I do have my uses,' he said smugly.

Of course, the thing is, he is a lawyer after all – so his main activity in life is wriggling out of tight corners, plus of course, defending the indefensible. It might come in very useful on Friday morning when we have to have a meeting with the Headmaster of Luke's school about a recent food-throwing incident.

Thursday 9th May

I didn't sleep very well at all last night, what with worrying about my interview, Tom's chemistry exam and all the other things going on. Two of the kittens are missing and no one had time to look for them this morning, I'd forgotten to iron anything for the interview, and Flora is spending too much time with Gaz.

Anyway, I needed to focus on the job in hand.

'That's an interesting top,' said Andrew, casting an eye over my blouse - 'is that wrinkle-look in fashion again?'

'No,' I said.

'Well, don't worry - no one can see you on the radio, can they! Good luck, Dora – I'm sure you'll be fine!'

I got to the studio with a whole hour to spare, because I was worried I'd be late, so I parked and found a café across the road and ordered a coffee. When I sat down, I noticed I had several texts on my phone from well-wishers:

'Don't worry Dora – you'll be great!' (Suzie)

Just relax – it's only 'Cheeky Chas', not Prince Charles!' (Andrew)

'Good luck Mum!' (Flora)

Jess tells me you're on the radio today! I've told all my friends to listen in!' (Mum)

'Don't forget to breathe,' (Jess)

*'Tuning in **now**! Just be yourself!' (Melanie)*

'Remember what I said – pretend you're someone else!' (Andrew again)

I switched off my phone at this point – my head was spinning. I decided to employ a self-help calming device by imagining I was floating on a lilo in the Pacific. I closed my eyes and with the warm sun on my face, imagined I was drifting over gentle waves with the soft splash of the water on the bleached sun-soaked sand behind me, and the bright, turquoise sea stretching out for miles towards the hazy horizon ahead….

'Bugger!' I said out load, waking up and looking at my watch - suddenly realising I only had ten minutes to get to the studio. How did that happen? I must have nodded off!

I got to the studio with seconds to spare. Red-faced and panting like a dog, just as Cheeky Chas was about to introduce me. What followed should most definitely be consigned to the cutting room floor, in my opinion. It was one of the worst twenty minutes of my life.

A busty girl called Wanda with blonde tresses and spades of make-up showed me in and introduced herself as Chas's Personal Assistant. She looked about twelve and made me feel about a hundred.

'Quick, get Mrs Loveday a chair!' she said to someone, taking one look at me.

'It's OK,' I said, - 'I'm just a bit breathless from running.'

'Glass of water, love?' said another twelve-year old.

Cripes, I thought, looking round at the photos adorning the walls of the studio – hundreds of grinning minor celebrities in baseball caps, weighted down with chain jewellery doing V signs and being cool, mocked my middle-aged irrelevance.

Cheeky Chas turned his gaze reluctantly from leering at Wanda's cleavage, to me. As the last few bars of '*How much is That Doggy in the Window*' faded out, grinning excessively, he introduced me.

'We're all wagging our tails here, we're so happy to see the lovely Pandora Loveday who's come to tell us all about her charity work for Pets' Haven. So, Pandora – or should I call you Panda?' he said, smiling at his own puerile joke.

It's Dora, actually,' I said.

'OK – great!' he said, his fixed smile slightly faltering. 'So, Nora, tell us about your little enterprise…'

'Well, my idea was to try and help people with animals who might have to go into hospital, or …'

'Cool! That sounds like my kinda charity,' said Chas. 'So, Nora – what's your favourite animal?'

'Um, well, I don't think I've got a favourite…'

'Mine's an elephant – don't you just love those huge tusks and long, squirty trunks? I always wanted my own pet elephant when I was a kid!' I noticed some of the staff looking a bit nervous at this point.

'My son has some stick insects,' I offered, lamely.

'Cool!' said Chas. 'It's so great to have you here in the studio, Nora – now let's play some more tunes!' He put on *'Nelly the Elephant'*. 'I lurve this – it's like I'm five again!' said Chas, singing along to it. Wanda rolled her eyes and pointed at her nose which seemed to generate a reaction from some of the others in the room.

'So, Nora, what do you think about rhino's and stuff – y'know, the animals that are becoming extinct in the world – sad, isn't it?'

'Well, yes of course, but I'm here to tell the listeners about my local charity Pets' Haven …'

'Sure, Nora – and what a fantastic job you're doing – we're all into animals here – I mean, did you see how *cute* those baby orangutans *are!* I mean, they're just adorable, aren't they! Let's have another tune.' He then played *'I Want to be a Monkey Like You'*.

I decided, whilst watching Chas do the actions to the song, that when the music ended, I would take charge of things and get my message across, or this whole thing would be a total waste of time.

As the Jungle Book music faded away, I took my chance, and as fast as possible so he couldn't interrupt, I said as much as I could and only stopped when I saw someone doing a throat-cutting gesture.

'Wow!' said Chas, - 'I think someone wants my job!' He laughed hysterically, played a perky jingle and then said, - 'let's take some calls!'

'What?' I said, looking at Wanda, who was filing her nails in the corner and looking bored.

'Yeah, we've got some listeners on the line eager to ask you some questions, Nora. I've got a Mr John Thackery on the line. Go ahead John…'

'I'd like to ask if there are any pets that Nora won't take.'

'So, what do you think, Nora – I mean, what if someone's got a pet giraffe or something?'

'Well, obviously that wouldn't be likely, would it?' I said. Chas was still grinning manically. 'Do you have an unusual pet, Mr Thackery?'

'Well, I've got several, actually – I've got three Carpet Vipers, four Crested Geckos, two African Tree Frogs and a Bearded Dragon.'

'I see. Well, initially, I'm afraid, we'll only be accepting normal pets – dogs, cats, rabbits – that sort of thing.'

'Oh,' said Mr Thackery, - 'that's very disappointing to hear.'

Chas moved on quickly and took another call.

'This is Philippa Snow – I'd like to ask if I'd be able to skype my dog if I was in hospital? He's all I've got, you see, and I'd need to know I could see his little furry face every day…'

'Well, Nora, what d'ya think? Would the old dear be able to see her precious pooch? I mean, it seems cruel not to …'

'I'm sure that could be arranged, Mrs Snow,' I said, looking at Chas whose eyes were beginning to glaze over. 'The whole point about Pets' Haven is that the charity is here to help owners as well as their pets.'

'We'll take our last call now,' said Chas, yawning. 'So, who have we got on the line?'

'Hello, my name's Jack,' said a familiar voice. 'Hello Dora!'

'Hello Jack,' I said nervously.

'So, you know each other?' said Chas.

'Yes – Dora used to work in my pet parlour.' Chas stopped yawning, his interest re-kindled.

'So, Jack – what do you think of Nora – I mean Dora's great new charity?'

'Well, to be honest, I was quite surprised when I tuned in this morning and heard who your guest was going to be. I've got a few reservations …'

I decided to have a massive coughing fit at this point. It wasn't going well and I had to save the day.

'Can I get you that glass of water now?' Wanda said.

Chas wound things up by saying: 'Well I'm afraid we've run out of time to hear about Jack's reservations – would that be 'wild animal reservations'? Who knows!' he said, laughing hysterically again. He put on another song – this time it was *Run Rabbit Run*.

'Let's get a quick photo,' said an assistant before I could escape.

'How did it go?' asked Suzie on the phone later.

'Badly!' I said.

'I'm sure it wasn't really. Melanie recorded it. I'm going there later to hear it. Are you coming?'

'No thanks – I think I'll just go and become a recluse. Honestly, Suzie, the whole thing was awful. I think there was something wrong with that Chas bloke. Anyway, that's the first and last radio interview I ever do.'

'OK, well I'll call you later – and don't worry, I'm sure it's not as bad as you think.'

'Well,' said Andrew,' when I got home, - 'that was interesting!'

'I suppose you heard all of it?'

'Absolutely! Cheeky Chas was on form, wasn't he! What an idiot! Actually, Dora, he must have been on something – don't you think?'

Wanda's nose-pinching suddenly made sense.

'What happened at the end, Dora? You sounded as if you were choking to death – I was really worried!'

'It was Jack on the phone – I had to do something – she was about to dob me in, Andrew!'

'By the way, Dora, I got a phone call from school reminding us we've got to go in and have a meeting with Mr Grimsby tomorrow morning.'

'Can't you go without me?' I said, - 'I'm feeling a bit fragile.'

'I'm not facing him alone,' said Andrew, - 'Luke's Headmaster takes no prisoners – we need to present a united front.'

'Can't we say we're ill or something?'

'No, Dora. We must face the music.'

'What does Luke say about it all?'

'Well, apparently Freddy Scarman started it by throwing a bread roll at Barny Butterworth, and it hit him in the eye. He says Barny then threw a spoon at Freddy and it missed him, landing in Luke's ham salad which went all over the floor...'

'Never!' I said, shocked.

'Well, it's not that hard to imagine!' said Andrew.

'No, I mean Luke eating a salad!'

'Oh, yes! Well, anyway, Freddy was laughing, so Luke threw a carrot at him and it caused Freddy to have a nose-bleed, apparently. So, Freddy's parents complained to the school about Luke.'

'For God's sake!' I said with exasperation. 'It would be Freddy Scarman, wouldn't it! Of all the boys, it had to be *that* one.'

Andrew's still got a red mark over his eye from the punch-up with Freddy's dad Jim, when they all fell out on the rugby pitch back in February. As far as I know, Jim is still barred from becoming a Governor at the school and, not unsurprisingly, is looking for ways to pay Andrew back for the humiliation. The trouble is, Andrew responds by escalating things – I mean, instead of secretly ditching a pile of rubble in Jim Scarman's driveway and therefore causing untold tribulation, he should have been the bigger man and just let it go. Anyway, calling each other very rude names over a silly game is frankly, infantile.

'It's not a '*silly*' game,' Andrew said at the time, - 'it's a well-respected time-honoured test of skill and strength, but that thug Jim Scarman and his moronic son don't understand the rules!'

Anyway, it's not just Freddy in this case, Luke always seems to be getting himself into trouble. I don't know why he can't just settle down and focus on his school work. Barely a week goes by when there isn't an incident of one sort or another.

'Perhaps we aren't giving him enough of our attention, Andrew.'

'Nonsense Dora. Only the other day I spent an hour practicing bowling with him for his inter-school cricket match next week. And you made all those croissants for his French class didn't you! No Dora, he's just being his usual silly self. It's time he learned to be a bit more responsible.'

After tea, we tried talking to him about being responsible.

'It wasn't my fault!' he said.

'The thing is, Luke, you could have decided not to respond by throwing the carrot,' said Andrew. 'Instead, you could have just gone and asked the dinner lady for another ham salad.'

Luke thought for a moment. 'But Dad, you didn't walk away when Freddy's dad punched you, did you! Anyway, Barny

Butterworth was crying, and Freddy Scarman just thought it was funny.'

'Oh, I see,' said Andrew.

'I found the kittens,' said Luke, changing the subject.

'Where?' I said.

'In my school bag.'

'Oh well, that's a relief. It's a good job you saw them before you went to school!'

'I didn't,' said Luke.

'What do you mean? You didn't take them to school, did you?'

'Yes.'

'I don't believe it! Luke, how could you be so daft!'

'It's not my fault, Mum. Anyway, it's OK – Mr Grimsby said I had 'surpassed myself' and that I was 'full of surprises' and then he took them away and put them in his office. I think he likes cats.'

I looked at Andrew, who had his head in his hands.

'It's quite sweet, isn't it?' I said to Andrew, at bed time, - 'you know – Luke defending another boy from being bullied.'

'Well, I suppose so, but look at the trouble it's got him into - and us!'

Friday 10th May

Mr Grimsby had the look of someone who'd just encountered a nasty odour. He shook our hands as briefly as possible and directed us to sit down opposite him.

'Well, Mr and Mrs Loveday, I'm sorry to say this, but your son Luke is causing us a great deal of concern.' He scowled at us from the safety of the other side of his vast, highly polished desk.

Thus, began his diatribe:

'Please help me understand why your son thinks he has no need to conform to the high standards of behaviour we expect from pupils attending *Our Lady of the Immaculate Conception*? Here at OLIC's we believe very sincerely in our school motto 'Bonitatem et Disciplinam et Scientiam, Doce Me' – Teach me Goodness, Discipline and Knowledge'. This revered and illustrious seat of learning was established 300 years ago by the Little Sisters of Perpetual Servitude. I don't need to tell you what that means to me, Mr and Mrs Loveday, do I?' Mr Grimsby looked wistfully out of his window towards the sports field where we could hear the boys playing cricket outside. 'It means,' continued Mr Grimsby, - 'that for centuries, boys like Luke have passed through the hallowed hallways of this most celebrated of schools and I have been here long enough to predict which of those boys will go on to make us proud to call him an OLIC's boy. I was an OLIC's boy, and my father before me was one.'

I tried not to look at Andrew at this point, because I could sense him trying to stifle a snigger. Mr Grimsby was not impressed.

'You may think it amusing, Mr Loveday, but I do not.'

'Sorry,' said Andrew.

'Now,' said Mr Grimsby, - 'there are several incidents I wish to share with you,' he said stuffily. 'The first is a matter of grave concern because it involves missile throwing which could have had serious consequences.'

'You mean the carrot flinging incident?' said Andrew.

'Yes,' said Mr Grimsby, 'I certainly do.'

'He was defending Barny Butterworth from that thug Freddy Scarman,' said Andrew crossly. 'And for heaven's sake – it was only a carrot!'

'ONLY A CARROT! Mr Loveday! As Benjamin Franklin said, and I quote: "A small leak can sink a great ship". Your son is an impulsive and foolish boy, and that's a dangerous combination, Mr Loveday. Now, the second thing I want to speak to you about is something that happened in Monsieur Bonheur's French class on Tuesday.'

Andrew looked up at the ceiling and breathed out noisily. I elbowed him sharply to stop him saying anything else.

'Monsieur Bonheur was holding a French Appreciation Day in the school, and he went to a lot of trouble to organise an interesting and informative event which we were all looking forward to.'

I dreaded to think what Mr Grimsby was going to tell us next.

'Unfortunately, your son Luke took it upon himself to arrange his own event at break time while Monsieur Bonheur was in the staff room. Apparently, he decided to hold a croissant-eating competition and was seen taking wagers from other boys to see who could eat the most in one go. Not only was Monsieur Bonheur most disappointed there was nothing left to spread his pâté canard on at lunch time, but his star pupil, Henry Goldbloom, was unable to finish his presentation on *'The Delights of the Dordogne'*, because he was taken ill half way through, and was sick all over Monsieur Bonheur's laptop. It later emerged that he had eaten eleven croissants in five minutes.'

'That could probably go in the Guinness Book of Records!' said Andrew, flippantly.

Mr Grimsby was unmoved. I noticed a slight twitch at the corner of his eye as he continued with his denunciations.

'The laptop is beyond repair, Mr Loveday – and this is not the first time Luke has been responsible for damaging school property. And, I don't need to remind you, I'm sure, how seriously we take illicit gambling in our school. Lastly, I don't know whether you are aware of the fact, Mr and Mrs Loveday, that animals are not allowed on the school premises. Yesterday, Luke brought in two kittens from your home without prior permission and certainly not with my approval. Apart from the obvious Health and Safety issues, it was a very irresponsible act and I'm afraid to say it is not the first time he has smuggled animals into the school.'

'Really?'

Nicola Kelsall

'Yes, Mrs Loveday – to date his teachers have had to remove two frogs, a collection of snails, a stick insect, and a large toad from his desk.' He glowered at us and paused for a response.

'Well,' said Andrew, - 'let's not get things out of proportion, Mr Grimsby. None of these incidents are the result of malicious or calculated behaviour   it's just that Luke doesn't consider the consequences of his actions. I mean, boys can be 'impulsive' and 'foolish', I agree, but it's not unusual, is it!' Andrew was trying to remain calm for once, which was a relief.

Mr Grimsby pursed his lips. 'Your son displays more than the average amount of idiocy, Mr Loveday – I am able to confidently say, that in all my years as Headmaster at this school, I have never come across one so prone to buffoonery, and certainly – no boy I ever taught was quite so reckless. Your son, I'm afraid, is heading for cataclysmic failure.' Mr Grimsby's eye started twitching again.

Andrew shifted in his chair, which was too small for him, and I detected an abrupt change in his demeanour. My heart sank.

'Look here, I don't believe you're being fair – Luke's got plenty of potential. You can't just write him off like that!' Andrew said, raising his voice.

'He's got a kind heart, Mr Grimsby,' I said, butting in, - 'I know he's silly and does daft things, but he doesn't mean to cause trouble.'

'My wife's right' said Andrew, - 'I remember being a bit of a wag at school myself. Don't you remember being a school boy, Mr Grimsby? Didn't you annoy your teachers at all?'

'No, Mr Loveday, I did not! My behaviour, I'll have you know, was exemplary! Any boy found wanting was quickly despatched, never to be heard of again. Spare the rod and spoil the child, Mr Loveday – at your peril! Which brings me to the main purpose of this meeting. You should know that I have placed your son on probationary status and I will be watching him like a hawk. If he steps out of line again, his future at this school will be seriously jeopardised. He's on very thin ice – do you understand my drift?'

'What a miserable old fart!' shouted Andrew, stomping back to the car. I followed him with the cardboard box the school receptionist had given me containing the two stow-away kittens.

'Let's just get home,' I said. 'I'm feeling exhausted by the whole thing.'

I'd just made myself a nice cup of tea, when my mother rang.

'Hello Dora! I just wondered if you were OK? It sounded as if someone was being strangled at the end of your interview.'

'Oh, it's fine, Mum. I just had a frog in my throat.'

'What a shame! I thought you'd be on for longer.'

'It was quite long enough, I can tell you!'

'That Chas is a bit cheeky, isn't he!'

'Yes, Mum, that's why he's called 'Cheeky Chas'. He's supposed to be like that – I didn't quite appreciate it until it was too late. Anyway, what did you think?'

'Well, there was one bit when you were gabbling and I couldn't make out what you were saying, but he played some jolly tunes and I liked his jokes.'

'But Mum, did the information about the charity come across well?'

'What charity?'

'Pets'Haven, Mum!'

'Oh, is that what it's called?'

I decided to change the subject. 'How are you anyway – what have you been up to?'

'Oh, I've been very busy in the garden – Reggie's been a real stalwart – I couldn't have managed everything without him. I've decided to give him a special treat tomorrow evening as a surprise for all his help.'

'Oh, that's nice,' I said, - 'what will that be then?'

'I don't know yet – I haven't decided. I might make him a nice steak and kidney pie – or we could go down to the Cat and Fiddle for a drink or two.'

'What, that rough old pub down by the chip shop?'

'It's not that bad, Dora – I've been in there a few times now - with Reggie, of course.'

At the dinner table this evening, things got a bit fraught. We told Luke about our meeting with Mr Grimsby and that we were a bit disappointed with his behaviour.

'But Mum,' he protested, - 'Freddy's lying about getting a nose bleed, and anyway he's a bully. And I was only trying to make the

French day more interesting. Monsieur Bonheur was making us watch boring videos and speak in French *all day*! It was *SOOO* BORING! Anyway, it wasn't my fault Henry Goldbloom was sick – he ate a whole plate of French cheese as well. And I didn't know that the kittens got into my bag – they must have been asleep because I didn't see them until I got to the cloakroom. I tried to hide them in the cleaner's cupboard, but Mrs Vickers saw me.'

'Oh dear,' I said, - 'that was unfortunate. Well, the thing is Luke, Mr Grimsby isn't going to give you any more chances – you've got to stay out of trouble from now on. Do you understand?'

Luke kicked the chair leg and scowled at the table.

'Well, I'm glad today is over,' I said to Andrew when we went to bed. 'I do feel a bit sorry for Luke, but he is his own worst enemy, isn't he!'

'That fusty old Headmaster's a Victorian throw-back,' said Andrew, crossly. He belongs in a Dickens novel. If he tries to get rid of Luke, he'll have me to contend with – I'll sue the pants off him. OLIC's boy, my eye! What a lot of tosh. I bet he was the school snitch when he was a boy. He's got that sneering creepy look about him, don't you think, Dora? Are you listening Dora?'

'Sorry, I was thinking about my mother.'

'Why?'

'She's going out on a date with Reggie tomorrow night. I don't like it.'

'What's wrong with that!'

'You know I think she's making a mistake, Andrew – I mean, Dad would never have gone for a night out at the Cat and Fiddle. It's full of old drunks and people with no teeth. We used to call it the 'spit and widdle'. Mum's lost her sense of decorum.'

'It's just a pub,' said Andrew, matter-of-factly.

'I wish my Dad was still here,' I said, sadly.

Saturday 11th May

'Aren't you supposed to be revising?' I said to Flora this morning, as she put on her jacket to go out.

'You said you weren't going to nag us any more about that!'

'Sorry – I just thought, well – you know, you've got an exam on Monday….'

'I'm going out with Gaz – I need a break.'

'OK,' I said, biting my tongue. 'Where will you go and how long will you be out for?'

'Dunno. See you later, Mum.'

'She's eighteen – you can't stop her,' said Andrew.

'I'm going to see Oscar,' said Billy. 'His Dad's building an underground den in the garden – it's really cool.' He shot out before I could tell him to come home for lunch. Then Tom said he and Luke were going to the park to play football.

'Well, this is rare!' said Andrew. 'Just you and me, I mean!'

'Yes, I know – it's weird.'

'Shall we do something?'

'What do you have in mind, Andrew?'

'I don't know – maybe I'll go and get a newspaper and we could sit out in the garden for a bit.'

'Or we could do some work in the garden, Andrew. The hedge needs cutting – I didn't get very far last time.'

'Oh,' said Andrew, pulling a face. 'Yes, I suppose I could do that. I'm still going to get a paper though. Life can't be all work and no play.'

When he came back, I made a pot of coffee and we went outside. I must say, it was very nice just to sit and read for a bit. That was until I unfolded the Citizen and saw what was on the front page.

'What is it?' Andrew said, hearing my sudden gasp of horror and nearly spilling his coffee. I showed him the picture. There in all her hairless glory was a huge photo of Queenie, with her owner beside her, looking as miserable as it is possible to look for a local paper running a tale-of-woe revelation. I could barely summon the courage to read the story. Andrew grabbed it off me and read it out.

DEVASTATED DOG-LOVER SUES LOCAL PET PARLOUR

A local dog-owner is suing Pooch Parlour (no.52 Shillingsworth High Street, Shillingsworth) for allegedly causing her prize poodle, Queenie, to lose all her fur practically overnight. Mrs Ava Bush, Queenie's distraught owner, says she left her beloved pooch with what she thought was a trusted dog groomer, only to discover later that her dog had not received the usual shampoo treatment, but something unnaturally harsh, possibly endangering the dog's life.

"When I got Queenie home, she began to shed fur immediately, and the next morning she looked like a moth-eaten carpet," complained Miss Bush (37) of 99 Fleece Avenue, Shillingsworth. "She had clumps missing all over her – I could have stuffed a mattress with what fell out! I don't know what they used on her, but it's ruined her career. How can I breed from her now!"

Miss Bush also said that she intends to sue the afore-mentioned grooming salon for defamation, saying that their counter-claim, suggesting that Queenie's ailment could be caused by separation anxiety and a personality disorder, was 'complete bo****ks'.

"My first-class bitch was a beautiful dog before they got their hands on her," says Miss Bush. "I will not rest until that place has been closed down. I don't want any more animals to end up like my poor Queenie!" Miss Bush would like any other disgruntled dog-owners to contact her at jb@terribleservice.com, or alternatively, they can visit her new Poodle Page on Facebook: 'JUSTICE FOR QUEENIE'. She urges people to please get in touch if they have had a similar experience at this salon.

'Who's written it?' I asked Andrew.

'Who do you think – Trudy Stoker, of course!'

'It would be her, wouldn't it! That Rottweiler reporter loves to sink her teeth into a juicy story,' said Andrew.

'Well, the salon's lawyer hasn't contacted you yet, Dora, so there's no point in worrying about it.'

So much for relaxing in the garden. I mean, how was I supposed to relax now? I couldn't, so I decided to get the shears out and trim the hedge myself. With hindsight, this was probably not the best idea when I was in such an agitated state of mind. Later, when Andrew finally lifted his head from the Sports section, he expressed his surprise at how industrious I'd been.

'Blimey, Dora!'

I surveyed my handiwork from a distance and realised that I'd been a bit over-enthusiastic. Where there had been a straggly overgrown privet hedge around the perimeter of our garden, a few dry sticks now stood naked and forlorn. Without its abundant foliage, the hedge could no longer be described as such.

'It'll grow back,' said Andrew. The obvious comparison to the threadbare Queenie was inescapable.

'Look at all the things you've uncovered, Dora,' said Andrew. 'There's Scratch's old flea collar, and Billy's Batman lunchbox.'

We went around, collecting up an interesting selection of previously lost household items, including several pairs of Mona's wind-blown undies from her washing line.

'What do you think this is?' said Andrew, dangling a thing that looked like a leather net with spikes on it.

'I don't know, but I've found a fingerless satin glove and a pair of crotchless knickers.'

'Amazing what you can find in your garden!' said Andrew. 'Do you think if we plant them they'll turn into bloomers?'

Sunday 12th May

Last night's meal with Andrew started out well enough. Flora agreed to look after Billy and when we left, all was quiet on the home front. It was a nice warm evening and we decided to walk, as it's only fifteen minutes to town from our house.

At Lorenzo's, we were seated near the window, next to an olive tree in a pot. Fabio, our waiter, came and lit a candle and brought us some wine. I felt myself beginning to relax – I had Andrew to myself, some very nice Chianti, and the atmosphere in the restaurant was quite romantic, with its soft lighting and unobtrusive, ambient music playing in the background. I looked at my husband in the flickering candle-light and thought to myself, *he's actually still quite a handsome man really, as long as you don't look at the bit in the middle.*

'What do you fancy, Dora? I'm going for the garlic mushroom starter with extra garlic sauce and then I think I'll have goat's cheese and parmesan pizza.'

Unfortunately, Andrew has the knack of dispelling any thoughts of romance in the blink of an eye.

He poured some more wine. 'Let's drink a toast to your future success Dora! It's going to be a fantastic project! I'm so proud of you! When you officially open on Friday, you'll be the talk of the town!'

'Thank you, Andrew. And I'm sure your book will be a huge success too!'

'Oh no!' he said, suddenly.

'Don't you think so then?'

'No, not that – look who's coming through the door! Quick, hide behind the menu and look out of the window.'

'Dora dear, is that you?' said a familiar voice.

'Hello Mum!' I said.

'Fancy you being here too!' she said. 'Reggie – look who's here! What a coincidence! Have you just ordered? Why don't we join you? It seems silly for us to sit separately.'

'Yes, of course,' said Andrew, gallantly.

The rest of the evening was an experience never to be repeated. Reggie had never been to a restaurant before, apart from frequenting the Fried Egg Café by the recycling skips next to the car park at Aldi.

'Reggie, you have to twist the spaghetti around your fork, like this,' I said, showing him, - 'rather than sucking it up strand by strand. Then you don't have to make any noise when you're eating it.'

'What's that stuff you're puttin' on your pizza Andrew?' said Reggie.

'Parmesan cheese, Reggie.'

'It smells like one of me old gardenin' socks, don't it Ruth, eh! Them ones that 'aven't been washed for a year!'

'Oh yes, Reggie, very funny,' said my mother. 'You're a laugh a minute, Reggie Bunion! Oh dear, I think you need a bib,' said my mother, tucking his napkin into the top of his vest.

'Oh, I'm a right mucker, eh Ruth!'

'Can't take you anywhere!' said Mum.

Andrew and I exchanged glances and I could feel myself tensing.

'It's very posh here, isn't it!' she continued.

'Yes, Mum, it is. I'm surprised you decided to come here. I thought you were going to the Cat and Fiddle?'

'Well, it was your friend Suzie who told me about it – I saw her yesterday in Marks and Sparks. We were getting Reggie a new pair of trousers.'

'Yes, me old ones won't stay up coz the zip's gone on 'em. Ruth says I can't go round with string tied round – she says I look like a tramp.'

'You'd better watch out, Reggie,' said Andrew, - women are never satisfied. The next thing you know, you'll be made to shave every five minutes, you won't be able to do what you want, and your life won't be your own!'

'Rubbish,' I said.

'Desserts?' said the waiter, seeing we'd finished our main courses.

'No thanks,' I said.

'Well, I'm having one,' said Andrew. 'I'll have a Double Chocolate Sundae with extra chocolate sauce, please.'

'Andrew is that a good idea?' I said, glancing at his expanding stomach.

'See!'

'Well,' said Mum, - I don't mind a bit of meat on the bones myself – a bit of padding is a good thing! I don't trust skinny people,' she said, - 'they don't know how to enjoy themselves.'

'More wine?' said Andrew to my mother.

'Don't you think she's had enough,' I whispered to him.

'Thank you, Andrew – yes I will!' she said.

'I'll have a pint of bitter,' said Reggie.

'Sorry sir, but we don't serve draft beer,' said Fabio.

'What – no beer! What about a bottle of stout then?'

Fabio looked blank.

'Reggie, just have some wine,' said Mum – 'this is a restaurant, not a pub, dear. I'll have one of those delicious ice-creams,' she said, pointing at the sweet menu.

I looked on dismally, as Reggie and my mother shared a huge Knickerbocker Glory, and Andrew tucked enthusiastically into his chocolate pudding overdose. Reggie and my mother were giggling like teenagers.

I suppose I should have been pleased that my mother had a nice evening out, and that my husband enjoyed himself despite being gate-crashed unexpectedly, but I just feel very irritated by the whole thing. I mean – is it too much to expect to have just one night out with your husband, and spend some quality time together without interference? Suffice to say, the rest of the evening did not improve. When we arrived home, the children were all still up and Billy was watching a dreadful and totally inappropriate werewolf film called *Fang*.

'I thought he'd gone to bed,' said Flora, when we got in.

'Well, how can you watch him when you're in your room with the door shut,' I said angrily.

'Chill, Mum – it's not like it's the *Exorcist* or anything!'

'This evening has turned into a total disaster,' I said to Andrew tearfully, on our way upstairs. I tucked Billy up and went to bed myself, feeling disgruntled and disappointed. The evening had not met with my expectations in any way.

Next day in the afternoon, we all went out with the dogs to the common, and for once, no one argued or had an accident, and the weather was warm and sunny. It all felt a bit surreal, in fact.

Later, Andrew told me he'd instructed them all to be on their best behaviour because their mother was a bit 'emotional'.

I don't know what's worse – a family of bickering adolescents, or a bunch of unnaturally well-behaved ones making weirdly polite conversation.

Monday 13th May

I arrived at the shop this morning to find another big pile of donated stuff, and rang Melanie to see if she was free to come and help.

'Dora,' she said, when I rang her, - 'did you see the Citizen on Saturday?'

'Yes.'

'Isn't that the same dog groomer's place where you worked?'

'Yes.'

'It's terrible, isn't it! That poor dog!'

I'll just have to grin and bear it, I suppose, but it's an awful weight on my mind. I wish I'd never set foot in that wretched salon. Oh well, as Andrew says, "there's no point in crying over spilt milk". I'm glad I've got my shop to think about. It's a good distraction from all the stressful things going on and I can just focus on getting it all in order for my Friday opening.

Melanie turned up mid-morning to help me.

'I don't know how I'd manage without your help,' I said gratefully.

'Well, I don't mind at the moment – it's all quite quiet at home with Geoff at work and the boys at school. To be honest, I don't have enough to do.'

'You could be a pet carer for Pets' Haven.'

'I could, except Geoff is allergic to cats and Peter is terrified of dogs. When he was eight, he was chased by our neighbour's poodle and he never got over it.'

'Oh,' I said, disappointed. 'Maybe Suzie could help.'

'I don't think so – she says Ping-Pong needs a peaceful environment because of his nervous disposition.'

'Really?'

'Yes – apparently he's got worse since he followed some other dogs into a freezing river and nearly got swept away.'

'Oh dear!' I said.

Honestly, I do sometimes think Suzie is a bit over-protective with that dog of hers. I mean, it wasn't my dogs' fault that Ping-Pong fell into the river and nearly drowned that day! Fudge and Cocoa were just playing a bit boisterously on the river bank, and Ping-Pong accidentally got catapulted into the water. Anyway, it was all OK in the end. He just got a bit of hyperthermia, that's all. He soon recovered.

'Have you checked your emails recently?' asked Melanie.

'No – I haven't,' I said. 'I've been a bit busy.'

'Well you might have some people interested in looking after pets now – you know, after the radio show.'

'You're right, Melanie – I'll check when I get home.'

We sorted through another load of bin bags and boxes and opened the shop door for some air.

'Look at all this!' said Melanie, holding up a familiar looking gadget. 'There are six boxes of these weird nutcrackers! Who on earth sent them do you think? They must be deranged!'

'Oh my goodness! I know exactly where they came from, Melanie! My old boss, J.R. Isn't there a note anywhere?'

Melanie searched round and found an envelope. She read out the letter inside: *Dear Dora, heard you on the radio the other day! AWESOME!! I've sent you some of my old stock as I'm discontinuing one or two items. Good luck with the charity! Keep in touch! J.R.*

'They're hideous!' said Melanie, attempting to crack an imaginary nut. 'Who on earth would buy a penis-shaped nutcracker with a scrotum for a handle?'

'No one! That's why he gave them to us. Well, we can't sell them here – I'll put them upstairs for now.'

'By the way, Dora, the press release goes out in the paper tomorrow, so fingers crossed for a good turn out on Friday! I've also sent private invitations to a selection of V.I.P's. We'd better get some fizz in, don't you think?'

'Yes, I'll ask Jess to make something as well. I'm looking forward to it now,' I said, - 'it's finally happening!'

Later, when I got home, I found Andrew in a flap.

'Dora, you're not going to believe this!' he said, looking worried. 'It's my parents – they're on the news! I saw them on 'Lunchtime Newsbite'! I was just tucking into my cheese and pickle sandwich and there they were, on the TV!'

'Really? Why? What's happened?'

'It seems there's been a government crack-down in Columbia, on drug barons. That bloke, Pablo Narco, is an international criminal. He's been recruiting people from all over the place with his organic health food scam. I'll put the TV on again, Dora, it's nearly time for the 6 o'clock News.'

Breaking news, said the tag line, running along the bottom of the screen. The camera panned across a vast canopy of dense vegetation. The view of the Chocó jungle in Western Colombia steamed and wobbled in the rising heat.

'I'm not sure I can bear to watch this,' I said, flinching. The film zoomed in on a desultory crowd of sweaty officials in tatty army fatigues on a rough track next to a clearing in the jungle. Bob and Barbara suddenly emerged with several other old hippies being forced out at gun point, and jostled into a truck with their hands tied behind their backs. The reporter was saying:

'A large group of British and French nationals have been arrested in Western Colombia. Official sources say that these people have been found in secret locations camped out in the jungle and are suspected of being part of

rebel forces operating illegally in this part of the country. A number of weapons and a large consignment of cocaine was discovered at the site, along with a facility for producing this dangerous and highly addictive drug, with a street value of twenty million pounds. The workers seen here being arrested will be taken to Bogotá for further interrogation. More on this story later. Now we'll go over to Leamington Spa where 80-year old Albert Finnigan has just completed his first half marathon ....'

'Oh my God!' I said, as Andrew switched off the TV. 'What do we do?'

'Well, I've rung the British Embassy in Bogotá, and there's nothing we can do until next week, apparently. All public workers are on strike until next Monday. So, all we can do is wait.'

'Oh Andrew, it's terrible!'

I must say, I found it very hard to get to sleep, thinking about poor Bob and Barbara stuck in some awful dark, overcrowded, hot, stinking cell, full of hardened criminals. It made me feel sick. God knows how we're going to get them out of there – they could be stuck there for years! Imagine that! International drug traffickers for parents! How do we explain that to the children?

Tuesday 14th May

'Good grief!' said Andrew this morning, when he saw how many emails I had.

'I know! I've been forgetting to check,' I said. 'There must be at least 200 here. I'd better get on and answer them.' I made myself a big mug of tea and got down to it. I trawled through them one by one:

Dear Nora,

Can I be a pet carer? I've got a couple of Rottweilers – they're OK with other dogs but not cats. Piggy ate a cat three weeks ago, so no cats. Regards, Jamie

Hi! I'd like to look after lots of cats because I luv them sooooooooooooooooooooooooooooooo much. I would give them lots of cuddles. Luv from Emma (age 8)

Hi! Do you take mothers-in-law as well as pets? Her bark is worse than her bite. Regards, N.F.

Hello Nora,

I heard you on the radio and loved the sound of your voice. You seem like a lovely woman – I'd like to get to know you better, if you're game! I am a youthful 60- year old, comfortably off, with a nice house and all my own hair. Let's give it a go! Yours, B.Grateful

'Andrew!' I shouted, - 'did you send me an email?'

'No!' he said, - 'why?'

'Nothing.'

Hi,

I am very interested in looking after pets – particularly our feathered friends. I have an aviary in my garden and two parrots called Errol and Flynn, so if you have any birds needing a temporary home, please call me. J.S.

Nicola Kelsall

Dear Naughty Nora,
I'd love to stroke your Pussy... (Oh for God's sake! <u>DELETE!!</u>)

Hi,
I have a dog called Jake who needs a new home – sorry to ask, but can you take him? He's great with people and most other pets, but he doesn't like chickens. Well – he <u>does</u> like them, but not in the right way, if you see what I mean. We keep chickens and since we got him, the numbers have decreased at an alarming rate. Yours, Jennie Blythe

Dear Nora,
I heard you on the radio and wondered if you could look after my cat Smudge next month. I am going on holiday for two months and the Sheraton doesn't take pets. Yours, Mrs Bently (For goodness' sake, Mrs Bently – if you can afford a five-star hotel, you can afford a cattery!!)

Dear Nora,
I'd like to be a pet carer. I'm very good with animals and I have lots of room plus a big garden. Kind regards, Mrs P. (at last – a sensible one!)

Dear Mrs Loveday, I will be going into hospital in a week or two and I have no one to look after my pet rat, Mr

Nibbles. Please could you be kind enough to consider having him – I may be in for two weeks. Thank you, Yours sincerely, Philip Potter

Hello,

I'd love to be a pet carer – my favourite animals are rabbits and guinea pigs but I don't mind other small pets. I'm not really allowed any large animals due to a mental health condition I have, which means I sometimes get amnesia and forget where I live and stuff. Anyway, It's OK, because the police know me now and bring me back to my flat if I get lost. From Shaun.

Dear Mrs Loveday,

I am writing to you to request that you please provide a witness statement to us ref. Messrs Fothergill and Shaft on behalf of Miss Jaqueline Branch (Managing Director at Pets Parlour, no. 52 Shillingsworth High Street, Shillingsworth).

Please respond as soon as possible and we will arrange a suitable time for you to come to our office to discuss the aforementioned statement. Yours sincerely, pp. J.M. Fothergill

'What's wrong?' asked Andrew, coming in with another cup of tea.

'Look,' I said, - 'Jack's lawyer wants to see me.'

'Oh, I see. OK, well, you just have to say exactly what happened, Dora. Don't worry – it's a storm in a teacup,' said Andrew, confidently.

I tried to pretend I hadn't seen that particular email and carried on sorting through the rest until I got to the last one which was from Cheeky Chas:

Hi Nora!

Great to have you on the show the other day! I've had lots of requests for a repeat interview – you've got fans, Nora! People love you! When can you come on again? Lurve Chas X

'Hey Dora, you should say 'yes' to that,' said Andrew, - 'it's great publicity!'

'I'm not sure I want any more publicity,' I said, dismally.

The phone rang at this point – it was Melanie. 'Dora, have you seen the press release?'

'No, I didn't get a paper today – why?'

'Well, there are a few typos, I'm afraid.'

'Oh – are they important?'

'Well, yes – I think they are. I'll come over.'

'Oh, not more trouble,' I said to Andrew.

'I'll distract you with an excerpt from my novel,' said Andrew, and he read out a short passage:

'The acrid smell of death hung formidably in the air like a toxic haw over the troubled town of Blackridge. It permeated every nook and cranny, burrowing its way resolutely into every living room, every back street and

hidden passage-way. The stench of it spread like lava; crawling, seeping, consuming everything in its wake. No one was untouched; life in that small insignificant town changed overnight as each and every occupant felt the ice-cold finger of fear enter their hearts. Like a poisoned arrow, that dark and heinous crime now polluted the very air they breathed: sleep would become a distant memory, as the people felt the heavy weight of it pressing down on their souls.'

'Well, what do you think?' he said eagerly.

I thought for a moment. 'Great!' I said.

'Not too over-the-top then?' he asked.

'Um, well – maybe just a little, umm flowery, possibly …'

'What do you mean 'flowery'?' he said, defensively.

'Well, only a bit,' I said, - 'perhaps you could tone it down just a tiny bit...'

'Mmm,' he said, looking a bit miffed.

'But it's really good apart from that,' I said.

Melanie knocked on the door and saved me from further remonstrations. I left him to ponder on the over-use of adjectives and offered her a cup of tea.

'Look, Dora!' she said, thrusting the paper in front of me. 'They've miss-typed the heading and most of the copy – it's not what I sent them at all! It *should* say *'Grand Opening of New Shop'!*

The article read:

GRAN OPENING OF NUDE SHOP

Pets' Haven *animal charity are delighted to announce the opening of their new slop in Shillingsworth High Street, on Friday 17th May. Anyone who would like to cull in will be very welcome. Dora Loveday and her assassinants will be there to beet you and shov you around. Cuntstomers will be able to see for themselves an inserting display of things for stale. Some people may have heard Dora on the recent badcast of 'Funtime with Cheeky Chaz' where she explained the idea behind this herrific new charity. Dora and her coneagues will be on hand to answer any questions.*

'Oh no!' I said, - 'they've attached a terrible photo of me as well, Melanie!'

'Well, it's not that bad,' she said, lying.

'Good God!' said Andrew, coming into the kitchen, - 'that's a terrible photo of you!'

I looked like a deranged beetroot – my face was bright red and matched my blouse, which on being photographed seemed to have acquired ten times the number of wrinkles it actually had.

'You look like a giant purple prune,' said Andrew.

'Well, the studio was hot and I had to hurry to get there, and I hadn't had time to iron anything…'

'Never mind,' said Andrew, - 'it's on page 63, so no one will see it anyway.'

'You'd think they could employ people who could actually spell. I mean, what's the world coming to?' said Andrew. 'Honestly, why can't the British media see what damage they're doing to the English language! It's outrageous! Thank goodness some of us are continuing to uphold high standards.'

Wednesday 15th May

'Mum,' said Tom this morning, in a rare moment of engagement, - 'after my exam today, I'm going to my mate's house.'

'Which mate?' I asked.

'Um, just someone you don't know.'

'Tom's got a girlfriend,' said Luke.

'Shut up!' said Tom.

'Girlfriend, girlfriend, Tom's got a girlfriend,' sang Luke, dancing round the kitchen to avoid Tom's long-armed punch.

'You two, that's enough!' I said.

'Tell him to get lost!' shouted Tom.

'I know who it is,' sang Luke, fanning the flames.

'I told you to shut up!' shouted Tom, throwing a Weetabix at Luke's head, which missed and broke into zillions of bits on the floor.

'For God's sake, you two!' I yelled at them.

'So, who is it then?' I asked Luke, when Tom had left the house in a strop.

'She's called Hillary – she goes to Flora's school.'

The name rang a bell. 'What's her surname,' I said.

'I don't know – but some of the boys call her Hilltops.'

'That's awful!' I said. 'Why do they call her that? Is she very tall?'

Luke looked at me with incredulity. 'No, Mum,' he said.

I told Andrew about Tom's girlfriend and he just laughed and said something about chips and blocks.

'Have you heard anything else about Bob and Barbara?' I asked Andrew over breakfast.

'No, I tried the Embassy again and got the same response. They asked if we had any money, Dora. I think we'll have to pay the officials in Bogota to release them.'

'Oh my God, it's a nightmare, Andrew. How much do you think we'll need?'

'I don't know. I could kill my father though! That's if someone else doesn't get there first.'

'Oh Andrew, it's terrible – those jails are hell on earth – I looked on the internet.'

'I'll tell you something, Dora, if they ever get released, I'm confiscating their passports permanently.'

Poor Andrew. His parents are bonkers. I mean, who would be daft enough to think that someone with a name like Narco, claiming to be a herbal remedy guru from Colombia, would be a person to trust! Not only that, but they actually thought that living in a tropical jungle in forty-degree heat would be 'fun'! If this experience hasn't given them a reality check, then nothing will.

'You'll never guess what!' said Suzie, when I met her at the shop later.

'What?'

'Violet doesn't want any wedding presents! It's ridiculous!'

'Did she say why?'

'She's decided that presents are decadent, and she wants everyone to make a donation to the Society for the Preservation of Kittiwakes!'

'That's unusual,' I said. 'Thoughtful though.'

'But Dora, she needs things for the house! She doesn't have any decent crockery – it's all from Argos! None of her bed linen matches, and God knows where she bought her cutlery from. It's so cheap, you could mistake it for tent pegs. Why doesn't she want nice things Dora! I just don't understand her at all!'

'Well, Suzie, her priorities are different I suppose. It's quite admirable, don't you think?'

'No Dora, I have no idea why she wants to give lots of money to some mangy, scavenging seagulls, when she could have some nice Orla Kiely hand towels or a decent selection of Dartington Crystal! I can't believe she's *my* daughter!'

'How's everything else going?' I asked, diverting her.

'Well, I'm assuming it's all in hand, Dora. I've had practically nothing to do with it! She was determined to do it all herself. By the way – that press release was awful wasn't it!'

'I know. I rang this morning to complain about it and they just said they didn't know what happened and it must have been a technical problem – "a computer software problem", they said.'

By the end of the day, we had the shop looking really good. Melanie came over and took some photos for posterity. I don't think we can do much more, do you?' she said. 'Tomorrow we should relax and do something else so we're fresh on Friday.'

'Good idea,' I said. 'I think we've thought of everything.'

Thursday 16th May

Where did you put all that stuff we found in the garden?' asked Andrew this morning.

'I took it to the shop – most of it wasn't really useful to us – why?'

'I've lost my camera and I've looked everywhere.'

'OK - I'll have a look for it next week – I'm not going in tomorrow. Why do you need it anyway?'

'Well, I've got some photos of murder scenes on it …'

'How on earth did you manage that? I said, horrified.

'From pictures, out of books and magazines, Dora, not real life! It's to help me with my novel.'

'Oh, I see,' I said, not really seeing at all. 'You don't really need to use material like that, do you? I mean, can't you just use your imagination?'

'No Dora – I've got to make everything as authentic as possible. Readers of today are well-informed, Dora. If you get anything wrong, they roast you for it!'

I suppose he's right, but it's all a bit too gruesome for my taste. I'd rather settle down with a nice rom-com and a cup of tea. Oh well, each to their own. As long as he doesn't let Billy or Luke read any of it – I don't want them becoming psychologically disturbed. Luke keeps coming up with ever more elaborate, macabre scenarios for Andrew to consider, and Billy keeps asking me why his Dad is writing about dead people. It's only a matter of time before Billy's teacher, Mrs Pincher, has cause to complain.

I know we were supposed to 'relax' today, but really – that's something I have no concept of. There's a gargantuan pile of laundry, and I haven't done any housework for ages. It's no use asking Andrew – he's immersed in his creative masterpiece and will just say he'll do it later, and then he'll forget to do it later and I'll just get annoyed with him. Then we'll have a row and I've got my anxiety levels to consider. Anyway, I don't want anything spoiling my big day on Friday.

'Hellooooo,' shouted Jess, opening the back door. I came downstairs to see her plonking a huge box down onto the kitchen table.

'What's this?' I said.

'It's for tomorrow, for your Grand Opening!'

I looked inside. There was an enormous chocolate cake. On the top, it said 'Best of Luck' in beautiful swirly silver writing.

'Oh, thank you, Jess. It's lovely!'

'Don't thank me. Terry made it,' she said, slightly taking the edge off it.

'Well, tell Terry he's a marvel! Have you seen Mum recently?' I asked her.

'I saw her last Sunday. She said she'd been out to Lorenzo's with Reggie and you two. That's getting a bit cosy, isn't it?' Jess sounded a bit peeved.

'Oh, it wasn't arranged, Jess. In fact, to be honest, I was a bit put out about it. Andrew and I were supposed to be having a night out together and Mum and Reggie turned up at the same restaurant. I couldn't tell them they couldn't sit with us, could I! Anyway, it wasn't the evening I'd had in mind at all.'

'Oh dear!' said Jess. 'Mum said they'd had a great time.'

'Well, I'm glad someone did.'

'Dora, I think we should intervene and introduce Mum to someone else – you know – someone a bit smarter. If she's going to go out on dates, she should be a bit more choosey.'

'I agree, Jess, but you try telling her that!'

'Well, I think we need to be more proactive Dora. I've got a plan. I'll tell you about it later.'

Flora brought Gaz home for tea today. Luckily Andrew was out. Last time Gaz stayed for a family meal, it was really hard work – 'stultifyingly tedious' was Andrew's description, which was a bit of an exaggeration, but he does have a point. Flora turns into a monosyllabic brain-dead clot just like him when she's with him. We've decided that it's either a weird form of flattery she's exhibiting by mimicking him, or she doesn't want to overshadow him with an actual personality.

'Maybe he suffers with socio-phobia,' I'd suggested. Andrew was having none of it.

'He seems to have extremely limited brain function, Dora,' he said, seriously. 'He doesn't seem able to communicate! When I asked him what kind of music he liked, he just stared at me and sighed! I mean, what kind of response is that!'

The trouble with Andrew, is that he's forgotten what it was like to be a teenager himself. Anyway, he went out with Geoff to the pub for the evening, so at least I didn't have to cope with him upsetting people with his provocative comments.

What's for tea?' asked Billy, as we sat down.

'Fish fingers,' I said.

'What sort of fish?' asked Flora.

'The usual sort,' I said, - 'why?'

'Is it line-caught?' she asked.

'Well, I don't know! It's out of a packet in the frozen food section in Tesco. I didn't look, and even if I had, I couldn't have looked anyway because I didn't have my glasses with me.'

'Gaz and I don't eat fish that's not sustainable. Sorry, Mum.'

'Right.' I said.

Flora shrugged and she and Gaz exchanged glances.

'Well, have some ham instead,' I said.

'What sort of ham is it?' said Flora.

'The one I always get – you know, the one you normally *like*.'

'Is it organic?'

'No,' said Tom, butting in. 'And it's made from mashed up pig's feet.'

Flora glared at him.

'So, Gaz,' I said, - 'you've decided to only eat organic food now have you?'

He nodded.

'I see. Well, I admire your resolve, but it poses a slight problem as you can see, most of the food in this house is mass-produced non-organic Supermarket fodder, so I'm not sure what you could have.'

In the end, I suggested an omelette. Flora's face was a picture when I dished out chocolate ice-cream for pudding and she couldn't have any.

'I suppose you could make your own,' I said, slightly mischievously.

'So, Gaz, what are you doing with yourself these days?' I asked him when everyone had finished eating. Flora rolled her eyes

'This and that,' said the riveting conversationalist. I looked at him expecting further elucidation. It didn't happen.

'Right,' I said.

'We're going upstairs now,' said Flora, and they beat a hasty retreat.

'He's got a job in Juicy Lucy's in town,' said Tom. 'I saw him in there the other day.'

'What's Juicy Lucy's?' asked Billy.

'It's where people buy weird drinks made of cauliflowers and beans and stuff,' said Luke.

'They taste of pond water,' said Tom.

When Andrew came in later, whistling to himself and clanking round the kitchen, I was already in bed.

'Do you have to make so much noise?' I said.

'Sorry, Nora,' he said, falling down on the bed to remove his socks.

'You're drunk!' I said.

'Only a smidgen,' he said, pulling off his sock and flinging it away.

'How was Geoff?' I asked.

'Great! He wants me to go camping this summer for a few days.'

'What sort of camping?'

'Wild camping, Dora. We're going fishing – it'll be marvellous. There's nothing like the great outdoors to make you feel alive! I can't wait. I'll need to get a few things though.'

Oh, good grief! Here we go again – another escapade involving buying expensive gadgets and equipment that will only be used once. It'll end in tears. The last time we all went camping, he complained all week about having to rough-it and couldn't wait to go home.

'You hate camping!' I said, as he got into bed.

'That's not strictly true,' he said. 'I hate *family* camping - that's different.'

'It's not that bad!'

'It is, Dora! It's tortuous. You have to pack the whole house up and fit it into the car along with all the squabbling kids, and when you get there your ears are ringing and it takes an eternity to work out how to put the tent up and unpack everything. The kids are miserable and un-cooperative because they have no internet, and spend the whole week sulking. The weather's always appalling and there's usually a leak somewhere – more often than not, on my side of the tent. The family in the tent next door are noisy and moronic and get up unspeakably early. Then you are forced to make polite conversation with people you don't want to get to know and you'll never see again anyway. ***Then,*** *(he was on a roll)* you have to traipse backwards and forwards with washing-up bowls and gallons of water, put up with cold, draughty showers, smelly toilets and other people's noisy ablutions. Really Dora, it's completely different going by yourself. You don't have to see anyone else. You travel light – you don't need anything with you except what you stand up in, a kettle and some matches, your tent and a sleeping bag - that's it!'

'And a mattress, and waterproofs, and warm clothing, and wash stuff, and a stove, and food – oh and all your fishing gear and a cooking pot to boil your fish in,' I said.

'Yes, all right – those things too.'

'Well, I hope you enjoy it,' I said. 'The proof will be in the pudding.'

'Dora, are you asleep?' he asked me after a minute of two.

I ignored him. I've got a big day ahead tomorrow. Anyway, I must say I really feel that he doesn't appreciate his family as much as he should – I mean, not all the camping trips were terrible. I've got some nice memories of at least two of them.

Friday 17th May

The morning was quiet in the shop and we thought no one was going to come, but gradually as the day wore on, we got busier. At lunch time, Melanie put out some snacks and opened a couple of bottles of plonk.

'Here's our first V.I.P.,' she said, waving at a familiar figure.

'Oh no!' I said, - 'it's Trudy Stoker! You speak to her, Melanie!' I disappeared upstairs to escape and waited for some more people to come.

'This is a big change, isn't it!' I heard her saying huskily. 'I bet it was a lot of work! Last time I was in here, the place reeked of aromatherapy oil and nail polish – it was wall-to-wall candy pink with fluffy cushions everywhere! I must say, you girls have really done an amazing cover-up job!' She laughed a deep throaty cackle and grabbed the stem of a glass of fizz with her heavily ringed fingers. 'I'm gasping for a fag,' she said, and went outside. I heard some more people come in and went back downstairs.

'It's a good job Suzie isn't here yet – she won't want to see her!' I said to Melanie. Throughout the course of the afternoon, I had more than one reason to disappear upstairs again. Jack had the audacity to turn up and I heard her asking Melanie where I was.

'I'd like to have a word with Dora if she's around,' she said to Melanie.

'Oh, she was here a minute ago,' said Melanie.

'Well, when you see her, please tell her that Ava Bush is after blood, and it won't be mine that gets spilt, if you get my drift!' And then she left, leaving Melanie a bit taken aback to put it mildly.

Well, honestly! And I thought Jack was a nice person when I first met her! It just goes to show how people can change! She's not being very charitable – I mean, it's not as if I deliberately tried to cause any trouble. Some people can be so unreasonable.

I'd only been back downstairs a few minutes when I saw Mrs Peake coming towards the shop and I had to bolt back upstairs again.

'Why do you keep hiding up here?' said Melanie, following me up the stairs.

'People I don't want to see keep coming in!' I said. 'I mean, who invited Mrs Peake, for God's sake!'

'I did,' said Melanie. 'She was on the list of people willing to look after animals – Mrs P. – she emailed you!'

'Oh,' I said, - 'sorry, Melanie.'

'Why don't you want to see her?'

'Um, well, it's just that something happened to her cat and she thinks it was my fault….'

Melanie looked at me quizzically.

'It's a long story,' I said, not wishing to elaborate.

'Well, she's gone now, so you can come down. Suzie's here, oh and someone called Ava Bush….'

Saturday 18th May

Well, after the events of yesterday, I'm beginning to wonder if this shop was really such a good idea, and that's an understatement. I know Melanie was just doing her job by inviting all those people, and she didn't know that half of them were not exactly on my Christmas card list, but she could have checked first! I mean, fancy inviting Mona and Roger! I didn't even know Roger was our local councillor. I suppose they could be categorised as V.I.P.'s, although it's scraping the barrel a bit. Melanie said she couldn't get the Mayor to come as he was busy opening a gourmet pie shop at the posh end of the High Street. That's probably why the press didn't stay long. Anyway, Trudy Stoker still managed to grill a few people for information. I just hope she writes something nice for a change. I must say, I was glad when everyone went away and I could relax – it's no fun trying to dodge people. Ava gave me a fright, turning up like that – I felt quite queasy for the rest of the day. Luckily, she didn't stay long. Jess's cake went down a storm, of course – unfortunately, there wasn't much left of it when the Citizen came to take photographs, which was a shame because that would have been some nice publicity for the bakery. Mind you, I couldn't face any cake, what with Mrs Peake and Jack turning up as well, and then the sight of Mona Knightly strutting about in her stretch-nylon mini skirt, fishnet stockings and gold plastic mules – that just finished me off. My mother told me that she saw Mona showing Trudy Stoker her latest tattoo which was on her thigh – a rabbit apparently, eating a carrot. That woman has no shame.

At least Reggie came looking a bit smarter for a change, in his new trousers - minus the string. I was a bit disappointed with Andrew though, since he only came for half an hour at the end. Apparently, Fudge and Cocoa escaped from the garden and he had to spend two hours looking for them. He said it was my fault because when I 'trimmed' the hedge, I exposed a gap big enough for them to get out. It's the second time they've got into Miss Pearly's garden (our next-door neighbour), and caused trouble.

Andrew said this time they dug up her roses, trod on her endives and peed on her water feature. So, I didn't think things could get any worse, but how wrong could I be!

'We need £5,000,' said Andrew, this morning when he opened a letter from the British Embassy. 'To start the legal process to release my parents.'

'Can't you do it?' I asked.

'No, Dora! It needs specialists in international law!'

'You mean people who know how to oil wheels.'

'Well, yes. Anyway, where the hell are we going to get £5,000 from! And that's just the start!'

I must say, I feel thoroughly depressed. A dark cloud of doom and despondency is threatening to engulf us. We haven't told the children because we don't want them to be upset, but Andrew is going around looking like the grim reaper and they have definitely noticed.

'Why is Dad so miserable?' said Tom at lunch time. 'I only asked him if I could borrow a fiver to go to town and he gave me a massive lecture about saving money.'

'Yeah,' joined in Luke. 'I asked him how much professional footballers get paid, and he started shouting and saying it's obscene what footballers get, and they should give fifty percent of it to charity or something…'

'Daddy's a bit stressed at the moment,' I said.

'What's he got to be stressed about?' said Tom. 'It's not like he's got exams or anything, is it? He just sits around writing stuff and watching T.V.'

Sunday 19th May

Have you seen yesterday's paper?' asked Jess on the phone this morning.

'No,' I said, - 'I forgot to get one.'

'Well, I've got two – I'll bring one round.'

'Did they do an article about us, then?'

'Not exactly,' said Jess.

I told Andrew that Jess was on her way. 'It sounds as if Trudy Stoker has done it again,' I said.

'I've been thinking about Mum and Dad's predicament,' said Andrew over breakfast. 'We might need Trudy to help us.'

'You are joking, aren't you?'

'No. We might have to do a publicity campaign to raise the money for them.'

'After everything you've said about her, Andrew, you can't be serious!'

'I am, Dora. Anyway, she doesn't know what I think about her. I have been perfectly civil to her, face to face.'

'If we do something like that, we'll have to tell the children,' I said to him.

'Yes – I know – sooner rather than later, I think.'

'Look!' said Jess, twenty minutes later, thrusting page four in front of us.

'Is that the cake?' said Andrew. Jess's cake, or what was left of it, stood on a table at the centre of the picture. Two enormous pink balloons hovered above it. Between the balloons, stood a large wine bottle. The effect was unfortunate to say the least.

'I don't remember any balloons,' I said.

'Put your glasses on, Dora!' said Jess. 'That's Mona!'

Next to the cake was a man appearing to leer at the balloons. Then I noticed the cake. All that was left of 'Best of Luck' on the remnants of the cake was an 'f' above the letters 'uck' making the obvious very rude expletive. Coupled with Mona's oversized chest, protruding phallus-shaped bottle and the leering man, the picture was, in a nutshell, obscene. A few lines beneath read: **'Exciting new shop opens for business.'**

'Is that all it says?' I said, staring at it. 'Good God, Andrew, that's you!' I said, suddenly recognising his face.

'Is it?' said Andrew.

'Yes! Look!'

'Well, I don't know how the photographer managed to catch me – I was only there for a few minutes…'

I rolled my eyes. Jess looked at me sympathetically.

'Well, whatever,' I said. 'Luckily you aren't mentioned, or I'd have to ask them to publish a disclaimer.

'Saying what exactly?'

'That you're not my husband, that I've never met you and I have no idea who you are.'

'It doesn't even mention the shop, never mind who's in the photo!'

'I suppose not, but who do you think is making the editorial decisions – I mean, that photo is shocking!'

Monday 20th May

I've decided not to open the shop on Mondays because I can't manage everything at home, plus running a shop, and although Andrew says he can help at home, so far that has been an empty promise. He just doesn't seem to be able to apply himself in a way that's useful. I've tried to explain to him that spending half an hour loading the dishwasher using his scientific space-saving technique is all very well, but I could have hand-washed it all in half the time. The same goes for laundry – by the time he's worked out the drying times of each individual textile and hung it accordingly on the drying rack over the boiler, I could have dried it all myself by blowing on it. He's worked out that you should only put 10 pairs of socks, 6 pairs of boxers, 3 bras and 4 pairs of knickers on a 'Delicates' wash in order to obtain maximum cleaning results. I mean, really! I haven't got time for that nonsense. I've got to stuff as much as possible into that washing machine without it spitting it all back out in protest so that we've all got something to wear the next day. And, don't get me started on cooking dinners! I mean, I've got a life to live! Out comes the recipe book, then he has to go to the shops to buy special ingredients we don't have in the house (because they're expensive), and then he uses every dish, saucepan, bowl and spoon to make whatever it is he's set his heart on. Afterwards, the kitchen looks like it had to provide dinner for the 5,000 and the washing up pile is bigger than Mount Vesuvius. Of course, he thinks that because he's done the magnanimous thing of providing the family with a nourishing meal, the washing up, drying up, and putting away is nothing to do with him. In fact, he's usually under the impression that he's done his bit for the whole week at least. And, on top of that, we all have to say how wonderful his efforts are and give him enough complements to make a beetroot blush.

Anyway, apart from the never-ending list of domestic chores, I had to go and collect Mr Nibbles for his holiday stay and take him to Suzie's - she'd agreed to have him because she can't have dogs and cats. She said she thought she'd be able to cope with a rat – I'm not convinced though. She's not the most tolerant of people when it comes to animals, apart from where Ping-Pong is concerned. He's spoiled silly, that dog.

Mr Potter's house wasn't far from mine as it turned out. He seemed a nice old chap and very attached to his rat. Frankly, I don't really see the appeal of rodents. He's got beady eyes, bad teeth, and lacks social skills, plus he smells.

'That's no way to talk about your clients,' said Andrew, when I got back from delivering him to Suzie.

'The rat, Andrew - not Mr Potter!'

'I rang the embassy this morning and got things rolling with the lawyers,' said Andrew.

'How?' I asked, thinking about the £5,000.

'I put it on the credit card.'

'Was there any room left on it?'

'I've extended the limit.'

'How will we pay it back though, Andrew?' I said, alarmed at the thought of our personal debt mountain rising stratospherically.

'I don't know, but what else can I do?' he said despairingly.

'What about the funding campaign?'

'That will take a while to achieve anything. I've spoken to the Citizen though, and they like the idea – they said they'd be happy to put it on the front page and support us, so I'm going to get on with the crowdfunding stuff and the Facebook page this afternoon. With any luck, we can get the national newspapers and the BBC to run something as well. My book is going to have to go on the back burner now – I won't have time to do any writing.'

At tea time we decided to tell the children about their Grandparents' appalling predicament, given that it would soon be plastered all over the papers. We wanted to pre-empt the unpleasant reality by giving them our version of events first.

'It's not fair!' said Tom. 'My friend Gary's brother Mick only had to do twenty hours' community service for growing some grass in his Dad's greenhouse. Why do Grandma and Grandpa have to stay in prison?'

'This is on a slightly bigger scale, Tom, and it's not 'grass' either.'

'Who is Gary, and why are you friends with him?' I interjected.

Tom shrugged.

'Gary Wheeler's a drug dealer', said Luke excitedly. 'He sells drugs to the other boys at school.'

'Really!' I said, shocked.

'It's OK, Mum, it's no big deal,' said Tom, nonchalantly. 'Loads of people are doing it.'

'Good grief, Tom, that's terrible!'

'Half the school kids in Britain are funding people like this guy Narco's lavish lifestyle,' said Andrew.

'Well I hope none of you lot are involved in drug-taking!' I said to the children.

'Course not, Mum,' they said in unison.

Tom and Flora gave each other a look that told me otherwise. 'It's very stupid to take drugs of any sort!' I told them.

'Well, what about Grandpa then?' said Luke.

'He's been smoking weed since it was invented – he's too old to change the habit of a lifetime,' I said.

'Anyway, just look where it's got him!' said Andrew.

I gave him a 'be careful' look. Well, I didn't want the children to be unnecessarily traumatised by graphic descriptions of Bogota prison.

'The thing is,' I said, - 'Granny and Grandpa have been arrested, and even though they are innocent of any crime, the authorities in Colombia have to keep them there until they are proved innocent, and in Colombia that process can take quite a long time.'

'So,' said Andrew, - 'we've decided to set up a campaign to raise funds to get them out sooner.'

'Were they on the news?' asked Flora, - 'because my friend Sonia said she thought she saw them and I said it couldn't have been them because they were on holiday in South America.'

Tom rolled his eyes.

'She said they would never get out of there – she said people don't come back from a place like that – she said they get their heads chopped off and made into footballs…' Flora's eyes filled with tears.

'No one's getting anything chopped off – OK!' said Andrew. 'Calm down, Flora, the British Embassy are doing everything they can to help us.'

'Are they going to be in the papers?' asked Tom, nervously.

'Yes, I'm afraid so,' said Andrew, - 'which is why we needed to talk to you all. The next few weeks are going to be a bit rocky to say the least. You two older ones have got important exams and we don't want them being disrupted – you've got to focus on that because it's what your Grandparents would want you to do. OK?'

Flora and Tom nodded.

'My friend Spike at school says his Dad's in prison and he's allowed TV and juggling visits,' said Billy.

'Juggling?' I asked, bemused.

'Yes – it's called that when he goes home to see Spike's Mum.'

'I think you mean *conjugal*,' said Andrew.

Tom sniggered, Luke said he thought that juggling was boring, and Flora burst into tears and ran upstairs.

Tuesday 21ˢᵗ May

I was glad to go to work this morning. I barely slept last night, worrying about everything. I mean, my whole family seem to be turning into criminals! When I said to Andrew last night how concerned I was about the children getting hold of illegal substances, he just said there wasn't much we could do about it.

'We could speak to Mr Grimsby!' I said.

Andrew pulled a face and said he didn't think that was a good idea.

'Why not!'

'Because there's no way he's going to accept that any 'OLICs boys would be selling drugs, and it'll only draw attention to our boys, Dora! Can you imagine what he'd say! He'd instantly suspect them of being involved.'

'Oh, Yes, I suppose you're right, but what can we do, Andrew?'

'We just have to hope our kids will be sensible.'

We're done for then, I thought gloomily.

'How's Mr Nibbles getting on?' I said to Suzie when I got to the shop.

'Well, he bites his cage a lot which wakes up Ping-Pong, so I put him in the garage.'

'Oh, OK,' I said. 'Mr Potter was hoping he would be taken out to play every day – he's used to being handled, Suzie.'

'I'm not doing that! Oh no, I couldn't touch it – not an actual *rat*, Dora!'

'Oh well, perhaps I'd better have him at our house – the boys will be happy to play with him, even if Flora won't.'

I collected Mr Nibbles on the way home, and when I got in, I heard an unfamiliar girl's voice in the conservatory with Tom and realised it might be his new girlfriend, Hillary. When I saw her, I could see the resemblance to her father.

'Hello,' I said, brightly, putting Mr Nibbles in the corner.

'This is Hillary,' said Tom, awkwardly.

'I guessed,' I said. 'Hello! Welcome to the madhouse!'

She gazed at me wide-eyed, and twisted her long dark hair around her fingers.

'Rats are unhygienic,' she said.

'He's a pet rat – they're quite clean, actually,' I told her. 'This is Mr Nibbles. We will have to be careful though – the cats would love to make *ratatouille* out of him, wouldn't you?' I said, as Scratch eyed him from a chair.

'What's ratatouille?' asked Billy.

'It's French – it's a vegetable stew.'

'Why would Scratch eat vegetables?' said Billy.

'It's just a joke, Billy.' Billy looked confused.

'Maybe some animals are vegetarians, Mum. Reggie's mouse fell in some pea soup, didn't he?' said Billy, remembering the awful incident.

'It was an accident, Billy,' I said.

'Fudge and Cocoa like carrots,' said Billy, 'but they like all kinds of things, don't they? They ate some squirrels once didn't they, Mum?'

'Yes, Billy they did, but let's not dwell on that now,' I said, smiling at Hillary.

Hillary continued to stare unblinkingly at me and said she preferred cats.

'Do you have a cat?' I asked her, wondering whether her parents had got another one yet.

'No,' she said flatly. 'My cat died.'

'I showed Hillary the kittens,' said Tom. 'She likes the white ones.'

'Well, we've got three left still, if you are interested, Hillary. Now, I must get on,' I said, finding her a bit unnerving.

Hillary proved to be an unresponsive, laconic girl with no sense of humour. At the tea table, she barely ate anything and spent a lot of time staring at me. The reason for this became obvious later.

When she'd gone home, Tom said that Hillary's parents had told her there was a mad woman living in our house.

'They said that she couldn't be friends with me!' said Tom.

'She obviously ignored their advice then,' said Andrew, smirking.

'Why did they say that though?'

'I don't know, Tom! I mean, your Mother's perfectly normal, as you know.'

'Why are you smiling when you say that!' I said, scowling at him.

I decided to put Tom out of his misery. 'When Hillary's parents came to look at the kittens, I was in the bathroom and Rufus – the ginger one – jumped on me and gave me a fright, and your Dad sort of told them I was mentally unstable.'

'What! Why did you do that?' said Tom, scowling at Andrew even more.

'Well, it was funny at the time – you had to be there…,' Andrew said, weakly. 'Anyway, we didn't know you'd be dating their daughter five minutes later, did we! It's just an unfortunate coincidence.'

Tom gave Andrew a look that could kill.

'Sorry, mate,' said Andrew. 'It was just a bit of fun…'

'I hate you! shouted Tom, - 'you're ruining my life!'

'Oh well,' said Andrew, when Tom had gone off upstairs and was out of earshot, - 'I didn't like her much anyway.'

'Me neither,' I said.

Wednesday 22nd May

Melanie offered to cover the shop this morning, so I could go and give my statement to Jack's lawyers. Andrew did ask to come with me but he would have made me more nervous than I was already. I could just imagine him sucking air noisily if I said the wrong thing, or worse, coughing indiscreetly. I must say, I felt like a criminal being interrogated like that! They were quite rude when I tried to explain the circumstances – they said I wasn't giving short enough answers. 'We only want the salient facts', Mr Fothergill had said to me, abruptly, when I tried to tell them about how complicated some instructions on packets are these days. Does he ever read the labels on things himself? It's a minefield, I tell you!

They expected me to remember exactly what happened on the day of Queenie's visit, which was quite difficult as so much has happened since then; it's all a bit of a blur, really. Mr Fothergill wasn't very patient at all. It's very difficult remembering 'salient facts' when you're a busy mother. I don't suppose he's ever had to do more than one thing at a time – he's a man, after all. Anyway, I did my best and they finally said I could go. Of course, I could have refused to give a statement, but Andrew said they could 'subpoena' me (whatever that means) and make me do one anyway. Oh well, I did my best.

'How did it go?' asked Andrew when I got back.

'OK, I suppose – but they told me it might go to court.'

'Well, as long as you told them exactly what happened, you don't need to worry,' he said.

'I hope you're right, Andrew – I tried to, but Mr Fothergill was very sharp with me and said he didn't want to hear anything about my private life or my 'suppositions', and told me to stick to the point!'

'Yes, Dora, I imagine he did!' said Andrew, smirking.

'It's not funny, Andrew!'

'No, Dora,' he said, still smirking.

'Well, I only said that I thought maybe Ava Bush had been over-grooming Queenie. Dogs can get 'psychogenic alopecia', apparently. I looked it up on the internet. I told him about how Scratch used to lick himself too much and he got a bald patch on his tummy. Mr Fothergill wasn't interested at all – that's when he said my personal opinions were of no interest to him!'

'The thing is, Dora, in a court of law, they have to stick to the facts. They can't take into consideration what us lawyers call 'conjecture', otherwise innocent people would be convicted just because their neighbours don't like them. Anyway, it probably won't go to court, Dora, these things usually get settled before then.'

'Oh, I hope so – I really don't want to have to stand in the dock with all those people staring at me, Andrew!'

'Don't worry, Dora, it'll blow over, you'll see. By the way,' said Andrew, - 'the lawyers in Colombia have made a bit of headway and they've visited Mum and Dad.'

'Oh good! What did they say?'

'Well, Mum and Dad are obviously upset, and they've been separated, so that's made it worse. Anyway, they cheered up quite a bit now they know people are trying to help them.'

'I hope they're being treated well,' I said.

'Well, apparently Dad traded his socks for some fags and Mum made friends with a prostitute who's getting a supply of extra food and toiletries from one of the guards for 'services rendered'.'

'Good grief, Andrew, the sooner we get them out of there, the better.'

Thursday 23rd May

'I made us some tea, Dora,' said Suzie, when I got to the shop today. 'You'll never guess what's happened now!'

'I don't know – what?'

'Warren says he wants to move!'

'Why now? You've been happy there for years!'

I know, but he says it's not the same any more – he says the area's gone downhill in the past few months.'

'It can't be that bad, Suzie! Perhaps the house just needs freshening up a bit.'

'Well yes – particularly when I can't seem to get rid of the smell of rotting vegetables – I don't know where it's coming from, Dora!'

'Oh dear!' I said, wondering what Bob and Barbara had managed to leave behind as a memento of their short but eventful visit.

'Warren says he's fed up with the neighbours complaining about disused vehicles and rubbish – he says he doesn't know what they're going on about. He even had a woman emailing him about market stalls in our garden bringing down the tone of the neighbourhood. I mean, what is it with these people! I don't see how anyone could mistake a gazebo for a market stall – we only put it up last week!'

'Er, no, Suzie…. look, don't take any notice of that – it's not worth worrying about. It'll all blow over, I'm sure. Anyway, why is Warren worrying about it – he's hardly ever here.'

'I know – I think he's thinking about retiring again.'

'Oh, I see.'

'I'd rather he didn't, Dora – I like things the way they are.'

'Yes – I can identify with that!' I said, thinking about Andrew being at home now. 'They need a lot of attention when they're at home don't they! Andrew is always asking where things are and accusing people of taking his stuff – then he finds it and it usually turns out it was his fault all along. His camera went missing last week, and I found it in his office drawer – it had been there all along! He complains about interruptions and noise - like the telephone, the dogs barking, people coming to the door, the postman, the bin men, the neighbours – he even complained about the ticking clock in the lounge the other day! He said it was disturbing his concentration. I mean honestly, the house isn't an office! I wish he was back at work, really I do!'

'Oh dear, Dora! Is his writing not going very well then?'

'It was, but he's now focusing on Bob and Barbara's case – we've got a Facebook page for raising money for them – look!' I showed Suzie on the computer. 'We've already raised £400, Suzie. There's going to be a news story on local news next Friday night, and Andrew got a radio slot with Cheeky Chas. The Citizen are going to run a front page about it too.'

'My God, Dora! Is that where they are being held? It's awful!' said Suzie, pointing at the photo of the prison. 'It looks like Alcatraz!'

'I can't bear to think about it,' I said, closing the laptop. 'Honestly, I think my family are jinxed, Suzie. Nothing ever goes to plan – there's always trouble looming.'

'I know how you feel – just look at Violet's wedding plans, for heaven's sake!' said Suzie.

'I'm not sure you can really compare Violet's eccentric venue choices with being banged up in a foreign prison, Suzie!'

'Well I know, but did I tell you what a logistical nightmare it is, organising transport from the Scottish Highlands on a Sunday?'

Friday 24th May

'I managed to write some more of my novel yesterday,' said Andrew at breakfast time.

'Oh good,' I said. He proceeded to read it to us:

Detective Inspector Drake Lucas surveyed the scene before him. It was not a sight for the faint-hearted…'

'OK, Andrew,' I said, butting in. 'I don't really think this is a good idea. I'm trying to eat, anyway.'

'Spoilsport!' said Luke.

'Yeah, Mum! We want to hear it!' said Tom.

'Well, I don't – not now, anyway.'

Andrew looked disappointed.

'Mum, what does repencible mean?' said Billy.

'What are you talking about?' said Tom.

'Well, we had to write about our favourite book at school, so I wrote about Dad's murder book and Mrs Pincher said it was 'repencible' that Dad was reading it to me. She said it wasn't age apro...apro ...'

'Age-appropriate,' I said, giving Andrew a hard stare.

'Billy's teacher is a twit,' said Andrew. 'She tried to stop his class from watching SpongeBob, Dora – she's gone crazy with her political correctness – a bit of healthy violence never did me any harm! These meddling idiots are all mad. Not content with banning Noddy books, I read in the paper last week that they've turned Denis the Menace into a pathetic wimp and stopped Gnasher from biting people – I mean, honestly! Give me Strength!'

'Mrs Pincher gave me 'The Cat in The Hat' to read instead,' said Billy, forlornly. 'I've read it four times already.'

'So, it's OK to teach kids to let strangers in to trash the house when the parents are out, then?' said Andrew. 'That woman is a bloody philistine!'

'What's a bloody philistine?' asked Billy.

'Now look what you've started!' I said to Andrew.

'Shall I ask Mrs Pincher?' said Billy.

'No!' we both said.

Later, after a busy morning in the shop, I met Jess for a quick lunch at the café opposite. She wanted to tell me about her plan to get Mum a new boyfriend.

'So, what have you got in mind?' I asked her when we sat down.

'Well, my friend Lavinia has started an on-line dating agency for oldies, Dora. I think we should put Mum on it.'

'I don't know if she'd agree to it, Jess. Anyway, she doesn't even know what 'on-line' is. When Andrew told her, we needed a new hard-drive, she said he was being silly to spend that much money when we can park on the road outside our house!'

'Well, I know Dora, but we can do it *for* her, can't we!'

'What – you mean, without asking her?' I don't know, Jess. I mean, I'm not sure we should go behind her back like that.'

'Well, I think if we ask her she'll say 'no',' said Jess. 'We need to present it as a fait accompli, Dora – it's the only way.'

'Is she serious?' asked Andrew, when I got home later.

'Well, yes I'm sure she is,' I said. 'She thinks we should set Mum up without telling her. I'm not sure it's a good idea at all. It's typical of Jess though.'

'Well, once she's got an idea in her head she usually can't be shaken from it,' said Andrew.

'I know,' I said, - 'she's like a rat up a drainpipe.'

Saturday 25th May

Where's Mr Nibbles?' I said this morning, panicking when I saw his cage was open.

'Luke had him in his room last night,' said Billy. I went upstairs and opened Luke's door. He was sprawled across his bed fast asleep with most of the covers on the floor. I opened the curtains.

'Mum!' he protested, - 'close them!'

'Where's Mr Nibbles?' I said, searching the room.

'I don't know,' he said half asleep, - 'I haven't got him, Mum – I put him back last night.'

'What's all the fuss about?' said Andrew, coming in.

'Mr Nibbles is missing,' I said.

'What am I going to tell Mr Potter?' I said forlornly at lunch, when we'd all searched the house several times to no avail.

'Can't we just get another one?' said Billy.

'How will we find one that looks like Mr Nibbles, Billy? Mr Potter will know it's not him,' I said.

'We could say he died of old age,' said Flora.

'But he's only a year old,' I said.

'We don't know what's happened to him – he might be fine,' said Tom.

'What, with ten cats and two mad dogs in the house! I doubt it!' said Andrew, ever the pragmatist.

'Well, I've got a week to come up with something,' I said, - 'so in the meantime, all of you keep your eyes peeled.'

Honestly, that's all I need – an escaped rodent in the house. I hope I don't come across a body anywhere. It's making me very nervous about doing any housework. What could be worse than accidentally hoovering up a half-eaten corpse, or putting your hand on something warm and furry when you least expect it! I've had my fair share of squirmingly hair-raising encounters over the years, I can tell you! Once, Cocoa brought in a decomposing hedgehog he'd found in the garden, and refused to relinquish it, running upstairs and dragging it all over the new carpet, finally depositing it on Flora's bed while she was still in it. That was a particularly ear-shattering experience, both for us and for anyone within half a mile of our house. Apart from the incident with the entrails during Aunt Alice's ill-fated visit recently, one of the strangest events of this nature happened one evening last autumn, involving a bat with poor navigation skills and a newly acquired patio heater. It was Andrew's idea to get one:

'It'll be great,' he'd said, - 'we can sit outside even when it's cold.'

'Why?' was my response.

Anyway, he got one and we were sitting having a nice glass of port after dinner one evening in October, when suddenly the poor animal flew straight into it. There was a horrible screeching noise and an awful smell of scorched fur, followed by the thing plummeting down and landing with a charred, smoky thud onto

Andrew's dinner-plate. With its dying breath, it flapped its wings one last time and expired, next to two gherkins and a selection of party cheeses from Tesco. It put Andrew off his food for several days, that did.

Anyway, Flora could be right. Mr Nibbles may have a strong sense of self-preservation. I will, however, be checking every cushion before I sit on it, just to be on the safe side.

Sunday 26th May

Jess rang me this morning.

'We need to get a good photo of Mum for her profile page,' she said. 'I thought we could go round there today.'

We found our mother in the back garden with Reggie, planting out tomatoes in the greenhouse.

'She's not dressed for this, Jess,' I whispered. Mum was in her gardening clothes with her hair scraped back behind an ancient yellow hairband.

'I agree,' said Jess, - 'we'll move to Plan B.'

'What's plan B?' I hissed.

'We look for a suitable photo in the house.'

'What brings you two here?' asked my Mum, surprised to see us.

'Just thought we'd drop by,' said Jess, - 'to see how you are.'

'Well, I'm fine,' said Mum, - 'Reggie and I are just getting the greenhouse organised, aren't we dear?'

Jess shot me a pained look.

'Have you got time for a cup of tea?' I said to Mum.

'You go in and I'll come in a minute,' she said, waving us towards the house.

'Excellent!' said Jess, when we got in, - 'now we can have a quick rummage.'

'That's a bit cheeky!' I said to Jess, but she was on a mission.

'She keeps all the photos over here,' she said, making for the old bureau. Jess got a pile of them out and started raking through them.

'What about this one?' she said, holding up a photo of Mum when she was about thirty.

'I think that photo is too old, Jess – she looks completely different now.'

'OK, this one then!'

'No, Jess – that's when she was thin.'

'So!'

'You can't give a false impression, Jess.'

'Well, there's nothing wrong with a bit of window dressing, Dora!'

'Jess, you'll set her up for a fall. What about this one?' I showed her a picture of our mother taken about five years before. She looked nice and summery and happy. 'I think this was taken when she was on holiday in Greece with Dad,' I said.

'That'll do,' said Jess, shoving all the other photos back in the drawer, just in time.

'Well, this is a nice surprise,' said Mum. 'I'll put the kettle on. Reggie, do you want one?'

'No, ta – I'm just goin' 'ome to let Tinker out. See you later Ruth.'

'I think Reggie finds you two a bit overwhelming,' said Mum.

'You could do with a friend who likes meeting people, Mum,' said Jess, once he'd gone. 'You know – someone you could go out with socially.' I looked at Jess. *Don't push it too far, Jess, I thought.*

'I know what you're suggesting, Jess!' said Mum. 'I'm quite happy as I am, thank you very much.'

'I don't know how you're going to persuade Mum to meet someone different,' I said to Jess on the way home. 'I mean, she's quite stubborn.'

'I'll think of something, Dora. I'm quite stubborn too,' said Jess. *Well, that's certainly true, I thought. Jess is nothing if not determined.*

Monday 27th May

Searching through Billy's blazer pockets last night, I discovered a note addressed to us from Billy's teacher. If I'd put the blazer in the washing machine without looking, I'd never have known about it – which would have been a good thing:

Dear Mr and Mrs Loveday,

I am very concerned about your son Billy. In my opinion, he displays an unnatural interest in death and the macabre, and I do not think this is healthy for a boy of his young age. Only the other day, during 'book-corner', he cited your husband's novel as his favourite book. I do not think that something entitled 'Death by a Thousand Cuts' to be a suitable choice for a six-year old. Furthermore, he seems to have a remarkable memory for prose, as he was able to recite the first paragraph without hesitation, deviation, or repetition in our class version of 'Just a Minute' for our speaking and listening session.

I am sorry to have to bring this to your attention, but I feel Billy could benefit from some more edifying reading material such as 'Swiss Family Robinson', perhaps, or 'Pippy Longstocking'. I have taken the liberty of attaching an Ofsted-approved reading list for your perusal.

Yours sincerely, Mrs A. Pincher

'Ridiculous!' was Andrew's response when I showed it to him.

'Well, I think she might have a point, Andrew,' I said. 'Billy should be reading more uplifting stuff. I found a book by his bed last night, all about how spiders kill their prey. Maybe Mrs Pincher is right, Andrew! It's a bit worrying, don't you think?'

'Nonsense, Dora! Billy is a perfectly normal boy. When I was his age I liked nothing better than a grizzly, murder story. Mrs Pincher is a stuffy old trout with the imagination of a wooden peg. Just forget it, Dora!'

Well, it's all very well for Andrew to dismiss these things, but I can't help but worry about the consequences of Billy being exposed to too much violence.

Today was the first day of the half term holiday. With it being my day off, I thought it would be nice to take the children out somewhere.

'Really!' said Andrew, when I mentioned it. 'But last time, we agreed it was a hellish experience, never to be repeated.'

'That was you,' I said.

'Well, anyway,' said Andrew, - 'where do you want to go?'

'Well, it's quite warm today – how about the boating lake down at the park?'

I could tell Andrew would rather not go anywhere.

'They'll say they don't want to go,' said Andrew, stating the obvious.

'I know, Andrew – we'll have to make them.'

In the end, we managed two out of four, so not bad. Flora said she'd come if she could meet Gaz there, and Billy was easy to persuade, being only six. We took Fudge and Cocoa, this time, keeping them strictly on the leads.

'We don't want a repeat of last time, do we!' said Andrew.

'No, we don't!' It was the aftermath of the allotment fiasco which concerned me the most – Andrew whinged on about his bad back for weeks after and still won't do anything around the house without a battle. Honestly, you'd think he'd had to re-landscape St James' Park single-handedly, the way he goes on about that day in Cyril's vegetable patch.

'Can we go in a boat?' asked Billy when we got there.

'Yes – that's why we came!' I said.

'I'll take him,' said Flora. 'Gaz and I are going to get a rowing boat.'

Gaz appeared, sloping along the path from the other direction, with his head bowed and his ear-phones in. He nodded a minimalist greeting without removing them and they went off to pay for a boat. To my relief, Billy was handed a life-jacket.

'Look after Billy, Flora, he can't swim very well,' I called as they got into the wobbling boat.

'They'll be fine,' said Andrew, confidently.

I watched them float off across the murky water and wondered how deep it was.

An hour later, Andrew and I wandered back to the jetty, having walked all around the park twice with the dogs. Flora and Gaz were just re-appearing.

'OH MY GOD, ANDREW!' I shouted, panicking, - 'WHERE'S BILLY!!'

'FLORA! WHERE'S BILLY!' I shrieked, hysterically. My heart began to thud uncontrollably. Andrew rushed up to the boat.

'WHAT'S HAPPENED!' he shouted at Flora and Gaz.

'Chill, Dad, it's fine,' said Flora. 'Billy wanted to explore the island over there, so we left him there for a bit.'

'What do you mean, Flora? Go back and get him NOW!' I yelled at her.

'I'll go,' said Andrew, snatching the oars. He rowed off at double speed towards the little clump of trees in the middle of the lake.

'What were you *thinking*, Flora?' I asked her, dumbfounded.

'We thought he'd be fine,' she said. 'Billy said he wanted to be like Bear Grylls on 'Celebrity Island'.

'Well, I hope for your sake, he's OK,' I said.

'God, Mum, you and Dad are *soooo* stressy!'

Luckily, all was well and Andrew found him happily building a shelter with sticks and leaves.

'Well, that was a relaxing afternoon,' said Andrew sarcastically, when we got home.

'Never mind,' I said, - 'Billy had a lovely time, and was completely unaware of all the fuss. Maybe we *are* over-anxious parents, like Flora says.'

'Just wait till she has kids,' Andrew said, - 'then she'll realise how hard it is.'

Tuesday 28th May

'Has Andrew mentioned the camping trip to you?' asked Melanie, in the shop this morning.

'Yes, he has!'

'Geoff's very excited about it! I'd like to be a fly on the wall, or rather the canvas! The last time Geoff went camping, he got bitten all over by mosquitos and couldn't sit down for a week!'

'Well, at least they'll be away for a bit,' I said.

'Is he driving you mad?' asked Melanie, smiling.

'Only a bit! Mind you, it means I can come here this week and he can look after the kids.

'But does he?' said Melanie. 'In my experience, the kids have to fend for themselves.'

'Well, I gave him strict instructions to keep an eye on what they're doing, but the truth is, Melanie, he'll be immersed in his book and oblivious to what's going on.'

Just then, a man came in with some bags of stuff for the shop. When he'd gone, we took it upstairs to go through it all.

'There are some really good things here,' said Melanie, surprised.

'Ooh yes, not bad,' I said, looking at a nice silver tea set and several pairs of very expensive shoes. 'Look at all these handbags – I mean, they look as if they've hardly been used! And all these designer dresses, Melanie!'

'Why would someone get rid of such nice things? They must have money to burn, Dora!' said Melanie, sifting through it all.

'Good Lord, Melanie!' I said, opening a large mother of pearl jewellery box. 'Look at all this!' Inside was a fabulous collection of gold jewellery, several diamond rings set with sapphires and rubies, two strings of pearls and matching earrings, some antique brooches and numerous necklaces.

'This is valuable stuff, Dora – we can't put it in the shop, can we!'

'I know. What should we do, Melanie? We've got no idea who that man was.'

'Is there a clue anywhere – maybe an address on something?'

We went through everything with a fine toothcomb but came up with nothing.

'We need to get some advice, I think,' said Melanie.

We decided to put it all back in the bags until we could work out what to do.

Later, when I got home, I was surprised to see that all was calm, there was a meal on the table and no one was arguing or fighting. How marvellous, I thought. Then my mother appeared from the lounge.

'I thought I'd come and give you a hand,' she said.

'Oh, that's lovely, Mum,' I said.

Sometimes there's no substitute for a mother's intuition.

Wednesday 29th May

Last night, my mother's visit was quite fortuitous – I managed to broach the subject of on-line dating without getting my head bitten off (partly helped by my children – without them realising, of course).

'Mum,' I'd said, during supper, - 'have you heard of internet dating?'

'Yes – it's all the rage, isn't it! My friend Margery did it. She met a lovely chap called Desmond. They're both in their 80's!'

'That's so sweet!' said Flora.

Tom made a vomiting action by putting both fingers in his mouth. I scowled at him to stop. Luckily my mother didn't notice.

'Yes, she was very lucky, I think. But you don't know who you might meet on the computer, do you? I heard that people can pretend to be anyone – there was that woman in the paper the other day, wasn't there? She had all her savings taken by some bloke who promised to marry her. After he took all her money, he disappeared without a trace!'

'Well, yes Mum, but he should have been vetted properly.'

'Well anyway, what would I want with a dating agency?'

'You might meet a really rich man,' said Flora hopefully – 'who'd take you on cruises and lovely holidays and buy you diamonds and stuff!'

'Yeah, Nan, that'd be cool,' said Luke.

'Then you could give us some,' said Tom.

I frowned at my eldest son, hoping he would desist. I tried another tack. 'Have you been to the cinema recently?' I asked her.

'No, Dora, I haven't. I wanted to go and see the new Bond film, but I didn't have anyone to go with.'

'Doesn't Reggie like films then? Andrew asked.

'Well, I managed to get him to go to see 'Brief Encounter' at the Golden Oldie Film Club, but he said he couldn't hear what was going on and he fell asleep after fifteen minutes. I struggled to hear the rest of it because of his snoring – it was a bit of a disaster, I'm afraid.'

'Oh, that's a shame, Mum – you love the cinema and the theatre, don't you!' Andrew looked at me – he could see where I was going with this.

'Yes, I do miss going. Your Dad loved to go out to things like that…'

'Don't you have any friends to go with?' asked Flora, innocently.

'No, not really, dear – they're all a bit busy anyway, with their own lives.'

'I could go with you!' said Billy, sweetly.

'That's very kind, Billy, but Nan needs a grown-up darling,' I said, smiling at him.

'I've been wondering, Mum, whether it might be a good idea to see if we could find someone for you to go out with who likes doing the same things as you. What do you think?'

'Well, that might be an idea… but I'm not sure where you would find them….'

'I might be able to, if you're open to the idea, Mum…'

'Well, I suppose so. I don't see why not.'

'Very good, Dora!' said Andrew, that night when we went up to bed.

'Well, I'm quite pleased with myself too, Andrew! Jess will be impressed!'

'The trick will be to keep her on side though, Dora. If you make a mistake, it'll be curtains!'

Thursday 30th May

This morning, I rang Jess to tell her about the break-through with Mum.

'She sort of agreed to it,' I told her.

'What do you mean?'

'Well, I just suggested we look for a companion for her – you know, just someone to share similar interests.'

'Fine,' said Jess, - 'that's all we need! Great work, Dora! I'll get on with it straight away!'

I'm still slightly uneasy about it, I must say. I just hope Jess doesn't go over-the-top with promoting our mother's attributes – a discreet little biography should be sufficient.

It's not much fun in our house at the moment. Tom and Flora are supposed to be revising, but I'm not sure how much they're managing to do in between phoning their friends and watching YouTube videos, and Luke and Billy are fighting a lot at the moment.

'This has got to stop,' said Andrew to them, sternly, - 'or I will start confiscating all your toys until you have nothing left to play with.' They agreed to a truce and gave each other a muted apology. It won't last, of course.

Andrew is always grumpy at the moment – well, it's not surprising, what with everything we're trying to cope with, but I think we could all do with something to look forward to. A weekend away would be nice. I think I'll ask Mum if her friend Margery still has her caravan available, up in Skegness.

Friday 31st May

I went to pick up a paper early this morning, as we are all keen to see what they had written. As I approached the newsagents, I could see the A-board resting on the pavement. The headline read:

LOVEDAY COUPLE JAILED FOR DRUG-SMUGGLING

When I got home, I laid it out on the kitchen table for Andrew to see. They'd used a still photo of Bob and Barbara being arrested, from the television report.

'They could have made the headline less misleading,' said Andrew, - 'it makes them look guilty!' He read out the story below:

LOVEDAY COUPLE JAILED FOR DRUG-SMUGGLING
(by Trudy Stoker)

A local family have been left devastated by the arrest of grandparents Bob and Barbara Loveday. The couple claim they were duped by a notorious drug-smuggling cartel based deep in the West Columbian jungle.

"Dr Pablo seemed such a nice man," Barbara Loveday told the police. "We thought we were helping to produce a revolutionary cure for arthritis – that's what he told us."

"We are completely innocent," said Bob Loveday. "We had no idea that these people were not who they said they were, until our arrest."

"We just want to go home," said Barbara Loveday. "We just want to go home to our family."

The family are no strangers to controversy, however. Bob and Barbara Loveday were evicted last year from Tepee

Valley Commune by the local council, along with a known felon, Stanley Mitton (a persistent law-breaker, responsible for more than 30 burglaries and 15 drug-related offences). In addition, only a few weeks ago, a family friend, Suzie Small (previously of Pampers Beauty Salon, Shillingsworth High Street), was implicated in the running of an illegal brothel and people-trafficking offences. Mr Andrew Loveday, (son of Bob Loveday) was instrumental in achieving an acquittal for Ms Small, as her personal lawyer and close friend.

A spokesman for the family said yesterday, "whether these people have genuinely been duped and are just very naïve, or whether they knew what they were getting involved with, they are in any event extremely foolish, and don't deserve to be in Bogotá Prison, which has one of the worst human rights records in the world."

If any of our readers want to help the family to secure Bob and Barbara Loveday's release, please go to their JustGiving Page www.helpingB&B.com

The family are grateful for your support and don't forget, kids – JUST SAY NO TO DRUGS.

'That bloody woman!' said Andrew.

'I told you she couldn't be trusted, Andrew!' I said.

'People will think I'm a dodgy lawyer, reading this! How on earth did she know about Tepee Valley and Stanley Mitton, for God's sake! And why on earth bring up that business with the salon again?'

'Because it sells papers,' I said.

'It's tainted our campaign for Mum and Dad – no one will support us now, will they!' he said angrily.

'Well, they might….'

'I don't think so, Dora! I'm cancelling my radio interview with Chas this afternoon – if he gets hold of this I'll be made to look a complete fool, and it'll just make things worse for Mum and Dad.'

The news story on the TV later was a bit better. They showed the same footage as before, followed by an interview with a roving reporter stationed in Bogotá. The reporter, a middle-aged, stern-faced woman called Joanna Ray, wearing thick-rimmed glasses, gave a succinct, but fair appraisal of the situation:

This couple are facing a harsh sentence if proved guilty,' she said, grimly. 'The Columbian authorities are claiming they are part of an international drug smuggling operation, which the couple deny. They claim they are innocent of all the charges and that they were hoodwinked by a notorious criminal gang and brought here under false pretences. The British Embassy is working with the police here, to try to get the situation resolved as quickly as possible. Bob and Barbara Loveday's family in the UK are campaigning for their release and have urged the public to support them.

The JustGiving information flashed up on the screen and then the programme moved swiftly on to the plight of a Premier League footballer with a twisted ankle.

'Well, that was an improvement on the newspaper coverage,' said Andrew, turning the TV off. 'What do you lot think?'

'I'm glad it's half term,' said Tom. 'Everyone at school will be talking about it.'

'You don't have to say you're related,' said Andrew.

'I wish I wasn't,' said Tom, miserably.

'So do I,' said Luke. 'Why can't we have a normal family like other people?'

'Yeah,' said Tom. 'It's not fair.'

'I know, boys, but this will be a distant memory soon, you'll see.'

'A *distant memory*! Are you kidding!' I said to Andrew later, when the boys had gone out.

'Well, what do you want me to say?' said Andrew. 'I'm just trying to play it down a bit – there's no point in us all getting hysterical about it, is there? That won't help anything.'

Luckily, Flora was out today and didn't see the local paper or hear the news story, thank goodness. I told Tom and Luke not to discuss it with Billy either. He's too young really to have any idea about the gravity of the situation. Thank goodness that he's currently obsessed with Oscar's den, which has kept him occupied all week. I'm not sure Tom and Luke realise how serious this is either – I mean, all they can think about is how embarrassing it is and what their friends will say.

* * *

JUNE

Saturday 1st June

L ots of people came to fetch their kittens today but we've still got two white ones, and Rufus of course. 'Do you think Hillary might like them? I asked Tom this morning, at breakfast.

'Dunno, maybe…'

'Well, you could ask her, couldn't you?'

'He's not seeing her any more,' butted in Luke. 'Tom got dumped.'

'Shut up, Luke,' said Tom, crossly.

'OK, OK, that's enough,' I said. 'I'm sorry about that, Tom.'

Tom shrugged and stared at his toast.

'Hillary told all her friends that you're a mad cat lady,' Luke continued. 'She said we have loads of cats and you feed them on rat stew and mouse soup, and that our family are all crazy.'

Tom looked as if he was going to leap up and punch Luke any minute. 'I told you to shut up!' he yelled at Luke.

'Luke, I think you should go and find something to do in your room now – OK?' I said, ushering him out of the kitchen. He left the room grumbling that he hadn't done anything wrong.

'Don't worry, Tom,' I said to him, seeing how upset he was. 'It doesn't matter that she said that about us – I really don't care.'

'It's not fair,' said Tom, eventually.

'Do you still like her?' I asked.

'I wish I wasn't in this family,' he said after a while.

'Well, I can sympathise with you on that one,' I said. 'The thing is, Tom, that no family is perfect. Every family has its troubles and its eccentricities – even Hillary's. You're stuck with us, I'm afraid, whether you like it or not.' I gave him a hug because he looked sad enough to allow it. 'I tell you what, Tom, she might think we're all mad but it's better than being boring, isn't it? I mean, who wants to go through life being boring?'

'The treacherous witch!' exclaimed Andrew, when I told him about Hillary. 'Is Tom OK?'

'Not really. He's upset, but I think he blames us.'

'Ridiculous!' said Andrew.

'Well, we do come across as a bit bonkers, I suppose, and the kids feel embarrassed by us.'

'There's nothing abnormal about us, Dora! She's obviously from a very dull family.'

'Well anyway, she's given Tom the elbow, so be nice to him for a bit, please Andrew.'

'What do you mean, Dora? Of course I will!'

'When's Suzie taking Rufus?' Andrew asked, when most of the kittens had been collected.

'Um, she isn't,' I confessed. 'I decided to keep him, Andrew. He's so sweet – I couldn't part with him.'

'You're worse than Flora!' he said. 'Oh well, I suppose one more won't matter – as long as someone takes the other two.'

He doesn't know yet, but we will have an extra dog, two more cats and two parrots staying with us next week, because I haven't got enough people on my books to look after all the Pets' Haven animals.

'What about Mrs Peake?' Suzie had said, - 'haven't you asked her?'

'No,' I said. 'I think that might be a bad idea.'

'I don't understand,' said Suzie. So, I had to explain:

'You know when I worked at Pooch Parlour? Well, Mrs Peake's cat, Fluffy, came in for grooming and well, it escaped and got a bit traumatised and then a couple of days later it sort of died.'

'Oh dear!' said Suzie, - 'that's terrible.'

'Yes, it is, and well, the thing is – she thinks it was my fault.'

'Oh dear,' was all Suzie could say.

'Anyway, that's why I can't see her. She'd recognise me.'

'What do you all think about a weekend away in a caravan by the sea?' I asked everyone at tea time.

'Brilliant!' said Luke. 'We can go surfing and snorkelling. When can we go?'

'Don't know yet,' I said. 'Hopefully soon.'

'Can I stay here?' said Flora. 'It's not really my thing.'

'Not *your thing*!' said Andrew. 'Don't be so daft!'

Flora scowled. 'I don't want to go – it's boring, Dad.' Andrew rolled his eyes. 'What about you, Tom – you'd like to go, wouldn't you?'

Tom pulled a face. 'Not really.'

'For God's sake, Tom! Stop being such a misery!'

'I'm going,' said Tom, stomping off upstairs.

'What's the matter with him!' said Andrew.

'Have you forgotten already?' I said.

'Oh, for heaven's sake,' said Andrew, - 'he can't be serious! He's only sixteen!'

'I know, but to him it's really important – can't you be a bit more sympathetic?'

'Yeah, Dad.' said Flora, - 'don't you remember being young?'

'Can we take Fudge and Cocoa?' asked Billy.

'No,' said Andrew.

'Yes,' I said.

'Can't we leave them with your mother?' Andrew pleaded.

'But they love it there,' I said. 'You can't deny them a beach holiday! You know how much they love the sea!'

Andrew looked disappointed, but I wasn't going to be swayed.

'I've had a communication from the lawyers this afternoon,' Andrew told me later. 'The negotiations are going quite well. Our lawyers think that the authorities would like to get rid of Mum and Dad quite soon if we can agree the release fee. They say that Dad is stirring up trouble in the jail.'

'I wonder what they mean by that?' I said.

'God knows,' said Andrew, - 'but knowing my father, I can imagine he's becoming a thorn in their side – can't you?'

'Yes,' I said, laughing, - 'even in there!'

Sunday 2nd June

Jess asked me to go over to her place this morning and see what she's written about Mum. It only takes twenty minutes to walk to her flat. Terry answered the door in his pyjamas and slippers.

'For goodness' sake, Terry!' scolded Jess.

'I don't care,' I said, - 'it's Sunday, Jess. How are you, Terry?'

'We're OK, aren't we, Jess?' he said.

Honestly, I'm beginning to wonder if Terry has a separate personality any more. Jess may have beaten it out of him.

'What do you think?' asked Jess, logging on the website.

'**RESURRECTION.COM**' appeared, big and bold. Beneath it, it read: *Never Too Old For Love*.

'Right,' said Jess, - 'I'll show you Mum's profile page. I'm so pleased with it, Dora – wait till you see it!' Frankly, I was dreading what I might see next – Jess is not one for discretion or prudence. She didn't disappoint.

'Oh my God, Jess!' I said when I saw our mother pop up on the screen.

'Do you like it?' she said, excitedly.

'I don't know what to say,' I stared at the image before me. Something wasn't right.

'Jess, that's not Mum's body, is it?' I said.

'No Dora, it isn't – it's good though, isn't it? You can't see the join at all!'

I peered at the screen. There was Mum's head attached to a slimmer, younger body, dressed in jeans and a T-shirt.

'Jess – Mum's face is all smooth and shiny, like a plum.'

'Isn't it amazing what you can do with Photoshop, Dora!' said Jess, pleased as punch.

Beneath the fabricated photo, Jess had written a short piece about our mother: '*My name is Abigail Fairfax….*

'Why did you call her that?' I said.

'We can't use her real name, Dora – you don't know who's looking at this, do you? We don't want her being stalked by perverts, do we!'

'Then why did you make her look thirty years younger, Jess? I mean, you're asking for trouble doing that!'

'Don't be silly, Dora – all I'm doing is enhancing her image a bit.'

'Why 'Abigail Fairfax'?' I said.

'I was trying to make Mum sound a bit more impressive, Dora. It has a certain *je ne sais quoi* about it, doesn't it?'

I read on: ***I am a 50 plus single lady, with a zest for life and a fit and active lifestyle…***

'What! You can't put that, Jess! She's knocking on for 77, for goodness' sake! And the only exercise she gets, as far as I know, is a bit of gardening and the odd saunter down the road for a pint of milk and a packet of Fig Rolls!'

'We've got to present her in the best light,' said Jess. 'Anyway, it would be good for her if she met someone who was keen to get fit, wouldn't it!'

I read the rest of it with a sinking heart: ***I'm a fun and energetic woman with a keen interest in the arts. I particularly enjoy the Theatre, going to the Opera, good food and plenty of foreign travel.***

I laughed at this point. 'Jess – she's never even been to an opera!'

'Well, she watched 'Madam Butterfly' on the telly and said she liked it,' said Jess in her defence. 'We've got to attract the right calibre of gentleman, Dora. We don't want any old riff-raff expressing an interest, do we?'

'No, I suppose not, but it seems a bit over-the-top, Jess'.

'It's fine, Dora – you'll see,' Jess said, confidently.

I walked home after a cup of tea and one of Terry's Viennese Whirls. Jess usually gives the impression she knows what she's doing, but on this occasion, I'm not sure. What she's done with our mother's image on *Resurrection.com* could backfire badly. I mean, it's one thing to dress something up, but she's made Mum look like a totally different person. I'm not sure if Mum would approve if she knew. And making out she's a theatre buff! That's really stretching things a bit. You can't describe someone who reads the *Reader's Digest* from cover to cover, dunks biscuits in her tea, and watches anything with Alan Titchmarsh in it, as high-minded, can you? Don't get me wrong, I'm not saying our mother doesn't possess an intelligent and enquiring mind, but I do think Jess is being a bit over-ambitious.

Monday 3rd June

The kids went back to school today. It's always a relief to see them usefully occupied, and to have the house back to myself – well, almost.

'Dora, there's a man at the door with two parrots,' shouted Andrew, just after all the children had left the house.

'It's Errol and Flynn!' I said, as I came downstairs. 'Quick, Andrew, put the dogs in the garden – I'd forgotten they were coming!'

'I'll just get their perch,' said Mr Sawyer, and he went back to his car, leaving each of us holding a parrot.

'I hope they're not going to be noisy', said Andrew, - 'I mean, parrots can be really loud, can't they!'

'***Really loud, really loud!!***' squawked one of them, flapping his wings and hopping on one leg.

'Oh no!' said Andrew, - 'now we'll have to watch everything we say, for God's sake!'

'***God's sake, God's sake...***' squawked the other one.

'This is going to be fun!' I said to a worried looking Andrew.

Mr Sawyer erected their perch in the conservatory. It'll be best in here, he said, - 'you know, for hygiene purposes.'

'How long do you think you'll be in hospital for, Mr Sawyer?' I asked nervously, as he handed me a long list of do's and don'ts for parrots.

'Not sure – maybe a couple of weeks. They said we have to play it by ear a bit. Sorry.'

'Oh, don't worry, Mr Sawyer, it's no problem,' I said brightly, showing him out.

'*No problem!*' said Andrew. 'Blimey, Dora – they're going to be a real handful!'

'They'll probably settle down,' I said, just as the dogs spotted them through the glass from outside, and started barking at them furiously. Errol and Flynn were not impressed and began squawking even more loudly. Andrew went away and shut himself in the study, but reappeared after ten minutes.

'I can't hear myself think!' he said. 'How am I supposed to write anything with all this noise going on. PD James didn't have to put up with this sort of thing! I need somewhere peaceful with no distractions!'

When the children came in from school later, they were very excited to see our new visitors.

'They're much more fun than Mr Nibbles!' said Luke.

'Don't remind me,' I said, - 'I feel terrible about losing Mr Nibbles.'

'Do you think Mr Nibbles is dead?' said Billy.

'Mr Nibbles is dead, Mr Nibbles is dead....' squawked Errol.

'Mum, they can talk!' said Luke, excitedly.

'Yes, they certainly can!' I said. 'I think we'd better teach them something cheerful – how about a song or something.' I went off to sort tea out and left them to it. I don't know how I'm going to tell Mr Potter tomorrow, that we've lost his beloved rat...

Tuesday 4ᵗʰ June

'What do you mean by *'gone missing'*?' said Mr Potter when I broke the news to him this morning.

'Just that, I'm afraid, Mr Potter – I'm ever so sorry...' Then I had a thought. 'Would you be interested in a kitten, or maybe two? We've got some nice white ones looking for a good home.'

'But Mr Nibbles was my pal,' said Mr Potter sadly.

'I know, and I really am very sorry, Mr Potter – I don't know what's happened to him, but perhaps you could consider a kitten as a replacement,' I said, hopefully.

He mulled it over. 'Well, I suppose I could…'

I went and found the two white kittens. 'They're good company and very entertaining,' I said, watching them chase each other up and down the lounge curtains.

'I'll miss Mr Nibbles,' said Mr Potter, sighing.

'**Mr Nibbles is dead, Mr Nibbles is dead,**' piped up Errol from the conservatory. I quickly scooted through the kitchen and closed the door.

'What was that?' said Mr Potter.

'Oh, we've got a couple of parrots here – they're a bit noisy,' I said, hoping he hadn't heard properly.

After a while, I could see Mr Potter warming to the idea of having the kittens.

'Great result!' said Andrew, when I told him. 'By the way, Mum and Dad are going to court on Friday for a hearing, so fingers crossed!'

'Oh good, it can't come soon enough' I said. 'Oh, and I just need to tell you,' I began, making use of his current good mood, - 'there's a sausage dog called Percy coming this afternoon, and two more cats this evening.'

'What! But Dora, we've only just got rid of two…'

'I know. Sorry. It's just that I haven't got enough people lined up to look after all the animals yet.'

Errol and Flynn chose this moment to start making lots of noise.

'What's that they're singing?' said Andrew, frowning.

'I don't know – something about clover – I can't make it out. The boys were trying to get them to sing songs yesterday.'

'Well, whatever it is, it's a bloody racket.'

'I've got to go,' I said to him. 'Sorry, Andrew, you'll have to be here when Percy comes – about three o'clock. Oh, and don't forget to walk the dogs, feed the parrots and put the dishwasher on. I've got to be in the shop in fifteen minutes. Bye!'

I left him, looking downcast. It was his choice to be at home though, wasn't it! Well, it hasn't turned out to be the peaceful haven he was hoping for when he decided to write a book, has it! I suppose I ought to focus on getting more people to help with the animals. I must say though, I thought Suzie and Melanie might have been a bit more willing to look after some of them.

'You don't fancy a couple of parrots for a week or so, do you?' I asked Melanie when I got to the shop.

'No, Dora, I don't.'

'No, I thought not.'

'My uncle had a parrot. It was noisy, smelly, and said rude things to people when they visited.'

'Mmm,' I said. 'I need to recruit more helpers, Melanie – my house is turning into a menagerie.'

When I got home later, Percy had already made himself at home in Andrew's favourite armchair, and the two cats (Gin and Tonic) were chasing Rufus all over the house and causing mayhem, and Fudge and Cocoa were in the garden barking at the parrots through the windows of the conservatory. Scratch was nowhere to be seen.

'Probably keeping well out of it,' said Andrew. 'I wish I could.'

'And I'm trying to revise,' said Tom. 'I can't concentrate with all the noise.'

'Me neither,' said Flora. 'We've got exams, Mum!'

'Well, I'm surprised they can hear anything above the music on their headphones,' said Andrew, once they'd gone upstairs.

'I'll try and sort something out soon,' I said, - 'but it's not easy finding the right people.'

I'm beginning to think I might have bitten off more than I can chew with this project. It's far more work than I envisaged. Perhaps I should take Chas up on his offer of another radio interview – after all, it did raise quite a bit of publicity last time, even though the whole experience was pretty disconcerting to say the least. I suppose, on balance, it can't do any harm…

Wednesday 5th June

Suzie has agreed to look after the shop until Saturday, and Melanie said she would share next week with her so that I can be at home. Well, I can't expect Andrew to cope with all the animals by himself, and now the shop is turning over enough money to pay a proper wage to them both, which is great. Anyway, I had to be at home today, to welcome a hamster and four gerbils. Hopefully, Andrew will be too busy writing to notice further additions to our collection of pets.

When the bell rang at 10 o'clock, I thought it was the hamster coming a bit early, but I was surprised when I opened the door to Fay Barker who asked if she could come in.

'For a word, Dora,' she said, in a low whispery voice.

'Of course,' I said, wondering what Billy had been up to. 'Would you like a cup of tea?'

'No thanks', she said, staring at me intently. I was suddenly aware of how enormous her eyes looked in her head, which was cocked on one side like a bird.

'I'll get to the point,' she said. 'I found these in Oscar's den – Oscar tells me they belong to Billy.'

She delved into a bag and with a gloved hand, held up two pairs of black leather thongs, one of which was attached to a horse whip. 'They were making catapults out of them, Dora.'

'I can explain….' I said, suddenly realising the implication.

'You don't need to, Dora. I don't want to know the details of your private goings on. Although, I must say I am disappointed to discover that a woman who allows herself to be subjugated in this manner, lives just three houses away from me. I am also deeply distressed that a poor innocent child has discovered these disgusting items just lying around in the house!'

'Hang on a minute, Fay – if you'll just allow me to explain…'

She sucked in her cheeks and blinked at me with her giant baby-blue eyes. Just then, Andrew came out of the study to see who was at the door.

'Good grief, Dora! Not more bondage gear! We ought to open a shop!'

'Andrew,' I said sharply, 'Fay thinks these are mine…'

'Oh, no – they don't belong to Dora – she prefers red ones, don't you, Dora!' he said, thinking he was being very funny. 'I think you'll find they belong to our neighbour. They ended up in our garden the other day. It was all Tinker's fault – Ruth wanted to try out their new bed, then he got over-excited and was out of control in the garden.'

Fay looked scandalised. 'I can't believe what I'm hearing,' she said. 'And I thought this was a nice neighbourhood. Whoever Ruth and this Tinker person is, they should be locked up – I mean, in broad daylight! It's unbelievable!'

Andrew started laughing.

'I don't know why you find it funny, Andrew! You've got young children to consider! I think you should go and tell those people to keep their activities strictly inside their own home. I'd be ringing the police if I were you!' She turned to leave, but not before Errol and Flynn could be heard singing, or rather squawking, "***Roll me Over in the Clover, roll me over in the clover and do it again….***"

'Oh, that's just the parrots…' I said.

Fay gave us a hard stare, shook her head, and marched off up the road.

'Andrew!' I said, crossly, 'Why didn't you explain properly! We've already annoyed our neighbours enough over the years. Now they will think we're sexual deviants as well as being noisy and messy! I want you to go round to the Barkers later and speak to them. And tell them about the parrots as well.'

'Oh, all right,' said Andrew. 'Hey, Dora, that's quite innovative of Billy, isn't it! It's a very effective sling-shot! Look, it works really well!' he said, firing a custard cream across the room.

Thursday 6th June

'Please teach those birds a different song!' Andrew pleaded with the boys this morning. 'I can't get it out of my head! They won't shut up.'

'Something nice, please,' I added.

'Billy was teaching them farting noises last night,' said Luke. 'It was so funny!'

Andrew looked at me despairingly. 'How much longer are they here for?' he asked.

'Another week and a half.'

Andrew groaned. 'I'm thinking of moving in with your mother, Dora. What do you think?'

'Does she know?'

'No, I haven't asked her yet.'

'If you go to Mum's, you'll be able to keep an eye on her and Reggie!' I said to Andrew, when all the children had gone. 'It could prove quite useful.'

'That's not why I'm thinking of going there,' said Andrew.

'I know, but it would be a good opportunity, wouldn't it?'

'I'm not going to spy on your mother, Dora. I need to focus on my book. I won't have time to '*keep an eye*' on her, or Reggie! I'm only thinking for a few days, Dora – just until the parrots have gone. I'm feeling extremely frustrated at the moment.'

'Suzie,' I said later, when I rang her at the shop, - 'Andrew's going to go to my mother's for a while.'

'Oh Dora…I'm so sorry.'

'No, Suzie, it's not like that. He says he's frustrated - he needs peace and quiet to write.'

'Oh, I see – well, he could always use my house if he wants – there's a proper study.'

'OK – thanks Suzie. I'll put it to him. How's the shop today?'

'Well, it's fine, except there's a group of people outside with a banner and it's stopping people coming in.'

'What does it say?'

'It says *Justice For Queenie'.* They're saying Pets' Haven is run by the same people who 'destroyed Queenie's career'. They're demanding to see the management, Dora. What shall I say?'

'Tell them the management lives a very, very long way away, Suzie – tell them that it's all run from abroad or something.'

'Don't go down there,' said Andrew, when I told him.

'What about poor Suzie though – I can't just let her deal with it by herself.'

'Oh, for goodness' sake, I suppose I'd better go and sort it out,' he said, sighing and putting his manuscript down for the third time this morning.

Andrew came back an hour and a half later.

'So, what's happening?' I said, as soon as he opened the door.

'Well, there's a bunch of about five people with a banner and some placards. Ava Bush was there and an odd collection of people. There was a blind man with a funny looking dog – I think it was one of those Chow Chows but it had been given a sort of Mohican! And there was a little round woman with beady eyes who had a nasty, moth-eaten Westie – it tried to bite me twice! Mrs Peake was there as well, with a blown-up photo of a Persian cat on a stick. Anyway, I called the police to come and break it up.'

'Really!'

'Yes – they were obstructing the pavement and access to shops. That photographer from the Citizen was there taking photos, so I expect there'll be another article in the paper soon. I'll try and find out what's happening with the case.'

'What if those people are there every day, Andrew?'

'I don't think so Dora. The police told them they'd be arrested if they come back.'

'Why weren't they protesting outside Pooch Parlour instead?'

'Well, the business appears to be closed, Dora. There's a notice on the door.'

The mystery of Mr Nibbles' disappearance resolved itself this evening – rather spectacularly, as it happens. I went round to Mona's house to return Billy's improvised weaponry to its rightful owner, and thought I'd be able to escape quickly after shoving the items through the letterbox, when she flung open the front door and caught me mid-shove.

Just returning some of your lost things,' I said. 'We found them in the garden the other week…'

'Thank God you're here!' she said, somewhat dramatically. Then she pulled me into the house. 'I need your help, Dora!'

'Oh…'

'Quick, in here!' She dragged me into her bedroom and pointed.

Sitting in the middle of her dressing table, chewing on a large, fluorescent pink hairbrush, was Mr Nibbles. He was quite unconcerned with Mona's shrieks of disgust and didn't move an inch.

'I'll catch him,' I said, - 'don't worry. You'll have to throw that brush away though – he appears to have chewed all the bristles right off!'

'It's not a brush, Dora – it's one of my new cherry-flavoured leisure accessories – I only just got them! I haven't even tried them out yet!'

'You're kidding!' said Andrew later, when I told him I'd found Mr Nibbles chomping on a giant dildo.

'She thinks he's been living in the pantry,' I told him. 'Roger's demijohns had been tampered with – he'd chewed right through the tubing. Mona said he'd nibbled her bacon bits, and there were tell-tale bite marks all round her skirting.'

Friday 7th June

'Mum, Dad!' shouted Luke this morning, as we came downstairs. 'Percy bit Rufus!'

'Where?' I asked.

'On his tail. I saw him do it.'

'Really? Are you sure? Percy's such a placid little dog, curled up on the chair like that – I can't imagine him being aggressive!'

'Well, he did it – I saw him!'

'Well, I expect Rufus was annoying him,' said Andrew.

'No, Dad, he wasn't – Rufus was sleeping and Percy just went up and bit him.'

'OK, well, animals can be a bit unpredictable sometimes, Luke.'

'Well I don't like him any more.'

Oh dear! And I thought Percy was going to be easy to have – he seemed such a sweet little dog. Oh well, the cats will just have to learn to avoid him, I suppose. Anyway, I've got too many other things to contend with at the moment, especially today. It's Bob and Barbara's court appearance, although I don't suppose we'll hear anything until next week. I must say, I am feeling quite at sea just now with everything that's going on. Flora and Tom's exams seem to be going on interminably, I'm worrying about Ava Bush's legal proceedings, Andrew's book is taking forever to write, and all these animals are giving me a headache. Jess has embarked on a mad enterprise for our mother which I am uncomfortable with to say the least, and poor Bob and Barbara's predicament hangs over us like a huge, dark thundercloud. There's a terrible sense of foreboding which I just can't ignore. Andrew on the other hand seems to be able to switch off from the potential direness of his parents' situation with relative ease.

'There's no point in fretting about it, Dora.' Andrew said this morning, when I told him how I was feeling - particularly about his parents. 'What will be, will be. We're doing our best to get them out, aren't we? I mean, I don't see what more can be done. Anyway, it's all in the hands of the lawyers now. Sometimes, you just have to let things take their course. I'm going to get on with my book. See you at lunch time,' he said, resolutely closing the study door.

'Dora, it's Jess,' said Jess, when she rang up a bit later.

'Yes…'

'Guess what!'

'What?'

'I've had loads of interest on Mum's profile at Resurrection.com! I need your help.'

'I can't leave all the animals, Jess – you'll have to come here.'

She was round within half an hour, and opened her laptop on the kitchen table. We perused the responding suitors with a range of reactions.

'Look at this one, Dora! It's hilarious!' said Jess. 'Let's rate them out of ten, then it'll be easier to eliminate some of them.'

'I don't know, Jess. I mean, you can't just dismiss people like that…'

'OK, listen to this then.' She proceeded to read one man's message out. *'My name is Jake Vantage. I'm looking for a lady like you for fun and frolics with no strings attached…'*

'See - he's obviously married,' said Jess.

'OK, I see what you mean,' I said. 'He's only a 'one' then.'

'Jess read on. 'What about this bloke – *'We could make great music together – let me be the bow for your violin, the keys to your piano, the wind in your cornett….'*

'Good grief, Jess, that's awful! No, he's definitely a 'one'.'

'OK, this one then – *You look like a charming woman with great sex appeal! I can't wait to meet you! I'm very open-minded, so feel free to bring a friend…'*

'NO!!'

Jess tried another one - *'I'll show you mine, if you show me yours…'*

'What's wrong with all these men! All they want is sex! Isn't there one that just wants companionship?' I said, sighing deeply.

'Well, there are one or two. What about this one then – *'If you like cooking and home comforts, you could be the woman for me…'*

'Maybe – seems a bit dull though. I'll give him a 'four'. What does he look like?'

Jess enlarged his photo. 'Well, he's no oil painting,' I said, peering at the rather dumpy, bald man in the picture.

'No, but look at his car, Dora!'

'Honestly, Jess, you're so shallow!'

'This one sounds better,' said Jess. 'He sounds like the sort of chap we're looking for.'

I read his message – *Dear Abigail, I've been widowed for six years now, but I've decided to stop feeling sorry for myself and get out more. I'd like to meet someone who will bring some joy into my life. My best friend is my adored dog Geoffrey who has been with me for twelve years. I liked your photo, and wondered if we could meet for afternoon tea? What do you think? Yours sincerely, Lawrence B. Fairchild.*

'Well, I'd say he's an 'eight',' I said, looking at the photograph attached. A tall well-dressed, dark-haired man stood in the driveway of a very large Edwardian house, flanked by a beautifully kept lawn and a golden retriever sitting obediently beside him.

'Look at *his* car!' said Jess.

'Isn't that a Bentley?' I said.

'Ooh yes! Right, let's arrange a date,' said Jess.

'Isn't that a bit quick, Jess? I mean, shouldn't there be a bit of corresponding first?'

'No! Strike while the iron is hot, Dora. There's no time to lose.'

'I think we should show Mum first, Jess. She hasn't even seen her own profile page!'

Jess sighed reluctantly and agreed to speak to Mum first.

'Well,' said Andrew, when I told him at lunch time, - 'I hope Jess knows what she's doing! For all we know, he could be a con man. His real name could be Terence Leaf, and he's just come out of the nick. I mean, that could be anyone's house, couldn't it!'

He's quite right of course. I think Jess is being a little hasty. Looks can be deceptive. Just look at Percy for instance. He looks like an adorable little dog, but he's obviously a wolf in sheep's clothing and we need to be on our guard.

Saturday 8th June

'So, kids – how's it all going?' Andrew said to Tom and Flora when they finally emerged at 11.30am this morning, bleary eyed and still in their pyjamas.

'OK,' said Tom.

'Yeah, OK,' said Flora.

'Well, how do you think your exams are going so far?'

'OK,' said Tom.

'Same,' said Flora.

'I think that's all you're going to get,' I told him, when they'd disappeared back upstairs with over-filled bowls of cereal and mugs of tea.

'I wish they'd be a bit more sociable!' said Andrew.

'Like you, you mean!' I said. Andrew looked surprised. 'Well, you haven't been particularly sociable yourself recently, Andrew! You shut yourself away in the study to work on your book and we only see you at meal times, or to complain about something!'

'It's not as bad as that, Dora – you're exaggerating. Anyway, I've got to work on it as much as possible if I'm going to finish it in six months – well, five now. You know how hard it is to concentrate here, Dora – there's so much going on in the house.'

'Actually, Andrew,' I said, remembering Suzie's offer, - 'Suzie suggested you use the study at her house. Warren is away again, so you would have it all to yourself.'

'Oh, that sounds like a great idea,' said Andrew, brightening up.

'But, I need you to come back at lunch times and help with the dogs – agreed?'

'Fine,' he said. I'm not sure he will stick to this plan, but time will tell.

'Can I go to Oscar's?' asked Billy after lunch.

'Yes, but you can't have the catapults you made,' I said.

'Why not! Oscar thinks they're awesome! We made a target on a tree and a proper scoreboard! I was winning!'

'Sorry, Billy, but the things you used belonged to someone else and I had to return them.'

Billy looked cross. 'It's not fair! Anyway, I don't see what use a bendy walking stick is to anyone, or those weird hairband things.'

'I'll get you something else to use, Billy, don't worry.' I went and found an old pair of Andrew's Y-fronts, took the elastic out and handed it to Billy. 'This'll be just as good,' I told him.

Sunday 9ᵗʰ June

I rang my mother today to ask her about Margery's caravan.

'I don't know if she's still got it, Dora. I'll ask her,' said Mum.

'Great. How are you getting on?' I asked.

'Well, Jess came over yesterday and showed me a photo of someone called Abigail Fairfax she's put on the computer – she says it's supposed to be a photo of me, but I don't know what to make of it, to be honest. I don't think it's a very good likeness. Anyway, she said I've got lots of admirers! Then she said I've got to call myself Abigail Fairfax to 'maintain my cover'. I'm a bit confused, Dora – I mean, what would Abigail Fairfax have to say about me impersonating her if she found out?'

Oh dear, I'm not sure if this plan of Jess's is going to go very well. If my mother can't grasp the rudiments of internet safety, this doesn't bode well.

'Mum,' said Billy, as I put the phone down, - 'Percy bit my hand – look!' He showed me a row of teeth marks on the back of his hand.

'Oh, goodness! You weren't teasing him, were you Billy?'

'No, Mum – he just got off the chair and walked over and bit me for no reason!'

'What should we do?' I said to Andrew, over breakfast. 'He obviously can't be trusted, can he?'

'Just find someone else to have him, and those beastly parrots as well! Just listen to them!'

They were making loud farting noises and squawking, **'better out than in…'**

'Was that you, Luke?'

'What?'

'The parrots – did you teach them that?'

'No, Mum! It was Dad!' said Luke.

'Why do boys have to be so disgusting!' said Flora, pulling a face.

'Billy, please don't put that dirty old tin on the kitchen table when we're eating,' I said to him.

'He's been carrying it around all week,' said Luke. 'He won't let me see what's in it.'

'Probably best not to,' I said.

'Give it here,' said Luke, suddenly lunging at Billy and making a grab for it. Billy held on to it, but it was finally wrestled from him by his bigger and much stronger brother. Unfortunately, the lid came off in the process, and the rest of the tin fell to the floor with an almighty clatter.

'AAAAAAHH,' shrieked Flora, dropping her toast and instantly leaping up onto her chair. Everyone else backed away hastily as we tried to avoid stepping on Billy's live spider collection.

'Don't kill them!' shouted Billy as Andrew batted them out of the way with his newspaper.

'You can't keep spiders as pets, Billy!'

'Why not, Dad? I like them. I've been feeding them lots to make them grow really big. This one's my favourite,' he said, scooping it up off the floor just in time, before it met an untimely demise beneath Andrew's descending shoe.

Monday 10th June

'I'm not coming in the kitchen,' said Flora this morning.

'There aren't any more spiders, Flora – they've all gone now,' I said.

'Except for Wolfie!' said Billy.

'Billy, that's really unhelpful,' I said, giving him a hard stare.

'Well, he's right there,' said Billy, pointing at the lampshade above the table.

'Wow, that's a whopper!' said Luke.

'See!' said Flora, from the safety of the hallway and she left without having breakfast, saying, 'I hate my brothers,' as she banged the door on the way out.

'He's my biggest one,' said Billy, balancing on a chair as he tried to flick him back into his precious tin.

'Put it in Flora's bed, Billy!' said Luke – 'that'd be *soooo* funny!'

'You boys will be in more trouble than you ever thought possible, if you do anything like that! Do you hear me?' I said, sternly. 'It's not fair to tease your sister.'

They grumbled a vague 'OK', but I'm not at all convinced. Poor Flora – it's not easy having three brothers.

We finally got the phone call we've been waiting for, mid-morning. Andrew called me through to the study and put the phone on loudspeaker, so we could both hear what the lawyers had to say. To cut a long story short, Bob and Barbara have been given a reprieve, thank God! The judge agreed that they were innocent of all charges and could go home (the undisclosed cash injection into a certain offshore bank account obviously helped). He did, however, order them both to stay away from the country and never set foot in it again. There was mention of serious political unrest and protest activities within the jail, but the line went fuzzy at this point and we got cut off. Anyway, they should be home by the end of the month.

'Well, that's fantastic news!' said Andrew, when he put the phone down. He quickly wiped away the tears of relief from his face and I caught a rare glimpse of the Andrew I loved and admired. 'Let's go out for lunch to celebrate!' I said.

Tuesday 11th June

Gin and Tonic have made an awful mess of my lounge curtains pulling all the threads out. I'll be glad when they get picked up later. Unfortunately, Percy doesn't go until tomorrow. We've decided he must be psychologically disturbed. After he bit Billy, I put him in the downstairs loo between walks, to stop him biting anyone else.

'How's it going in the shop?' I asked Melanie, later on.

'Well, I wasn't going to tell you this, Dora, but well, we've had a bit of a problem this morning.'

'Really? What?'

'Well, when Suzie and I came in today, we saw that someone had vandalised the sign above the shop.'

'Oh! What did they do?'

'Well – instead of saying, 'Pets' Haven', someone added an 'S' so it now reads 'Pets' *Shaven*' and there's a photo of Queenie stuck on the window and someone has painted a giant arrow pointing at it. We've managed to get rid of the arrow and the photo, but it's taken us all morning. I think we'll need Andrew to come with the big ladder and take the shop sign down, Dora, so we can clean it up.'

Honestly, some people just can't be rational, can they! What's the point in being so unreasonable! Whoever's doing this must be a bit unhinged – I mean, it's a bit over the top, isn't it? Those dogs will all get their fur back to normal soon, apart from Queenie possibly, but it's all getting a bit out of hand if you ask me.

After Melanie's phone call, I felt a bit despondent and decided to take the dogs out on the common, including Percy. Well, even a miscreant like Percy needs exercise. Anyway, he'll be going back to his owner tomorrow.

It was a lovely sunny day, which always cheers me up. We went down to the river so they could splash about. After about half an hour, I was just thinking about going home, when who should I spy but Ava Bush coming towards us with Queenie. I suddenly realised that Queenie was no longer bald – in fact she looked almost normal! When she saw my dogs in the water, she rushed in to play with them. Ava struggled to hold onto her, but Queenie dragged her down the bank into the cold, scummy water with her.

'Are those your dogs?' Ava shouted, climbing back up the bank dripping wet.

'Yes, they are.'

'This is all your fault,' she said, crossly.

'It's not my fault,' I said, indignantly. 'Anyway, they're just playing – you can't stop them from having fun!'

'It's you!' she suddenly said. 'It's you, isn't it? Dora Loveday! From Pooch Parlour! I might have known!'

'I don't know what you mean by that!' I said, - 'come on Fudge, Cocoa,' I shouted, - 'we're going!'

I nearly forgot Percy in my rush to escape, until he suddenly ran up to her and bit her on the ankle.

273

'Aaarrgh!' she yelped, hopping round on one foot. A man came over to try and help. 'What's going on?' he asked.

'That dog attacked me!' shouted Ava, pointing at Percy. Percy sat there looking innocent.

'Really!' said the man, - 'he looks so innocent!'

Ava scowled. 'You won't get away with this, Dora, – you'll be hearing from my lawyers'. She hobbled off with Queenie, who looked very put out not to be allowed to play any more.

Wednesday 12th June

'Did you get a photo?' asked Andrew, when I told him about Queenie's newly restored fur.

'No, I was too busy trying to make sure Percy didn't bite anyone else, Andrew – it was a very fraught situation. Anyway, never mind that – she's threatening to sue me because Percy bit her! What am I going to do?'

'Calm down, Dora! It wasn't you who bit Ava, was it! Listen – she's been saying Queenie's career is over – but if her fur is growing back, we need to get some photographic evidence to disprove her claim – do you see?'

'How are we going to do that, Andrew?'

'Well, she obviously goes to the common a lot, so take my camera and try and get a decent photo, or video.'

I rang Melanie at the shop today and told her.

'Oooh, that's very interesting, isn't it! Fancy still pursuing a claim against Pooch Parlour when her dog is fine!'

'Well, I'm not very happy about Andrew's idea, Melanie. I mean, she's bound to see me trying to film her and the dog, isn't she!'

'OK – I'll do it,' said Melanie. 'It'll be fun!'

Thursday 13th June

'It's my last exam today,' said Flora, this morning.

'Thank goodness for that,' I said. 'I mean, good luck, Flora darling. I'm sure it'll go well.'

'I'm seeing Gaz afterwards – I won't be back till later,' she said.

When she'd gone, Andrew expressed his disappointment at her continuing attachment to the gormless Gaz.

'It'll probably run its course eventually,' I said, - 'and they'll go their different ways – especially if Flora goes to university. I don't think we need to worry too much.'

'Well, I hope so,' said Andrew, gloomily. 'She needs someone a lot more intellectually challenging – someone who'll inspire her a bit and get her interested in other things.'

'Well, he's got a job at least, Andrew.'

'You can't call putting a few vegetables through a mangle, a proper job, can you, Dora! A monkey could do it!'

'That's a bit harsh, Andrew.'

'Well I'm sorry, but I want Flora to have some ambition in life.'

'I want her to be happy,' I said.

'Mm, well – she won't be happy if she doesn't aspire to better things.'

'Are we happy, Andrew?' I said, suddenly wondering.

'Of course we are!' said Andrew.

Am I? Am I happy? I don't know. I don't have time to think about it, do I? I'm so busy with everything I have to do, my life just whizzes past and I never consider whether I like it or not, and anyway, even if I came to the conclusion that I don't like my life, then what? I can't just pack up and go. What would my children do? They'd have to live on Andrew's awful cooking – they'd never have clean clothes and they'd become obese and ill through lack of fresh air and exercise, including the dogs. Especially the dogs. No, I can't possibly start thinking about whether I'm happy or not – it's not practical.

Friday 14ʰ June

'I'm feeling very pleased with myself today!' announced Andrew, as he got dressed.

'Are you?'

'Yes, Dora. I've finished the first chapter of my book and it's going swimmingly – being at Suzie's house has made a big difference already.'

'I'm glad to hear it,' I said.

'Yes, I'm particularly pleased with my last paragraph, Dora – can I read it to you?' He didn't wait for my answer:

Lucas slowly and cautiously, made his way along the dank, dark, dismal alleyway leading to Forceps Street. A thin relentless drizzle spattered down onto the filthy, rubbish-strewn pavement beneath his feet.

'This should be an open and shut case,' he muttered to himself. 'I've got to find something….'. He knew in his guts Levi Valdis was guilty. He flicked his half-smoked cigarette contemptuously into the gutter, turned the corner and stopped in the safety of the shadows. He could see the front door from here; its peeling paint and kicked-in doorframe starkly visible in the orange glare from the street lights. 'I'll get you Levi Valdis. All men make mistakes. You'll make a mistake Levi, and when you do, I'll be right there. I swear you will not get away with it – not while I'm alive and kicking.'

'What do you think, Dora?'

'Great!' I said. 'Gripping! You're getting the hang of this writing business, aren't you!'

'Is it gripping enough?'

'Oh yes,' I said, - 'definitely! Now, on another note, Andrew – we had some things delivered to the shop the other day, and the thing is – well, it's valuable stuff and we don't know what to do with it.'

'What do you mean by 'valuable'?'

'Jewellery and expensive clothes…'

'Maybe you should contact the police in case anything like that has been reported stolen.'

'Oh yes, good idea.'

'If it hasn't, then you could put an ad in the paper. By the way, have you found any more people to look after the pets?'

'Yes, I have. I'm going to interview a couple of them today actually.'

'Good,' said Andrew, just as Errol and Flynn started up again.

Saturday 15th June

Jess rang up this morning with the latest on Mum.

'I've managed to get her to agree to meet this chap Lawrence on Wednesday, Dora!' She sounded very pleased with herself.

'Well done, Jess. How did you manage it?'

'Oh, just my powers of persuasion, you know!'

Yes, I do know! Our poor mother probably just gave in to shut Jess up. I hope she isn't being bullied into it.

'Is everything OK at the Bakery?' I asked, with slight trepidation.

'Mostly. Ruby Bunion is still causing trouble. She keeps ringing the police, apparently. The nursing home have had to take her phone off her.'

'Why is she calling the police?'

'To tell them people are trying to kill her, Dora. First it was the tarts, then it was the cake, and now it's Reggie – she told them Reggie was stealing all her possessions and stashing them at Pets' Haven.'

'They don't believe that, do they?'

'I shouldn't think so, Dora – she's potty.'

After Jess hung up, I rang our mother.

'Oh, hello Dora! I can't be on long – I'm going in the garden in a minute.'

'Mum – Jess tells me you're seeing Lawrence on Wednesday.'

'Oh yes, I am. Apparently, he's very keen to meet me. According to Jess, he felt a real connection with me when he saw my photograph.'

'I see,' I said, - 'that's interesting! Where are you meeting him?'

'Well, he suggested a walk by the river, followed by a pub lunch.'

'That sounds nice. Which pub?'

'The Sailor's Tryst – by the river. We're meeting in a public place, Dora – it'll be fine.'

'We could be near by – just in case, Mum.'

'There's no need to spy on me,' said Mum. 'I'll be fine.'

'How can someone feel a connection to a person who doesn't really exist?' I said to Andrew this evening. 'That photo is mostly made up!'

'I've no idea,' said Andrew. 'Maybe he meant her personality.'

'Mm – well, I'm going to keep an eye on things – from a distance, of course.'

'You can't follow your own mother about like a stalker, Dora.'

'I don't see why not. I've only got her interests at heart, Andrew – what's wrong with that?'

Sunday 16th June
(Father's Day)

Billy woke us up at an ungodly time this morning, and I was just about to tell him off when I noticed he was holding a tray with what looked like breakfast and a card for Andrew. Then it dawned on me.

'Happy Father's Day!' said Billy, balancing the tray on our bed. He'd made a card at school with half the back end of a moose on the front of it.

'That's an interesting card, Billy,' I said.

'It was a racing car, but I put the glue on the wrong side.'

'I see. Look, Andrew – Billy's made you a card.'

'What time is it?'

'Six o'clock.'

'Any chance you could come back later,' said Andrew.

Billy looked offended.

'Come on, Andrew – he's made you a nice breakfast – look!'

'Oh, all right. Thank you, Billy - that looks delicious.' Andrew propped himself up and inspected Billy's offering. 'Fantastic! Ketchup sandwiches! Just the thing,' he said, gallantly.

Billy looked chuffed. 'I've made some tea as well.'

I took a sip and discovered it was cold, milky and lumpy, and didn't taste of tea. 'What did you make this with?' I asked.

'That brown stuff in the box that says 'tea' on it.'

'Andrew,' I said, - 'I'd give it a miss if I were you,' I whispered.

'Why?'

'Because it's gravy granules.'

'Come on, kids,' I said to them all later on. 'It's Father's Day and we should spend the rest of the day with your Dad. What shall we do?'

In the end, we settled on going to the pub for lunch and the kids played pool afterwards while we read the papers. To make a good day even better, Mr Sawyer came in the evening and took Errol and Flynn away.

'I hope they've not been too much trouble,' he said, putting them in the back of his van.

'Well, they were certainly quite noisy,' I said. 'I'm afraid they've picked up a few unusual phrases while they've been here... My sons have been teaching them one or two things...'

'Well, I'm thinking of selling them soon, so it won't be my problem anyway! Thanks for helping me out,' he said, waving as he drove off.

'Hey, Mum – can *we* buy them?' said Luke, as we watched Mr Sawyer disappear up the road. 'Pleeeeease!'

'Absolutely, categorically NOT!' I never want to see those two feathered fiends again!'

Monday 17th June

I gave Melanie Andrew's camera this morning and asked her to try and film Ava and Queenie as well as taking a few pictures.

'Ooh, I feel like an undercover detective! It's quite exciting, isn't it, Dora!'

'Just don't let her catch you doing it,' I said. 'By the way, Andrew says he thinks we should phone the police about all that stuff.'

'Might be a good idea – we don't want to be accused of anything dodgy, do we?'

'No – not on top of everything else.'

'Has Andrew heard anything from Fothergill and Shaft?'

'He says they're still gathering information from some of Pooch Parlour's customers - so obviously, they are still pursuing the case.'

'Well, the sooner we can get the evidence we need, the better. I'm going to start straight away!' said Melanie.

Thank you, Melanie – you're a star!'

When I got back home, Andrew had spoken to the lawyers about Bob and Barbara. 'They've visited them in prison again, to keep their spirits up and take some things for them.'

'How are they?'

'OK, I think. They've lost a lot of weight, apparently, but they are both OK. Anyway, it won't be long now – about ten days. I've arranged flights for them. They'll have to stay with us again for a while.'

Oh, help! Well, I knew this would have to happen, of course, but now the time is coming closer I'm slightly dreading it. I know it sounds a bit mean, after all they've gone through, but they are very difficult to live with.

Tuesday 18th June

'Dora, I can't find any pants that actually work,' said Andrew this morning.

'What do you mean?'

'Well, they seem to be bereft of their elasticated waistbands, rendering them useless as functioning underwear.'

'Oh well, you must have worn them out...'

'What, all fifteen pairs at once?'

Then it dawned on me. 'I think it was Billy. Sorry, Andrew – you'll have to wear your swimming trunks or something. I'll get you some more.'

'What on earth possessed Billy to destroy some perfectly serviceable underpants?'

'I'll explain later,' I said, as I was saved by the bell – literally. To my surprise, two policemen asked if they could come in and 'have a chat'.

'Oh, yes, of course,' I said nervously. 'What's it about?' We went into the lounge and sat down.

'Well, Mrs Loveday, we'd like to talk to you about a lady called Ruby Bunion. Are you acquainted with her?' I nodded.

'We're just following up one or two things. How do you know her?'

'Well, she's my mother's friend's mother…'

'I see.' One of the officers started writing in a notebook.

'I recently went to the nursing home where she lives – for her 99th birthday celebration,' I told them.

'Are you aware, Mrs Loveday, that Ruby Bunion has made several complaints about her possessions going missing, possibly stolen, and that she fears her life may be in danger?'

I laughed at this point, but the officers weren't joking.

'We're not joking you know, Mrs Loveday!'

'I'm sorry,' I said, - 'but she's a mad old lady who thinks people are trying to bump her off.'

'This is a very serious matter.'

'OK,' I said.

'Now – we need to know if you have any information which will help us with our enquiries. Can you tell us, for instance, if you have been in possession of any of Mrs Bunion's property?'

'Well, I suppose I have, but none of it is worth anything.'

'That's for us to decide,' they said.

I suddenly remembered the things in the boot of my car. 'I can show you some of it now,' I said, taking them outside to my car. I opened the boot, and the smell nearly knocked us over. They staggered back holding their noses.

'Sorry,' I said, - 'that'll be the hamster cage - I forgot it was still in here.'

'We will be taking possession of these items, I'm afraid,' said one of them.

'Really? Do we have to?' said the other.

I watched them remove all the things destined for the dump, which would now become police property – the blow-up doll, the revolting commode, the hideous lampshades, the monkey's head on a stick, and last, but not least – the extremely noxious hamster cage, which was practically radioactive.

'We'll be in touch,' they said, opening all the windows and driving off with their booty.

Wednesday 19th June

It's Tom's last exam today. He seems to think they've gone quite well. Either he's cleverer than we thought, or he's in denial. I'm inclined to go with the latter, but I may be being unfair – we'll just have to wait and see. It would be a shame if Aunt Alice is proved right after all. I suddenly realised, when he left this morning, that both he and Flora will be hanging around the house until September with nothing to do except eat all the food and play loud music. I must talk to Andrew – we need a plan.

At around eleven o'clock, I took myself off down to the common to meet Jess. At first, I didn't recognise her.

'Why are you wearing a poncho and a bobble hat in this weather?' I said.

'Well, why are *you* wearing Andrew's mac that's much too big, and a baseball cap?'

'Well, I thought I'd blend in better in beige.'

'Mm – well I know this get-up looks a bit odd, but I couldn't think of anything else,' she said. 'Hopefully Mum won't notice us anyway – her eyesight isn't very good at the best of times. Let's go and see if we can spot them – they were supposed to meet at the bench by the river at eleven.'

'Mum will be so cross if she sees us, Jess – we'd better be really careful.'

We began walking down the hill. 'Why are you limping?' I asked Jess.

'I thought It'd be a good disguise,' she said.

It wasn't long before we spotted them walking along about two hundred yards ahead of us.

'His hair is grey,' I commented, - 'not like the photo.'

'And he looks older,' said Jess.

'Well, I expect he thinks the same about Mum!' I said, hoping his eyesight was as bad as Mum's.

We sauntered round and walked parallel to them. They were deep in conversation, and seemed to be getting on fine.

'I think we should just leave them to it,' I said to Jess.

'Not yet. I want to make sure they go for lunch. I know, let's check out the carpark for his car!'

We wandered back towards the pub and looked around at the cars. No Bentley. Jess was disappointed.

'Well, maybe it's in the garage getting an MOT, or something, 'I suggested.

'Mm,' said Jess. 'I'm definitely sticking around for a bit longer.'

I must say, after a while, spying on someone is *really* boring.

'I'm getting hot in this poncho,' said Jess, while we sat in the pub garden, waiting for them to come in.

'Yes, I know what you mean – I'm getting warm myself. In fact, I'm feeling a bit faint.'

'Well, try to stay upright, Dora – look, they're coming in.'

Mum and Lawrence sat down at a table nearby and ordered some lunch.

'We'd better order something,' I said to Jess. 'We can't just sit here.'

'OK,' said Jess in a funny voice. 'Excusez moi!' she said to the waitress. I gave her a funny look. 'I'm being French,' she said, - 'it's part of my disguise. Deux café s'il vous plait.'

'Coffee?' I said, - 'I wanted something cold!'

'Sorry - I can't remember any other drinks in French,' said Jess.

Mum and Lawrence took so long eating their lunch, I was beginning to really regret this whole spying idea. I was sweating like a pig in Andrew's fur-lined mac, and beginning to hallucinate due to rapid de-hydration.

'Do you think we could go now, please?' I said to Jess.

'Wait, Dora, Mum's getting up.' Mum disappeared into the pub and Lawrence took out his phone.

'I want to hear what he's saying…'

We strained to listen in on his conversation. When he hung up, we decided to make our escape.

'Did you hear that!' said Jess, excitedly.

'Something about giving money to some cooks, or something – I don't know. Maybe he owns a restaurant…'

'*Coutts*, Dora! He was moving money into his account at Coutts!' Jess was smiling like the cat that got the cream.

'I don't think we need to worry about him.' she said.

Thursday 20th June

Suzie rang up in a terrible flap this morning. 'Dora, come quickly! The police are here. They've got a search warrant and they're upstairs right now!'

'What are they looking for?'

'I don't know.'

I got my jacket and jumped in the car. 'Where are you going?' asked Andrew.

'The shop – Suzie says the police are there.'

'I'd better come too,' said Andrew.

When we arrived, there were two police cars parked outside the shop.

'What's going on?' I asked one of the policemen.

'We'll let you know in good time,' he said.

'I bet it's to do with Ruby Bunion,' I said. 'I can't believe you've taken her seriously! She's an old lady who's gone doolally – she's always accusing people of things!' The policeman just smiled and said he couldn't comment on sensitive matters.

'Best not to say anything else, Dora,' said Andrew. 'Just let them do their job.' We sat there for an hour and a half until they eventually came downstairs with about six bags of stuff.

'We're removing some items for further investigation,' said one of them. 'We'll require you all to be interviewed at the police station – we'll call you tomorrow.'

'I wonder what they took,' I said when they'd gone. I went upstairs.

'All that expensive stuff has gone, and Ruby Bunion's old clothes - and they've taken Andrew's camera!' said Melanie. 'I left it up here on the table!'

'Honestly!' I said to Andrew when we got home, - 'that was ridiculous.'

'I know, but they have to be seen to do their job, don't they? I expect it'll all calm down once they've established Ruby's accusations are nonsense.'

I decided to bite the bullet and phone the radio station. Since Chas is still keen to do another interview, I thought I might as well try and see if we can't find the stranger who donated the jewellery. I've been given a slot next Tuesday morning.

Afterwards, I went straight round to my mother's house. 'Reggie's very upset,' said Mum, when she opened the door.

We went into the kitchen and she put the kettle on. 'Ruby told the police that he's hiring people to get rid of her!'

'Mum, they surely can't be taking her seriously – it's utter nonsense!'

'Well, yes, but don't you know? Ruby has gone missing from the old people's home. So now, the police are taking it *very* seriously, Dora. Poor Reggie had to go down to the police station yesterday evening to be interrogated. They showed him a load of stuff and asked him what he knew about it. Some of it was Ruby's old rubbish, but most of it he'd never seen before. He said some of the things were downright peculiar! They showed him a giant inflatable doll and a decapitated monkey's head, of all things! They asked him if he knew anything about Voodoo rituals and sacrificial rites! And they asked him about a large quantity of jewellery as well. Of course, he told them he knew nothing about any of it.'

'Oh, Goodness!' I said. 'This is terrible. Where can she be?'

'No one knows. The police have been looking for her since last night. Poor Reggie has got absolutely nothing to do with it - he wouldn't hurt a fly. Anyway, the silly old biddy doesn't have two pennies to rub together, so why would he bother to do away with her! By the way, Dora – Margery says you can have the caravan at the end of the month if you want.'

In the evening, we put on the local news, and Ruby Bunion's impervious wrinkly old face filled the screen. The

Presenter was saying: *"A local woman went missing under suspicious circumstances late last night, from a well-known nursing home in Shillingsworth. The staff noticed Mrs Ruby Bunion was missing when she failed to appear for her usual evening cocoa and buttered toast at around 9pm. The alarm was raised immediately for Ruby, who is 99 years old and very frail. She was last seen in possession of a Zimmer frame, wearing pink fluffy slippers, a purple dressing gown and carrying a bright orange shopping bag."*

'I wonder where on earth she is?' I said to Andrew. 'She can't have gone very far, can she, not dressed like that?'

Friday 21ˢᵗ June

'Dora, it was terrible!' said Jess, when I picked up the phone this morning, - 'and it's all your doing!'

Oh no, here we go again…

'I explained to the police that you're incompetent in the kitchen, and that we weren't even there that day! I told them about the mix-up with the curry. They wouldn't believe me, Dora! Anyway, the evidence has long-since gone, so nothing can be proved either way, but they made us feel like criminals, Dora! Insinuating that we deliberately tried to poison an 'innocent old lady'! I mean, really! Have they *met* Ruby Bunion!'

'I'm sorry,' Jess,' I said, - 'but it's not my fault she's a mad old woman, is it? Anyway, she's a *missing* mad old woman now, which is an entirely different matter.'

I must admit, my head is spinning at the moment – I'm fighting battles on all fronts, and it's exhausting. I'm not sleeping well at all. Ava Bush keeps appearing in my dreams. Last night she turned into a giant spider and I kept trying to chop her legs off with the hedge clippers, but they grew back again, bigger and stronger every time! And then Ruby Bunion appeared like the Grim Reaper, laughing like a drain and wielding a big, rusty scythe in my direction. I woke up in a cold sweat just as she turned into a giant parrot and tried to eat Billy.

'We've got to go down to the police station this afternoon,' said Andrew, when I got off the phone.

'You'll be interviewed separately,' said the policewoman, later on, as they took Andrew away into another room. 'Now, Mrs Loveday, just answer our questions as clearly and simply as you can,' she said, turning on the recording equipment.

An hour later, they let us both go home.

'Gin?' said Andrew.

'Yes, definitely,' I said.

'They asked to see my manuscript, of all things!' he said, pouring a large one.

'Why?'

'Because, when they discovered the camera was mine, they suddenly decided I might be a suspect – you know – the photos of the murder scenes…'

'No!'

'Yes. They wanted to know how long I've been interested in homicides.'

'This whole thing is getting completely out of hand. They asked me about all that jewellery again. I told them a stranger donated it, but I could tell they didn't believe me. Then they started asking me about Mum's relationship with Reggie. They think we're all in it together, Andrew. It's ridiculous!'

'Let's just hope Ruby turns up soon,' said Andrew, pouring another gin, - 'or we're all up the creek without a paddle.'

Saturday 22nd June

We're almost back to normal now on the animal front. The gerbils and hamster have been collected, so now we just have Mr Nibbles, who would have been staying with us permanently, except he's gone missing again. Luckily, the people I took on last week have turned out to be really good and can take most of the animals we get. Andrew is relieved about this. The children, on the other hand, are a bit disappointed.

'Aren't we getting any more animals now?' asked Luke.

'Not at the moment,' I said.

'Peace at last!' said Andrew, happily. Luke scowled.

'Dora, I've got some good news,' said Melanie, when I answered the phone to her today. 'I've managed to get a film of Ava and Queenie.'

'That's brilliant news!' I said. 'How did you manage it?'

'Well, I saw her in the park. I used my phone and I actually asked her if she minded me taking a picture of her lovely dog! I was filming instead and I asked her all about Queenie. If you come round, I'll show you.'

'I will,' I said, - 'right now!'

'That's a wrap!' said Andrew, when I showed him Melanie's film later on.

'This means it's over doesn't it, Andrew? Ava can't continue with her claim now, can she?'

'I doubt it, unless she wants to carry on saying her dog's been emotionally traumatised, but I don't think it'll be worth it. I expect the lawyers will all settle out of court. Job done!'

'Oh, thank goodness,' I said, - 'what a relief!'

Sunday 23rd June

I'd arranged to go to visit my mother today, and Jess suggested we all go out for lunch, so I left my family to fend for themselves, with Andrew at the helm of course.

Mum seemed in a very good mood when I arrived. 'Isn't it a lovely day!' she said. 'I've just been watering my roses – they're coming along a treat. Now, where are we going, do you think?' Jess suggested the Sailor's Tryst again.

'Well, this is very nice, just the three of us, isn't it girls?'

'Yes,' we said.

'It's lovely to get away from everyone once in a while,' I said.

'Well, Mum,' said Jess when we'd ordered, - 'spill the beans!'

'What do you mean, Jess?' said Mum.

'You know – Lawrence! What's he like? We're dying to know!'

'Well, he seems very nice. We chatted about our families – he's got three grown-up children, he's an accountant, and he likes playing golf. He says he loves travelling and wants to go to Australia next.'

'That sounds good,' said Jess, the pound signs almost visible in her shining eyes.

'Does he live nearby?'

'No, not really, but he doesn't mind a bit of driving – anyway, he says he has a chauffeur because he's often working whilst travelling.' Jess's eyes widened more. I elbowed her in the ribs.

'Has he travelled a lot then?' I asked.

'Yes, he has – an awful lot. He says he's got an apartment in Florida, and one in Spain, but he says he's getting bored of that one and might sell it soon. He says he wants to buy a villa in Tuscany. 'Oh, here are the drinks, girls!' she said, seeing the waitress coming. Jess smiled and gave me a sideways look that said; *see; it **was** worth it!*

I changed the subject. 'Mum, how is Reggie? Any news about Ruby?'

'No, no news. Reggie is terribly upset, of course. I told him not to worry – I'm sure she'll turn up soon!'

'You don't think he did her in, then?' said Jess.

'Of course not, Jess! What an awful idea!'

'Well, she is a bit of a pain,' said Jess.

Mum scowled at her. 'Don't talk like that, Jess. He's an innocent man, and don't you forget it!'

'Well, if you say so,' said Jess. 'But I think it's the only explanation. I'd watch myself if I were you, Mum.'

Monday 24th June

'I'm a bit worried about Mum, Andrew,' I said, when we got up this morning. 'Something Jess said made me think – well, you know – if Reggie *did* do something to Ruby, then Mum's in danger, isn't she!'

'Don't be daft, Dora! Reggie is no more a murderer than I am! Do you seriously think that blundering old codger capable of a violent crime like that! It takes a steely, calculating, vicious mind-set to carry out something evil like that.'

'I hope you're right, Andrew.'

'I am,' he said, confidently. 'Now, I'm off to take this video footage to show Fothergill & Shaft, as soon as I've had my breakfast.'

'I thought Melanie was brilliant, didn't you!'

'First class!' said Andrew. 'That bit where she says what a lovely coat Queenie's got is priceless.'

'I think we should get Melanie and Geoff over for supper soon, to say 'thank you',' I suggested.

'Yes, great plan,' said Andrew. 'Geoff and I can discuss our fishing trip.'

'Oh, yes, I'd forgotten about that. Are you still going then?'

'Does a fish swim? Of course I'm going Dora. I've already bought a new tent for it.'

'What was wrong with the old one, Andrew?'

'It was mouldy, Dora. And anyway, it took ages to put up. I've got this brilliant one that springs up by itself – it takes seconds to pitch – no faffing about with poles and guy ropes any more.'

'Don't spend too much money on things for this trip, Andrew,' I said. 'We're supposed to be on a budget.'

'It's fine, Dora. I've got it covered. That website, Xpertatlaw.com, are paying me quite well for legal advice at the moment.'

After Andrew left, I had to get Luke and Billy off to school – never an easy task, especially now that Tom and Flora have finished.

'It's not fair, Mum – why do they get to stay at home.'

'Because they have finished their exams,' I said for the tenth time.

'But we have to sit tests too!' said Luke.

'Yes,' said Billy – 'I had a spelling test on Friday, and it was really hard.'

'I'm sure it was, Billy. When you are Tom's age, you will be allowed to have early holidays after your GCSE's as well.'

'Do I *have* to do GCSE's?' said Luke. 'They're so stupid and boring.'

'Yes, you do,' I said. 'It's the law.'

'The law is stupid.'

'Don't let your father hear you say that,' I told him. 'Anyway, you'll appreciate having been made to go to school when you're older.'

'Never,' said Luke.

'No, never,' said Billy.

I decided to walk the boys to school, just in case they got any ideas, and then I went to Suzie's for coffee and a catch-up.

'I'm not sure I can work at the shop any more, Dora,' she said, as we took our coffee out onto the patio in the morning sunshine.

'Oh, why not?'

'Well, it's nothing personal, Dora – I've just got to concentrate on Violet's wedding now – it's only three weeks away, you know.'

'Oh, of course. Yes, I see,' I said. 'Well, don't worry – I'll sort something out.'

'And of course, there's the house to think about – Warren still wants to move. By the way, I found where that awful smell was coming from.'

'What was it then?'

'Well, you'll never believe it, but under the bed in one of the spare bedrooms I found some boxes with bin liners round them. The smell was disgusting, Dora! I didn't even look – I just chucked them straight in the bin.'

'Oh, I know what that was – I think it was Bob's Albino Asparagus – it needs complete darkness to grow. I suppose it must have rotted off by now.'

'You're telling me! I got through five cans of air freshener trying to get rid of the pong!'

'Sorry, Suzie.'

'Oh, well – it's all fine now. I can get the Estate Agent round again – he said it was unsellable before.'

Tuesday 25th June

I must say, I was already regretting my decision to go on the radio again as soon as I set foot in the studio. The plasticated Wanda had been replaced with the even more plasticated Chenaya, Chas seemed almost as drug-crazed as before, and I hadn't prepared properly this time – which was immediately apparent.

'The lovely Nora Loveday has graced us with her charming presence here in the studio today to talk about her cherished charity, Pets' Haven,' he gushed. 'So, Nora, my love, howz it going?'

'It's Dora,' I said, to no effect. 'Um, well – it's going really well, thanks Chas.'

'OK, Nora - any stories you'd like to share with us?' Chas grinned his vacuous grin.

'Well … we've had quite a lot of pets in the last few weeks. We had a couple of parrots, some gerbils, a hamster, some cats and a couple of dogs, and a rat called Mr Nibbles. Unfortunately, he's gone missing - at the moment.'

'Oh dear, Nora – that's sad, isn't it! Someone's pet going missing! If anyone out there sees a rat called – what was it?'

'Mr Nibbles.'

'OK – please get in touch with Nora. What does he look like?'

'Brown and white with a long white tail and pink eyes.'

'So, look out, people! Just remember, folks – Mr Nibbles could be just five feet away from you at any time of the day or night! They breed like crazy too, don't they!' He put on a record - *Rat Trap* by the *Boomtown Rats*.

'I want to appeal to your listeners for help with something else,' I said to Chas, as the track faded.

'Sure, Nora – go ahead – be my guest!'

I told everyone about the donated jewellery, and needing the person to come forward.

'Sounds like it could be stolen goods, Nora!' said the gleeful Chas. 'OK, listen up, all you people out there – Nora needs to find the person who left the hot goods in her shop! Call in if you have any information – we don't want poor Nora here being done for handling stolen goods, do we!' He then decided to play *I Fought the Law* by The Clash.

'Well, at least you got your message out to the public,' said Andrew, later. In an attempt to cheer me up, he added, - 'loads of people listen to Fun Time FM, don't they!'

Wednesday 26th June

Melanie's been helping me a lot in the shop recently, but now Suzie's not available, I decided to stick a sign up in the window for a new employee. By the end of the day we already had four CV's.

'This one looks quite good,' said Melanie, - 'look, she's worked in shops before, and with animals.'

'What's her name?' I asked, - 'I've mislaid my specs.'

'Liberty Beadle. She's twenty-six and lives in Shillingsworth. She came in while you were upstairs. She seemed quite nice.'

'The others are all 18-year-olds. I think I'd rather have someone older with a bit of experience,' I said.

'Well, you'll get some more before the end of the week, so you can decide later, can't you? At least you can probably stop worrying about Ava and her dog now.'

'I hope so, Melanie. We're waiting for Fothergill and Shaft to contact us. She threatened to sue me over Percy biting her as well though! He only grazed her slightly anyway. I wish he *had* sunk his teeth into her!'

'That woman needs to take a chill pill,' said Melanie.

'I can't wait for Friday – we're off to the caravan at Skegness for the weekend. Flora and Tom aren't keen, but it'll be nice to get away.'

'Couldn't you leave them behind?'

'Well, we could, but I'm not sure if we can trust them to be sensible, Melanie.'

At bed time, I told Andrew about Melanie's suggestion.

'Is she mad!' he said, straight away. 'Can you imagine what would happen if we weren't here! They'd probably have one of those parties where the house gets trashed or torched! No way are they staying here by themselves!'

'But Flora's 18 now, Andrew!'

Andrew just frowned and grumbled something about house insurance.

Thursday 27th June

I went to get the key for the caravan at lunch time from my mother's, and was surprised to see Lawrence there.

'We're going out to lunch and then on to the theatre to see *Run for Your Wife* at the Playhouse,' said Mum. 'I'm just popping upstairs for a minute to get my bag.'

'Hello Lawrence. Nice to meet you,' I said, shaking his hand.

'And you,' he said, - 'although, you are familiar to me, actually,' he said, winking.

'Really?' I said. 'How?'

'Well, let's just say that baseball caps and macs are an odd choice of attire for a summer's day, and your sister's get-up was even more amusing. I do hope her leg is better now – that was a terrible limp she had the other day!'

'What's the matter, Dora?' said my mother when she re-appeared, - 'you look a bit flushed.'

'I'm fine Mum,' I said, - 'don't let me hold you up – off you go and enjoy yourselves.'

'Au revoir,' said Lawrence as they left, - 'à bientôt!'

'Jess! It was *so* embarrassing!' I wailed, when I saw her at the Bakery at lunch time. 'He knew who we were – he saw us following them.'

'How?'

'I don't know! Anyway, he made me feel about two inches tall! He was laughing, Jess! He thought it was funny!'

'Well, I suppose from his point of view, it was,' said Jess. 'Oh well, on the positive side, he knows we are watching him, doesn't he! So, if he is at all dodgy, he'll think twice about trying any funny business, won't he!'

'I suppose so...'

'Has Ruby been found yet?' she asked, changing tack.

'No, Jess, she hasn't. It's very worrying – I mean, where can she have disappeared to? It's not as if she's inconspicuous, is it! Someone must have seen her.'

'Well, not if she's been bumped off and stuffed down a drain or something, Dora!'

'For goodness sake, Jess! You don't really think that, do you?'

'I've had my suspicions about Reggie Bunion ever since he befriended our mother – there's something fishy about him, Dora. His eyes are too close together.'

'Jess, you're being absurd!'

After lunch with Jess, I went back to the shop so Melanie could go home. 'Tomorrow,' she said, - 'why don't you stay at home and pack for your weekend away – I can manage here.'

'Thanks, Melanie – that would be great. Any more CV's to look at?'

'No.'

I decided to give Liberty a ring and invite her in for an interview. I needed to find someone quickly, and she did seem quite a likely candidate. Luckily, she was available in the afternoon. Anyway, when she walked in through the door, I recognised her straight away!

'Oh, it's you, Bertie!' I said, surprised.

She grinned. 'Sorry – I thought that if I let on, you wouldn't interview me.'

'Well, I suppose it could be a bit awkward – what about Jack?' I said.

'She's given up Pooch Parlour and gone to work on her sister's farm. The salon is shut now, for good.'

'Oh dear…' I said.

'Don't worry, Dora – it wasn't because of you – the place was getting run down and losing money way before you came along. Jack was talking about moving away last year. The business over Queenie just made her do it sooner, that's all.'

'Oh, what a relief it is to hear you say that!' I said. 'Thank you, Bertie, you've taken a weight off my mind, you really have. Let's have a cup of tea. My sister gave me some nice biscuits from the Bakery – I'll just fetch them.'

'Well,' said Andrew, when I told him about Bertie at tea time, - 'that was a piece of luck, wasn't it!'

'Honestly, Andrew, if it wasn't for Ruby, I'd be feeling so much better about everything now.'

'Kids,' I said, when they came and sat down, - 'please pack this evening, because I want to get away as soon as possible after school tomorrow.'

'Can I take my stick insects?' asked Billy.

'What will happen to the cats?' asked Flora.

'Your Nan is coming over here while we're away,' I said.

'I want to stay here,' said Tom.

'Me too,' moaned Flora.

'Well, I don't know if we can trust you,' Andrew said, bluntly.

'Please, Dad, we'll be really good!'

We looked at each other. *Should we take the risk? I suppose we've got to start sometime.*

'Mm – well … if we did agree, you have to be on your best behaviour,' said Andrew. 'No parties, no crowds of

305

mates, no fires, no power tools, no loud music, and NO boozing or smoking. And, clean up after yourselves!'

'YEAH! Thanks, Dad,' said Flora, cheering up instantly.

I rang my mother and, despite my reservations, told her she was off the hook.

Friday 28th June

'What made you change your mind?' I asked Andrew last night as we got ready for bed.

'To be honest, it was the thought of the pair of them whinging on for two days and spoiling our weekend away. I still think it could be the most foolish thing we've done for ages.'

After the children left for school, I got on with packing. It's amazing what you need to take, even just for two days. Andrew always thinks I over-pack. But, you don't know what the weather will throw at you, do you? It's been known to snow in June before now!

'Must we take wellingtons *and* sandals!' Andrew complained. 'And, why do you want to take all that food? There are shops there you know.'

'Yes, but we need breakfast stuff, coffee and tea and snacks and dog food ...'

Andrew left me to it. It's the worst aspect of going away – we always bicker over what to take. If it was left to him, we'd go with nothing but what we stood up in, spend a fortune on fast food, and waste valuable holidaying time having to buy things we should have brought with us.

By the time the boys came in from school, I had finished all the packing and was ready to go.

'I just got off the phone to Fothergill and Shaft, Dora,' said Andrew, coming out of the study. 'Ava Bush has agreed not to pursue her claim! I've also spoken to the lawyers about Mum and Dad, and they're flying into Heathrow on Wednesday afternoon.'

'That's fantastic, Andrew! We'll be able to meet them off the plane and get them home in time for next weekend!'

'Well, I'm not sure – the lawyers said that they are being put up in a hotel by a national newspaper.'

'Oh, really?'

'Yes – they must have sold their story to the papers.'

'I hope they know what they're doing,' I said.

'Highly unlikely,' said Andrew. 'Anyway, it's too late now.'

'Right, well, we'd better get going,' I said. 'Tom and Flora – I've left you lots of food in the fridge, OK?'

'Yes. Thanks, Mum.'

'Please don't just eat pizzas and crisps.'

'No, Mum.'

'You know they will!' said Andrew, as we drove up the M1 in the late afternoon sunshine.

Saturday 29th June

'Isn't it exciting to wake up in a different place!' I said to Andrew this morning. The warm sun was streaming through our caravan windows, and we could see the bright blue sea beyond – well, almost.

'When you said, 'caravan on the coast',' said Andrew, - 'I imagined a few nicely spaced mobile homes with attractive landscaped green areas where the kids can play - not this!' he grumbled, pointing at the vast numbers of caravans crammed together within spitting distance of each other. 'This resembles a factory forecourt – it's utterly soulless!'

'It's only for two days, Andrew. You'll just have to put up with it.'

We'd promised the boys we'd go to Fantasy Island today.

'I thought this holiday was supposed to be relaxing,' said Andrew, as we approached the giant multi-coloured mass of steel spaghetti, flashing lights, and thousands of screaming kids.

'I want to go on the 'Volcano' ride,' said Luke, - 'and the 'Beast'!'

'Dad, you'll come with me, won't you?' said Luke. Andrew's face turned pale, as he read the description of the 'Beast' ride: ***The 'Beast' is an exciting, stomach-churning experience! Spinning and twisting in every direction imaginable - this ride will leave you feeling totally disorientated.'*** Then he looked at the description for the

'Volcano': ***The frightening suspense builds, as you wait to be shot 183 feet at an amazing 50mph!'***

'Wouldn't you prefer the 'Log Flume'?' Andrew said, weakly.

'Nah, Dad! Come on, or you're a chicken!' goaded Luke.

I went with Billy on the Dodgems and that was hair-raising enough for me.

Several rides, ice-creams and candy floss sticks later, we made our way back to the caravan and to Fudge and Cocoa.

'I need to lie down,' said Andrew, disappearing behind the curtain and getting into the bed.

'Dad was sick in a bag!' said Luke, as we walked down to the beach with the dogs.

'Poor Daddy!' I said. 'Us oldies don't have strong stomachs for fairground rides, not like you youngsters.'

'I bet him he couldn't go on the 'Volcano' three times in a row!' said Luke, fiendishly.

'Well, your Dad shouldn't have risen to the bait,' I said.

Honestly, what is Andrew like! Is he ever going to admit he's getting older? He'll be 50 in September! I hope he realises he can't keep up with his sons like he used to. He needs to just give in sometimes and let them win. I suppose the alpha male in him refuses to lie down and die despite what his body is trying to tell him!

Sunday 30th June

'I want to dig in the sand,' said Billy, grabbing the bucket and spade after breakfast.

'It's quite chilly, isn't it!' said Andrew, as we marched along the seafront in the stiff breeze.

'Yes, well, Skegness isn't known for its tropical climate,' I said.

'So, 'Costa Del Skeggy' is a slight misnomer then,' he said.

'It's a free holiday, Andrew, so you can't complain.'

'Bloody English weather,' he said. 'I wish I'd packed my duffle coat.'

Down on the beach we sat huddled under my coat, while the dogs raced in and out of the water with the boys. After a couple of hours of walking up and down to keep warm, we bribed the boys away from the icy waves with the promise of fish and chips for lunch.

'Isn't it amazing how kids don't notice the cold,' said Andrew, as we rubbed their navy-blue legs dry with a towel. We left the dogs in the caravan on a blanket and went to find a chippy.

'There's nothing like fish and chips by the sea, is there!' I said, as we sat on a bench overlooking the beach, eating our delicious, hot and vinegary haddock and chips. 'It's so nice to get away from it all,' I said to Andrew. 'We can forget all our troubles for a bit.'

Just then, we heard a loud voice from further down the promenade. There seemed to be a bit of a kerfuffle going on.

'I know who you are!' said the voice. 'You can't fool me! I don't care what you say – I know what you're up to!'

'Why is that lady bashing that man with a stick?' said Luke.

'Get off me, you silly old bat,' the man was protesting – 'I don't know what you're going on about!' A crowd was gathering, and the shouting was getting louder.

'Look, Mum,' said Billy, - 'she's wearing pyjamas! And she's got her slippers on! Did she forget to bring her clothes on holiday with her?'

'Don't stare, Billy,' said Andrew, - 'it's not nice. She's probably not very well. I expect someone will come and take her back to her house soon.'

'I know who sent you!' shouted the old lady at the man running in our direction. He was carrying a tray of ice-cream tubs. 'You're trying to poison me! I know what you're up to. If you think I'm going to fall for it, you've got another thing coming!' she called after him.

'What on earth was she doing here?' said Andrew, as we sat waiting in Skegness Police Station.

'I don't know, but thank God we found her!'

'Mr and Mrs Loveday…' called the receptionist. 'Ruby will be taken back this afternoon to her nursing home. Do you have contact details for her family?'

'Yes – her son Reggie can be contacted through my mother.' I wrote down the number. 'How did she come to be here though?' I asked. 'I mean, it's miles away!'

'Well, apparently, she got on a bus in Shillingsworth with an OAP's holiday trip to Skegness and just followed them into the same hotel. She's racked up quite a big bill at the Seaview Plaza, I'm afraid. She likes her brandy, doesn't she!'

'Oh, poor Reggie!' I said to Andrew, as we strolled along the prom. 'I mean – where on earth is he going to find nine-hundred quid from?'

We spent the rest of the afternoon in the Aquarium before heading back to the caravan to pack up. We had one last walk on the beach with Fudge and Cocoa, and then headed home, tired but happy.

When we got back, Flora and Tom had plainly done as little as possible to tidy up or clean up, but I was too tired to worry about it. The main thing was that they appeared to be fine, and the house was still standing – so a good result all round!

'Mum, there were some messages for you,' said Flora. 'Granny and Grandpa left a message to say they are looking forward to coming home next week, and that they're OK – they said not to worry about the money because they'll be able to pay all the legal fees with the money from their story in the papers, and Cheeky Chas rang up and said that the donor of the jewellery is someone called Berny Bush. Apparently, he's divorcing his wife because she loves her dogs more than him, so Berny got rid of all her stuff in a fit of rage. Oh, and the police rang and asked if we had a dog called Percy here. Apparently, he has a Control Order against him and is supposed to wear a muzzle.'

Well, honestly! It beggars belief what some people are like! I must say, this pet caring lark is already wearing a bit thin – I mean, how do some of these people sleep at night! I might have to re-think the whole thing now. It's all been a bit of a strain, and I don't mind admitting that if I'd known what lay in store, I would have thought twice about the whole thing. I think Andrew would probably agree.

'Oh, and there was another message,' said Flora, suddenly remembering, - 'it was from Melanie. She says don't throw away the monkey head – it's an antique walking stick and it's worth £2,000'.

'Well!' said Andrew, - 'that's a turn up for the books, isn't it! What a lucky find! That puts a different spin on things doesn't it Dora! It makes all your efforts worthwhile! I think we've just found Reggie's nine-hundred quid too, don't you?' He went off upstairs whistling a happy tune to himself, and all was right in the world...

Of course, it's all very well for Andrew to think things are fine, but I can't help worrying about all sorts of things. Pet's Haven is rapidly losing its appeal to me now - people just don't seem to appreciate my efforts at all. And then there's Jess, with her bull-in-a-china-shop attempts at re-invigorating our mother's love-life. I mean, God help us if that goes wrong. My husband seems to be in a world of his own, dreaming about fame and fortune, whilst I live in fear of something terrible befalling one, or all of my children at once. And God knows what Bob and Barbara's story in the Daily Rag will be like – I dread to think! Then there's poor Suzie, grappling with Violet's insane wedding plans…

So, who knows what the next few months will bring?

* * *

ABOUT THE AUTHOR

Nicola Kelsall is an artist and writer, living in a little village in the Cotswolds with her own chaotic and noisy family, plus their latest addition, Chester the dog. She has loved being an artist and writer from childhood. She trained at Edinburgh College of Art, later becoming an artist and illustrator. Over the years, she supported her life as an artist by working in a wide variety of other professions.

Her eclectic assortment of jobs have included; Chambermaid, Barmaid, Driver, Shop Girl, Secretary, House and Pet Sitter, Child Minder, Dresser for the Royal Scottish Ballet, Printer, PA, Designer, Illustrator, Singer in a Medieval Banquet, Event Organiser, Teacher, PTA Queen, and most importantly – wife and mother extraordinaire.

"I used to worry that some of the dead-end jobs I did, represented huge amounts of wasted time and often felt trapped and frustrated. Now of course, I am grateful for all the interesting experiences and funny characters I've met along the way. Having a family has given me another very different perspective on life, and luckily inspired this series *Diary of a Stressed Out Mother.* I've enjoyed every minute of writing these books and I hope my readers love them too!"

For more about Nicola Kelsall:
www.facebook.com/stressedoutmother
@StressOutMother

Printed in Dunstable, United Kingdom